SAINTS PURGATORY MC

See Evil, Hear Evil, Become Evil, Purge Evil

UNHOLY SOUL

ANDI RHODES & LACY ROSE

See Evil, Hear Evil, Become Evil, Purge Evil

UNHOLY SOUL

ANDI RHODES & LACY ROSE

Cover Artwork and Formatting - © Dez Purington at Pretty in Ink Creations

For our husbands, and the men who came before them - Without you, we wouldn't be able to write the stories we love so much. Thank you for your encouragement, your support, and your unwavering love.

And for Grandpa Tom - You left this world too soon and are missed every second of every day. Love you!

A NOTE FROM THE AUTHORS

The Saints Purgatory MC is a work of fiction. It is not a commentary on our thoughts or beliefs about religion or the Catholic faith. Unholy Soul, like most MC romance stories, deals with difficult topics, and may be triggering for some. If you would like more information regarding specific triggers, feel free to reach out to either of us via email or social media. We're more than happy to discuss them further!

Now, buckle up and get ready! You're about to go on one helluva ride.

Much love,
Andi and Lacy

SEVEN DEADLY SINS

Sloth

Pride

Lust

Greed

Gluttony

Wrath

Envy

Sloth is a person's extreme laziness or the failure to act and use their talents.

Sloth is cured by placing the interest of others above a life of ease and relaxation.

Saints Purgatory MC Motto

See Evil, Hear Evil, Become Evil, Purge Evil

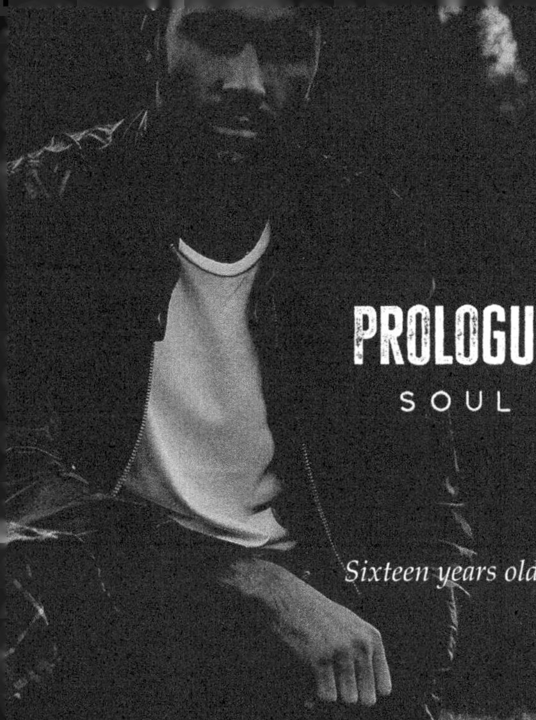

PROLOGUE

SOUL

Sixteen years old…

"Forgive me Father, for I have sinned."

My chest hurts as I sit in this tiny confessional booth. It's something I do every week. Not because I want to, but because my parents expect it. You see, my twin, Mary, and I have been raised to be devout Catholics. And everything would have continued down the path our parents wanted if things hadn't started happening… bad things.

"Please, go on," Father Brine encourages.

I ball my hands into fists as they rest on my lap. Words are clogging my throat, vowels and consonants clinging to one another to form a giant ball of vitriol that wants to be catapulted from my tongue to paint the walls of this booth in the rage I feel.

I close my eyes and take a deep breath.

"Whatever it is, my son, it's not insurmountable. Our God is a forgiving God."

"Is he?" I spit, unable to control the flash of temper that would have my parents tanning my hide for showing any amount of disrespect. "Because what I saw yesterday makes me question if our God isn't a vengeful God who doesn't give a shit about his children."

"Language," Father Brine warns from his perch beyond the mesh grate that separates us. After another moment, he sighs. "Son, start from the beginning, and we'll work through this together."

"I…" I swallow down the evil words I want to say, let them swish around in my stomach acid to form something more appropriate, and then spit them out. "I failed to help someone who was being hurt."

"And who was being hurt?"

I don't want to tell him. It's not my secret to tell. But isn't that the problem? That no one ever speaks up? What I witnessed yesterday between Deacon Block and my friend, Paul, is something we've been taught is wrong and a sin like no other. But it's not the first time I've seen something like it happen, and no consequences have ever been doled out.

"If I tell you, what will you do about it?" I counter.

"Well, Son, I don't know. Confessions are confidential. Without knowing what you witnessed, I can't give you a precise answer."

And this is the exact moment I make a decision that will alter the course of my life, and the lives of others, for all of eternity.

"Wrong answer, Father," I snipe as I rise from the wooden bench and shove open the door.

Storming out of the church, I ignore my parent's asking me where I'm going. I ignore my sister's stare, the one that tells me she's mad that I'm leaving her to face the rest of the morning on her own and I'll pay for it dearly.

Paul and our other friend, John, chase after me, their footsteps thudding on the pavement as I race to my hand-me-down blue Nissan Altima.

"Matt!" Paul calls to my back. "What the hell, man?"

"I gotta get outta here," I shout, anger seeping into my tone. I don't bother turning around and signing my words for John's benefit. I know Paul will make sure he knows what I said.

When I reach my car, I yank the driver's side door open and climb in. As I start the engine, my two best friends jump in and slam their doors. I peel out of the parking lot and flip the bird in the direction of the church, not giving a single damn that the Priest is standing on the steps watching my departure.

"What is going on with you this morning?" Paul asks as he spins in his seat so John can see his hands flying.

I stop at the stop sign down the block, and John taps me on the shoulder. When I turn, he signs, "You've been weird since yesterday."

I don't respond, focusing instead on getting home and as far away from hypocrite central as I can. Paul tries to ask more questions, but I tune him out.

I thought what I saw yesterday could be forcibly removed from my memory if I tried hard enough to block it out, but I knew the second I saw Paul walk into the church with his parents and younger brother, Mark, that there was no way in hell I'd ever forget.

When we reach my house, I park the car at the curb, allowing space in the driveway for my parents' car. Paul and John follow me inside, each helping themselves to a bottle of water in the fridge. We trudge down to the basement, silence punctuating each step we take.

Paul and John sit on the old couch and watch me pace until John stomps his foot several times to get my attention.

"What?" I snap, forgetting to sign.

He angrily signs the word 'talk' before sitting back and waiting me out. After several more passes over the area rug, I stop in front of my two best friends and look them square in the eye.

"We don't have secrets, right?"

Paul averts his gaze while John shakes his head. I huff out a breath, needing to calm myself down because as infuriated as I am, I can't imagine how Paul is doing. Not only does he have secrets, but they're awful ones.

Rather than push him, I decide to drop it. I'm still pissed and don't for a second regret hauling ass away from the church, but something tells me I need to tread carefully. If I were in Paul's shoes, I wouldn't want anyone to know.

The rest of the week goes by very slowly. It's close to the end of the school year, so Mary, John, and I spend most evenings studying. This is one of those times none of our parents push us to go to Mass, our education is just as important as our religion. Paul is oddly absent from our sessions, and I suspect I know why, but there's never a good time to question him about it.

Sunday rolls around like it does every week, and when I pull into the church parking lot, a sense of foreboding washes over me. I can't explain it even if I tried.

"What's wrong?" Mary asks me from the passenger seat.

"Nothing."

"Matt, we're twins," she huffs out. "I can tell when something's wrong with you. Besides, you've got that crease between your eyes, the one we both get when we're worried about something."

Heaving a sigh, I rest my forehead against the steering wheel so my face is hidden. Mary's right. She, more than anyone on the planet, can read me like an open book. As frustrating as it is, I can't say that I hate it. She's my twin and for some reason, it brings me comfort knowing that she gets me.

"Hack anything lately?" I ask her in an effort to change the subject.

It's her turn to huff. "We're talking about you," she snips as she throws her door open.

I quickly follow after her and grab her arm to swing her around when I catch up. Mary glares at me, but I don't miss that telltale sign she was so quick to point out.

"You've got the crease too," I accuse, tapping a finger between her eyes. "What are you worried about?"

She glances around the lot as more cars start to trickle in, and then she grabs my hand and practically drags me the rest of the way to the door.

"What's going on, Mary?" I ask, my worry now compounding.

"Shhh, not here."

My twin drags me down a series of halls but comes to such a sudden stop that I run into her back. Her body goes rigid, and her eyes are fixated on something in front of us. I lift my head to see what it is and freeze.

At the end of the hall, John is looking through the small window of a door. His face is red, but that's not the alarming part. No, what has us both frozen is that he's yanking at his hair with both hands and grunting incoherently.

I race around Mary to see what has my friend so upset, and the minute he feels the vibration of my footsteps, John turns. The anguished look on his face tells me everything I need to know. There's no need for me to look in the room, but I do anyway, in the vain hope that I'm wrong.

"Fuck," I whisper harshly when I see the same thing I saw a week ago: Paul being hurt by Deacon Block. Only this time, they aren't alone. Standing in the corner, with a sadistic grin on his face and his dick in his hand, is Father Brine.

"Jesus Christ."

I whip my head to the side to see Mary staring at the same horrific scene I'm looking at. And despite the shock in her tone, I can't help but notice that she doesn't look shocked. It doesn't take a genius to figure out why… or in our case, it doesn't take more than a twin.

"You knew about this," I seethe.

Mary lifts her eyes to mine and tears begin to form. "I hacked the security feed for the church. I didn't mean to, but I was bored and…" She shrugs, knowing there's no need to try to explain to me the why of what she does. My sister is brilliant and school is a cakewalk for her. And when her mind isn't challenged, she challenges it.

John is still losing his shit, but he's getting louder. We need to take this conversation somewhere else. I tap him on the shoulder and duck out of the way when his fist flies at me. I hold my hands up in front of me and within seconds, John's demeanor relaxes slightly.

"We're gonna make this right," I sign. I don't bother saying the words out loud because Mary also knows American Sign Language, or ASL. "We have to make this right."

"How?" John's hand shakes.

That's the million dollar question, isn't it?

"I don't—"

The door opens, cutting me off. Father Brine and Deacon Block give us each a pointed look before turning to Paul, who's still inside the room pulling up his pants.

"We'll continue our lessons tomorrow," the Deacon says.

Rage boils my blood and courses in my veins to burn a torturous path through my body. I lunge at Deacon Block, but John wraps his arm around my waist to stop me. John drags me into the room and slams the door, cutting off the laughter of the two most unholy holy men I've ever met.

John shoves me into a chair, holding me there until I stop struggling. Once I do, he squats in front of me and fixes his dark penetrating eyes on mine.

"This isn't about you or me," he signs. "It's about him."

John points toward Paul and that's when I notice that Mary's in the room. She's quietly talking to our friend although I can't make out what she's saying. I nod my head at John to let him know I agree.

Rising from the chair, I walk toward Paul and Mary. Paul's eyes are hard, unforgiving, but they're also dim like the light has been snuffed out.

Fuck that!

I rest my hand on his shoulder, ignoring how he startles at the contact, and squeeze.

"We'll fix this," I promise him. "They will pay."

John grunts, which tells me Mary must have

signed for him because I didn't. Several minutes pass by, the tension in the room a tangible thing.

Finally, Paul locks eyes with me and lifts his hands. "The only way to fix this is to take them down. And then we get the fuck out of here and away from the church."

"I'm in," Mary quickly says.

I look at John and he gives a curt nod.

"Done," I finally respond.

For the next twenty minutes we plot and plan, excitement building with the notion that we can stop these two men and others like them. I don't know if we can pull it off, but we're sure as hell going to try.

When it's time for confession, we each go our separate ways. I have no clue what the others will confess to, if anything. But it doesn't matter. I'll confess all of our sins… even the ones yet to be committed.

Once I'm in the all too familiar small booth, I become aware of things I never would've given a second thought to. I know it's Father Brine on the other side of the screen because of his cologne, which does not mix well with the smell of frankincense permeating the air. I know it's him by the way he clears his throat, waiting for me to begin.

But I make him wait. The sound of rustling fabric, of him swallowing several times like he's uncomfortable, mixes with my heartbeat thundering against my ribs. Every single one of my senses is on high alert.

I recite the seven deadly sins in my head: sloth, greed, envy, lust, wrath, gluttony, and pride. For some reason, they're knocking around in my brain, refusing to be ignored. Father Brine is guilty of them all. He preaches against them, dishes out Hail Marys like the prayer is a pill one can swallow to rid them of the sins they commit. But does he ever atone for his sins?

Highly unlikely.

Father Brine clears his throat again. I grin. He wants me to confess? Fine, I'll confess. But something tells me he's not going to like it.

I take a deep breath, and my grin widens.

"Forgive me Father, for I am going to sin."

CHAPTER ONE

CECE

Twelve years later…

"Mom, I'm here!"

The bell above the door jingles as I stride inside our shop, The Naughty/Nice Boutique.

"About time. You're only five minutes late today. I'm impressed."

I laugh to myself as I lock the door behind me and head toward the back of the store. I'm always fifteen minutes early for everything so arriving five minutes late will have mom teasing me all morning.

"The new styles arrived today. Let's try and get everything put out on the new display models before we open," Mom tells me as I take my purse and hang it on the office door.

"That works for me. I can't wait to see if these new styles are popular with our regulars."

We both carry a box toward the display and get started. Mom and I opened the boutique after I received my business degree last year. Our combined fashion sense and my business mind together came up with The Naughty/Nice Boutique. The women's clothing slash lingerie store is our baby. The naughty side features black tones with ice blue and white accessories to highlight the more risqué clothing. The nice side features white tones with ice blue and black accessories to highlight the more women's professional clothing. Anything from jeans and hoodies to cocktail dresses and pant suits. We only sell items we can get from size triple zero to plus sizes, so finding your perfect size isn't a factor. Every woman has the right to feel sexy in the clothes she wears and what she wears underneath.

Today's shipment consists of lacy boy shorts in five different colors for the nice side, lace crotchless thongs for the naughty side, and matching bras for both. What girl doesn't like a matching bra and panty set? I grab the last pair of panties to put on the shelf as Mom unlocks the door.

Looking around the shop, I can't help but think about how far we've come the last eight years. It was hard coming to grips with Dad's death and opening up to Mom about it. We went to family counseling to deal with our grief, which made a huge difference. Mom and I grew closer, and now she is one of my best friends, along with Carmella, who I've known since grade school.

When Mom and I came up with the idea to open the boutique, it seemed like the perfect thing for us to do together. Between my business degree and Mom's fashion sense, we've built quite a legacy. Looking around, I'm incredibly proud of all we've accomplished.

"Are you ready for your camping trip with Carmella?" Mom's question drags me out of my reminiscing.

"Oh, you mean our glamping trip?" I roll my eyes. "You know I'm going to ask you to borrow the RV. There is no way in hell me or Carmella will sleep in a tent on the ground."

"You can borrow the RV if you promise to send me pictures so I can live vicariously through you." Mom tries to keep a straight face, but ends up laughing at her little joke. "I'll stay here and make sure we still have a business for you to come back to."

The Naughty/Nice Boutique is one of the busiest stores in our little town. People drive from Las Vegas to Boulder City just to shop here. We have one helluva reputation. Sure, we're not immune to hard times, just like every business owner, but we stay up-to-date on the latest trends and marketing, so I'm not too worried. My dad was a meticulous records and finance keeper, and his knowledge rubbed off on me. We were also able to use his life insurance payout to put me through business school, buy the building, and have the start-up costs for the boutique. Two years later, we're in the black. We aren't rich by any means, but we live comfortably enough.

The bell rings to announce our first customer of the day. I'm not surprised when I look up and see Mary, one of our regulars. I grin as she walks toward me.

"Damn, you're out early," I tease.

"Things to do, people to see." She pulls the fabric of her tee away from her body, no doubt to cool off. "It's hotter than a devil's tit out there and it's only ten in the morning! Why the hell I continue to live in this godforsaken state is beyond me. I need seasons! I should move to Oregon," Mary rants. Mom coughs to cover her laugh, but Mary notices right away. "I know, I know. *It's a dry heat.* What the fuck ever. It's hot! Oh, sorry Mrs. Parker."

"Mary, I've told you a million times, call me Barb," Mom says, exasperated. "Cece, tell her to call me Barb."

Mom hates being called Mrs. Parker. Not because she didn't love my dad, they had a timeless romance that every girl dreams of. Mom just hates being called that because it makes her feel old and as she says she has a lot more miles left on her tires.

"Ooooh, new stuff!" Mary ignores her and runs over to the new display.

I shrug and follow her over to the new items. Mary is one of our best customers. She is a big believer of supporting local businesses and avoids big box stores whenever she can. Big corporations are the bane of her existence and they are greedy bastards....her words not mine. She normally buys more comfortable clothing, like oversized t-shirts and yoga capris, so I'm shocked when she asks what I would recommend for a club.

"One of my friends is insisting I go with them to Vegas tonight to a new night club," she explains, as she rolls her eyes. "Ugh, I just want to stay home and veg but no, I have to be a good friend and drive to Vegas for overpriced drinks, stupid valet parking... you know they'll scratch my car and that'll just piss me off, and did I mention crappy techno music? I have nothing to wear. You have to help me. I'm begging you." She's rambling so I decide to take pity on her before she's on the floor groveling.

"First, if I was going somewhere I didn't really

want to go, I'd tell that friend that *she* is footing the bill. *She* drives, pays for valet, and even buys the first three rounds of drinks." I look over at her and see her nodding. "Second, we find you a badass outfit."

"Not too much skin though but yes, definitely badass." Her eyes light up.

"I know just the outfit."

I've always had the feeling that there's more to Mary than meets the eye, but I keep my comments to myself. Mary is beautiful, with her purple-streaked black shoulder-length hair and huge hazel eyes. Underneath those oversized shirts you can tell she has a killer body.

I decide to pull out a pair of black skinny jeans and an off-the-shoulder emerald green shirt to play off her features. Not to be out done, Mom hands her one of our new lacy lavender strapless bras and matching panties. She takes the clothes I picked out and makes her way back to the dressing rooms.

Mom whispers to me, "I think there is more to Mary than we know."

"I was thinking the same thing."

After a few minutes, the door swings open and Mary strides out to stand in front of the three-way mirrors with a stunned expression. "I look fucking hot!"

"Yes, you do!" I say laughing.

"Oh shut up. You two are miracle workers. I love this outfit, especially the pretty lingerie." She turns to walk back into the dressing room, but pauses with her hand on the doorknob. "Hey, can you grab me a couple pairs of the yoga pants and t-shirts I normally buy?"

"You know I can." I roll my eyes. "I'll grab them and meet you at the front."

I make my way over and pick out the items she wants and wait for her at the register. Mary comes out of the dressing room and walks up to pay.

"I don't suppose you have any shoe recommendations?"

"We just got a new shipment in that will be perfect." I laugh at her. I run to the storeroom and come back and slip the shoebox over the counter to her. "Let me know what you think."

"Yes, yes, yes, this is exactly what I am talking about!" she yells as she pulls out the shoes. Mom is standing behind her laughing.

"What? Why can't she be comfortable and sexy?" I say. I picked a pair of vintage Havana tennis shoes that are black with sparkling emerald stars on the side.

"This is so fucking perfect. I'll be more comfortable in tennis shoes than those neck killers women wear to look taller. I'm already five foot eight, I don't need to be any taller."

I ring up her purchases and wave to her as she runs out the door, promising she will tell us all the details next month when she comes back in for more. The morning continues on with customers coming in steadily. Around lunch time I offer to go and get some food from the deli across the street.

"Cece!"

I don't even have to look back to know it is Carmella yelling at me. I keep walking, knowing she will follow me to the deli. We go through this song and dance almost everyday. "Cece! Don't ignore me hooker!"

I try not to laugh when she catches up to me.

"Why don't you ever fucking wait for me?" She acts like she's mad but I know better.

"You know you love to give everyone a show running down the road in your heels and skirt… fucking diva." I look her over, and sure enough, she's in three-inch heels and a pencil skirt with a v-neck sleeveless satin shirt. How she manages to run in that getup without breaking a sweat, or her neck, baffles me.

Carmella is five foot five with beautiful Hispanic features. She has deep mahogany hair and rich brown eyes. She's currently working as a legal aid for Jim Staten, Boulder City's most used attorney.

"Whatever slut. You're just waiting for me to fall and break my neck," she huffs.

"If you fell and broke your neck, what would Mom and I do for entertainment?"

"You are an evil, evil woman," she says once we're inside. "What are we having today?"

"Mom wants the club, and I think I'll stick with the turkey avocado." We get in line and wait to order. "What about you, Princess?"

"I think I'll get the club too. Are we going back to Naughty/Nice to eat?" she asks as we step up to order.

"Nah, Mom told me she would handle the store for a bit as long as I brought her back a sandwich and some chips." I finish ordering our food and follow Carmella to a seat by the window.

"So, I've been thinking. The bar exam is in two—"

"Oh no you don't. You promised you would take a week off from studying before you take the bar and go camping with me," I interject. "You will not try to get out of this or I will sic mom on you."

"Okay, okay… put away your claws," she concedes. "You know I hate it when you pit your mom against me."

The last time I had to get Mom on her case, it was because Carmella was on a seventy-two hour studying bender and was so exhausted she was hallucinating. Mom came to our apartment and handled the situation the way only a mother could. Ever since then, Carmella knows I mean business when I threaten her with Mom.

"I do know, which is why I still do it," I tease her. "Anyway, we will drive to Mom's house bright and early on Saturday morning and head out. Mom is helping get the RV stocked and ready on Friday, so I won't interrupt your last minute cram session."

"You know me too well."

"Fucking right I do."

CHAPTER TWO

SOUL

"THIS SHIT NEVER GETS OLD."

Paul 'Malice' Grandon, the Vice President of Saints Purgatory MC, straddles his Harley and fires her up. For a man who harbors so much rage, he's surprisingly calm after we finish a job. Probably because, like the rest of us, he's drunk on the knowledge that the world has one less fuckstick wasting air.

"Let's hope it never does."

As the President of Saints Purgatory, I lead my brothers in the fight against evil. We see it, we hear it, we become it, and then we fucking purge it. It's been this way since the night the last of us turned eighteen and we eliminated Father Brine and Deacon Block. The look of unfettered satisfaction on Malice's face now matches the one he wore back then.

I'd tease him about it, but the last time a brother did that, they wound up in the hospital with a broken arm, two fractured ribs, and a busted nose. I may be one of Malice's oldest friends, but even I'm not immune to the demon lurking beneath his skin.

Lost in thought, I miss our Enforcer straddling his Harley, so when he revs the engine, I'm startled and whip my head around to glare at him.

"Don't look at me like that," Grim signs, his fingers moving swiftly. John Dunn is a giant of a man who doesn't let the fact that he can't hear stop him from leaving a path of destruction in his wake. "You should be more aware of your surroundings."

I flip Grim off and then begin to sign as I speak. "We need to head to Purgatory. Rogue is already being a pussy bitch because he had to cover tonight."

Purgatory is our club-owned bar, and Rogue is the club's treasurer. Rogue does *not* like being cooped up inside. He prefers the freedom of riding out in 'the great wide open' as he puts it.

"Then what are we waiting for?" Spike, our Road Captain asks. The chains he always wears clang as he straddles his Harley. "Let's roll."

Malice and I simultaneously rev our engines before we tear across the desert. Spike, Grim, and Thorn follow behind us. Two of our prospects, Justin and Asher, are staying behind to bury the body, and Grim will ride back out tomorrow to make sure they didn't fuck up.

It takes almost three hours to get to Purgatory. We're always more careful of our speed after a job in an effort to limit the risk of drawing attention to us. None of us like the slower pace, but it's necessary and has kept us on the outside of a jail cell.

After parking in the back lot, we all head inside. Grim makes a beeline for the front to take up his post as unofficial bouncer. We don't need a bouncer as bikers tend to be scary enough to keep the bullshit to a minimum, but Grim insists on standing guard.

Malice and I slide into the corner booth. Even as busy as the bar is, it was empty because everyone knows it belongs to us. Thorn and Spike go straight to the bar, downing the shots Rogue hands them before he stalks toward us.

"About fucking time you got here," Rogue shouts to be heard over the music as he sets four full shot glasses and two half-full whiskey glasses on the table.

"You're just pissed because you didn't get to hurt anyone tonight," Malice taunts before downing his first shot.

"Damn right I am." Rogue levels his gaze on me. "We need reliable staff, Prez. I'm gettin' all twitchy being in here."

"How the fuck did you ever work in an office?"

Rogue was an accountant in his previous life.

Suits and ties every Monday thru Friday. Fortunately for us, he's Grim's cousin and assisted Grim with some *unsavory* tasks while the rest of us who grew up together entered the military. When we returned, Rogue was one of us and the suits and ties were enthusiastically burned to ash.

"I jumped at the chance to participate in murder and mayhem so that should tell you something," he deadpans.

"Yo, Rogue!" Thorn hollers from the bar. "Quit slackin' and get your ass back to work."

I cough to cover my laugh when Rogue's expression becomes homicidal. Lifting my hands in mock surrender, I say, "Interview for new bartenders, and I'll fire the others once we have replacements."

Rogue nods before retreating back to the bar, where Thorn and Spike continue to antagonize him. Outsiders would look at the three of them and probably worry about Rogue's ability to handle Thorn and Spike, but then outsiders have never seen Rogue in violent action. Bastard can take care of himself, even with the Clark Kent vibe he's got going on.

Shifting my attention to the small dance floor, I stretch my arm across the back of the black leather booth. A few women are dancing, but only one catches my eye. She isn't exactly a take home to mama type, but she's perfect for a take home for the night type.

My cock stirs to life as I watch her, and when it becomes painful against my zipper, I adjust myself.

"You're a dirty fucker, ya know that?"

I arch a brow at Malice as I tip my glass to my lips before returning my stare to the half-naked chick writhing to the music. The top-shelf whiskey goes down smooth and is just what I need after a long day.

"What the hell's that supposed to mean?" I question, although I have a pretty good idea.

Malice points to the woman I've been eye-fucking. "There is no way in hell you're looking at her and not imagining all the ways you—"

"Do *not* finish that sentence."

Malice and I turn to take in my sister, who I somehow missed walking up to our booth. She smacks Malice upside the head before sliding in beside him. My twin is the only person safe from Malice's temper, and she takes advantage of that particular perk every chance she gets.

Malice smirks at her. "What sentence?" He tilts his head. "The one where I give your brother a hard time because he's looking at that chick like he wants to bend her over a table and fuck her five ways to Sunday?"

"I don't know why you bother, Mary," I say. "You know he's—" I press my lips together when she narrows her eyes at me. "Sorry… Jezebel," I correct. For as long as I can remember, she's hated her given name, so when she started hacking, she took on her online handle.

Jezebel beams a smile at me. "That's better."

"Fucking hell, Soul," Malice gripes. "You have no problems giving orders, wreaking havoc, and basically being an all around master at all things brutal, but Jez gives you one sharp look and you turn into a eunuch."

My sister bumps him with her shoulder. "It's a twin thing. You wouldn't understand."

Malice twists to face her, but before he can get a word out, I slam my glass down on the table.

"What are you doing here, Jez?" I ask.

"Since when do I need a reason?"

"You don't. It was just a question."

She rolls her eyes. "I'm meeting someone."

Arching a brow, I lean forward. "Someone?"

"Yeah, someone," she says evasively. "So, how was work today?"

"Changing the subject isn't gonna work, Jez," Malice says. "Who are you meeting?"

If I didn't know any better, I'd be concerned about how protective my brothers are toward her, but she's off-limits and they all know I'd kill 'em if they touched her.

Jezebel huffs out a breath. "He's just a friend."

"He?"

"Yes, *he*," she snaps. "I'm twenty-eight, not twelve, so quit acting like you have to watch out for me like a little kid."

Malice lowers his gaze to take in her outfit and then looks at me and shakes his head. "No way in hell is she wearing that for 'just a friend'."

"Ya know what?" my sister says as she stands up. "I'll meet him outside, and we'll go somewhere else."

Before she can walk away, I lean out of the booth and grab her arm. "Sit down." Jezebel stares at me, but does sit. "Look, you wouldn't be meeting this *friend* here, in *our* bar, unless you wanted him to be seen. That tells me you're not sure about him and wanted us for backup." Her forehead wrinkles. "And *that*," I say, pointing at her tell-tale sign of worry. "Confirms my assessment. So, who is he?"

She crosses her arms over her chest, pushing up her cleavage in a way that makes a brother very uncomfortable. "Answer my question first."

"Work was fine. The job's complete." I lift my now empty glass. "Hence the alcohol. Who. Is. He?"

"Jesus you're impossible." She grabs Malice's whiskey glass out of his hand and downs the remaining liquor before setting it on the table in front of him. He glares at her, but she carries on as if she doesn't notice. And trust me, she notices. "I met him online in a hacker chat room. His name is Dan, and I did a thorough background check before agreeing to meet him in person so you can keep your weapons put away."

"Dan?" Malice asks, still glaring at her about his alcohol.

"That's what I said."

Malice turns to me. "The dude's name is Dan. He probably drives a Volvo and drinks warm milk to fall asleep." He snorts. "We have nothing to worry about."

Jezebel opens her mouth, but before she can get a word out, Grim steps up to the table. He hitches his thumb over his shoulder toward the door and signs to me, "He says he's here for her." He nods toward Jez.

I look in the direction of the entrance and see a forty-something man, wearing khakis and a button-down, craning his neck to find my twin. I lower my eyes to take in his shoes and smirk when I see loafers.

"Yep," I sign back. "That's Dan. He's Jezebel's date."

Seeing what I signed, Jezebel's eyes widen, and she whirls around to take in her 'friend'. Her shoulders stiffen, and several long seconds pass before she turns back around. Grim faces her so she can see his hands.

"Need me to take care of him for you?"

"I'm never going to live this down, am I?" She doesn't look at anyone other than Grim as she signs, but she speaks so we can hear her.

Grim shakes his head.

"Not a chance," I say.

"I've got material for months with this one," Malice jokes.

"Get rid of him," she instructs Grim.

Our Enforcer walks away, but none of us pay attention to how he handles Dan. As long as Dan doesn't become a problem, he's relatively safe.

Jezebel's face scrunches up as she props her chin in her hand. It would be so easy to give her a hard time about this, but the wrinkled forehead tells me she's beating herself up enough without us adding fuel to the fire.

"Any new jobs for us?" Malice asks, no doubt sensing the same thing I am. He's a dick, not a monster.

Jezebel shakes her head. "You know you two are the first to know when I have something."

Rather than respond, Malice lifts his hand and signals to Rogue to bring us another round of drinks.

The rest of the night passes in a blur. Brothers come and go, Malice and Jez get hammered, and I return my attention to the chick on the dance floor.

As image after image flies through my mind of all the ways I would fuck her, I can't help but think Malice was right.

I am a dirty fucker.

CHAPTER THREE

CECE

"ARE YOU FUCKING SERIOUS RIGHT NOW?"

Carmella is currently giving Mom the highlights of our camping trip. I don't normally care if my mom knows all the nitty-gritty details of our adventures, but we don't need to rehash the *incident*.

"And of course, she can't pick the easy trail… no, Ms. Adventure over here picks the harder trail," she continues.

"I don't think Mom needs to know *everything*, Mel."

"Your mom has a right to know," Carmella insists. "So here we are, walking a four-mile hike to White Owl Canyon because you know, we are 'bird watchers' now, and Cece is pointing out shit like she thinks she is Coyote Peterson." Mel struggles to catch her breath as she continues. "She's so busy looking up and instead of watching her feet, she trips over a tumbleweed, stumbles in slow motion, arms flailing like the wacky inflatable-arm man, and lands on top of a shrub."

"I'll gut you," I threaten.

Embarrassed, I duck my head, but can't help giggling at Carmella as she demonstrates my fall onto the loveseat by the dressing rooms. Mom doesn't even try to hide her laughter.

"Oh, it gets better. Cece starts screaming at the top of her lungs, *'Help me! The bush is up my ass'*."

Mom starts clapping at Carmella's theatrics as Mel gets up and bows in our direction.

"I'm pretty fucking sure I didn't say the bush was up my ass, diva."

"Hooker, you said it. "It's not my problem you were too busy freaking out to remember." She flips her hair over her shoulder. "My work here is done. I've gotta head to the office. You ladies have a fantastic day."

Carmella winks at me as she walks out the door, and I work on plotting my revenge.

"So… You and bush, huh?" Mom is still laughing. "Bet it didn't even buy you dinner first."

"Ha, ha, ha. You and Carmella are so fucking funny. You know I'll get you both back for this, right?"

"I look forward to it."

I unlock the door to the boutique and settle in for

the day. It's Monday so I'm not surprised that we aren't super busy. Mom decides to tackle our online orders, while I straighten up some displays. When I look at Mom a few minutes later, she's shaking her head and rubbing her temples.

"You, okay?"

"Yeah, I have a headache all of a sudden."

"Mom, I told you, you need to go to the damn doctor for your physical."

"I know. It's scheduled for next week. I wanted to wait 'til you got back from your trip," she explains. "You know I hate leaving the others here without one of us just in case there's an issue."

I understand where she's coming from but I have been on her for weeks to get checked out. She's been having issues with blurred vision and headaches popping up out of the blue. I've been concerned but didn't want to push her either. I walk over to the counter where she's putting together the last order. The package is addressed to 'Jezebel', who's been a long-standing customer for over a year. A last name has never been included on her monthly orders, and the only address used is a PO Box. She has great taste and tends to buy some of our more risqué items.

"Mom, why don't you go sit down or head on home? I'll finish up the order and wait for Gus to do the pickup." Our regular UPS guy runs his route like clockwork, and he won't be here for a while.

"No, it's okay. I took some Tylenol and just need it to kick in."

"Are you sure? We only have an hour left. I can handle closing up."

"Cece, I'm fine. Let me–"

Mom crumbles to the ground.

"Mom!"

I crouch down beside her, pull my phone out of my pocket, and dial 911 when she's unresponsive. While I'm answering the dispatcher's questions, I continue to try and wake Mom up.

"Mom, Mom, please wake up… You're scaring me. Wake up, damn it!"

I don't know how much time lapses before I am startled by a police officer and pulled aside as two EMTs kneel beside Mom.

"What happened?"

"I don't know. One minute we were talking, and then she just collapsed. She was complaining about a headache before she went down."

"Let's start an IV and get her on the gurney. We're going to head to Boulder City Memorial," the first EMT tells me. "You can meet us there."

"I want to go with her!"

"I'm sorry, we know this is hard, but we can't let you ride with us."

"Ma'am, we have to go. Meet us at the hospital when you can," the second EMT starts walking the gurney toward the door.

As they load Mom into the ambulance, I grab her hand and tell her I love her. I run back into the store and lock up before I race to my car, praying she'll be okay.

Two Weeks Later

Two words.

Exactly two words that will forever haunt me.

Brain aneurysm.

One minute we're talking and twenty minutes later, Mom codes and is pronounced dead on arrival at the hospital. The doctors explained that there wasn't anything they could've done. There was only a fifty-fifty chance of her surviving.

"Girl, I know you're grieving but you *have* to get out of this apartment."

Carmella has walked on eggshells around me since the funeral. I know she's worried that if she doesn't start pushing me to get out of bed I will continue to wallow. I am grieving, but that's not what is wrong. I haven't been honest with Carmella because I don't want her to worry, but I've felt sick.

"Back the fuck off."

"Look, I just want to he—"

"I know I need to get the fuck out of here," I interrupt her. "I don't fucking feel right."

"What's the matter?" Now concern mars her face, which is exactly what I was trying to avoid. First, it was pity and now, concern, neither of which I want to deal with.

"It's fine, I have a headache. My body hurts, and I am so tired." I rub my temples trying to relieve some pressure.

"Why didn't you say something? How long has this been going on?"

"Started a couple of days after Mom passed away."

"And you're sure it's not just grief getting you down?"

"This is one of the reasons why I didn't tell you. Poor little Cece doesn't know the difference between grief and being sick." I roll my eyes.

"Hooker please, if you're sick, you're sick. I'm

sorry you think I'm not a good enough friend to confide in." Carmella shakes her head. Now I just feel like an ungrateful bitch. "Do you want me to take you to the doctor?"

"I was going to go in the morning if I wasn't feeling better, but this headache only seems to be getting worse."

"We can blame your brain for your bitchiness then." Carmella laughs and waves her hand toward the bathroom. "Go get ready, and I will drive your ass to the clinic."

"Thanks. And Mel? You *are* my best friend. I don't know what I'd do without you." I give her a quick hug and walk into the bathroom.

"And don't you forget it!" she calls out as the door clicks shut.

An hour later we're walking into the urgent care clinic at Boulder City Memorial. Our town is small so the hospital, ER, and urgent clinic are all in the same building. It's a short wait until I am called back by the nurse who starts taking my vitals and asking me what's going on.

After I explain my symptoms, the nurse says, "Dr. Franklin will be right in. He's head of the ER, so you're in good hands."

As soon as the nurse opens the door, the doctor walks through. He appears to be in his mid-thirties, has blond hair, and a swimmer's build. Even though I don't feel well, I can appreciate he's a good-looking man.

"I'm Dr. Franklin," he says, shaking my hand. "What seems to be the problem tonight, Ms. Parker?"

"I've had a headache, some body aches, and I've been really tired."

He glances at the tablet in his hand. "Your vitals look good and no fever." He lifts his head. "When did you start experiencing the symptoms?"

"In the last week or so."

After looking at the chart again, he locks eyes with me. "Could you be pregnant?"

"Um… no, you have to have sex to get pregnant," I glance over at Carmella who's trying hard not to laugh. "Not that I don't have sex. Damn it! That's not what I meant."

My face heats and Dr. Franklin simply chuckles at my mouth's inability to shut up.

"Any major stressors in the last week?"

"Her mom passed away two weeks ago," Carmella interjects before I can respond.

"Ah, well that makes more sense then," he begins. "You're just grieving."

"I don't think I'm *just grieving*. I lost my dad when I was younger so I know how that feels."

"How old were you when you lost your dad?"

"Fifteen."

"And now you're… twenty-three, twenty-four?" he asks.

"Twenty-four, so?"

"Well Ms. Parker, that was seven years ago."

"And?"

"Ms. Parker, the emotions of a teenage girl versus a grown woman are going to manifest differently. Your mom was also your last living parent so obviously, you are going to have a stronger reaction."

Dr. Franklin just became Dr. Fucktard. Is he really trying to convince me that I don't know the difference between grief and being sick?

"I'm sorry, but I think I know the difference, *Dr. Franklin*."

"*Ms. Parker,* I am the one with the medical degree and the head of the ER. I'm pretty sure I know what's going on. My suggestion is for you to go home, fill the prescription I'm going to give you, and join a support group for people who have lost their parents."

"Are you fucking kidding me? You're not even going to run any tests?" I start shaking.

"Dr. Franklin, I believe what my friend is trying to say is that she would feel more comfortable with your diagnosis if you ran some tests," Carmella says, trying to diffuse the situation.

"I'm telling you that we are busy tonight and don't have time to run unnecessary tests because *your friend* doesn't want to deal with her emotions." Dr. Franklin says and refocuses on me. "I'm sorry for your loss but in my *expert* opinion, you're suffering from grief. If you'll excuse me, I have other patients to see."

"Are you fucking kidding me?" I yell. "Did that just really happen?"

"Unfortunately, yes." Carmella stares at the door with a dumbfounded expression.

We pause our conversation when there's a knock on the door, and the nurse from earlier walks in.

"Dr. Franklin asked me to give this to you. It's a prescription for Percocet, it will help with the pain and hopefully, let you get some sleep." She hands me the paper. "Oh, and here is the number to a support group. I'm very sorry for your loss."

I grab the prescription out of her hand and look at the card for the support group.

"Tell Dr. Fucktard I don't need a support group," I say as Carmella and I walk out the door.

CHAPTER FOUR

SOUL

As I roll over to turn off my alarm, I groan. I've never been a morning person… even the military didn't fix that for me. After I kick my legs free from the comforter, I get up and stride into the bathroom to take a leak.

The stone floor is cold, and at times like this, I wish we would've put in heated floors when we did the renovations on the decommissioned government site. Our needs are met, and then some if I'm being honest, but there are some luxuries that never even crossed my mind.

I brush my teeth, take a quick shower, and then air dry while I dig through a laundry basket to find something clean to wear. There's nothing on the club's agenda today, other than the weekly church session.

Once I'm dressed, I trudge down the hall and pound on the door of each of the club officers.

They're the only ones required to attend the weekly meeting, and if we're going to start on time, they need to get their asses up.

"It's too fucking early," Malice shouts a second after I bang on his door.

"Too fucking bad," I yell back.

Given half a chance, Malice will continue to argue, so I continue through the long corridor. The Saints Purgatory MC clubhouse is underground in the middle of the desert, and it is beyond huge. There are sections we haven't even begun to use, but I know we'll fill them as we expand.

When I step into the kitchen ten minutes later, my senses are overwhelmed by the scent of Abyss, our secretary, cooking. The man is good at every fucking thing he does, and a genius with food.

"Coffee's fresh," he says without looking up from the stove. "Breakfast should be done in a minute."

I step up beside him and inhale deeply. Abyss smacks my knuckles with his wooden spoon when I reach out to grab a piece of bacon.

"Dammit," I mutter. "I swear there isn't a person in the world who would know I'm the president of this club if they saw how you treated me."

Abyss twists to look at me and grins. "You might be my president, but you'd fucking starve if it weren't for me."

Asshole's right, so I keep my mouth shut and pour myself a cup of coffee. The first sip is hot, but it gives me the caffeine jolt I need to function.

"My mouth started watering down the hall," Thorn says when he walks in. "Jesus, what are you making?" he asks Abyss as he leans over his shoulder to get a whiff.

"Whatever it is, it smells better than any pussy I could bury my face in," Rogue comments when he steps through the door.

"Damn right it does," Abyss says proudly.

"Seriously, A... What is it?" Thorn asks again.

"A giant omelet with cheddar and swiss cheese, peppers, onions, and steak tips. I also fried up some bacon and sausage." Abyss slides a giant platter closer to the stove so he can transfer the food to it. "If you want toast or anything, you're on your own."

The four of us take a seat at the table and dig in, not bothering to wait for the others. It's common knowledge that if you snooze, you lose where Abyss's cooking is concerned. It isn't long before Malice and Grim walk in, but by the time Spike arrives fifteen minutes later, the only thing that remains is sausage. And Spike hates sausage.

"You're a bunch of fucking cock suckers," he snaps.

I push up from my chair and walk toward our

road captain to slap him on the back. "You know the rules. Last one in, last one out."

"That's what she said," Spike jokes, waggling his eyebrows. "Hence why I wasn't here earlier. Nikki just wouldn't let—"

A bang on the table has both Spike and me whirling to face Grim, who has a habit of using his fists on solid surfaces to get people's attention.

"No one gives a shit about which wiener cleaner you used last night," Grim signs.

Spike levels his gaze on the others at the table. "Which one of you was signing for him?" he asks.

Malice tips his chin. "That'd be me."

"Must have been some magic pussy because you're forgetting all the rules this morning," I say to Spike. "Fifty dollar fine due to Rogue at the beginning of church."

"Seriously?"

"If you speak when Grim is in the room, you sign," I remind him. "That's been the rule from day one, so don't act like you didn't know."

Spike pulls his wallet out of his back pocket, causing the chain connecting it to his jeans to rattle. He slaps a few bills on the table in front of Rogue. "There, it's paid. Now get the hell out of here so I can clean up after you sorry sacks of shit."

"Church in twenty," I say as I walk out of the

kitchen and head down the corridor that leads to the business wing of the clubhouse.

There are five main wings to our underground fortress, and three of those break off into multiple corridors. Two are for the living quarters, which house patched members, prospects, and club bunnies. Prospects and bunnies share a wing, and each individual bedroom has an attached bathroom. They're more like suites.

The corridor housing club members also has a separate space for our theater room and a smaller common area. There's a wing for business, which houses the room for church, offices for the club officers, our security rooms, and a conference room. The fourth wing houses the medical facilities, as well as a full-sized gym. The last wing houses all of the unused space and breaks off into four other corridors.

The center of the site is divided into three sections: main common area with a bar, pool tables, couches, and a large television mounted on the wall, the kitchen and dining area, and a more relaxed area where members, prospects, and bunnies can visit with anyone who's cleared to enter the site.

Like I said, the clubhouse is huge.

I enter the sanctuary, which is what Grim dubbed the room where we hold church, and flip on the lights. Saints Purgatory club colors, black and purple, grace every inch of the space, from the ceilings to the floor. A skull with roses and curlicues covers the expanse of one wall, while our motto, *See evil, Hear evil, Become evil, Purge evil,* is painted in large blocky lettering on the opposite wall.

My boots thud on the shiny black floor, which is identical to the rest of the clubhouse floors. Just as I'm about to take my seat at the head of the table, the snap of a lock disengaging alerts me that I'm about to have company.

Malice, Rogue, and Abyss stroll in and take their seats. The four of us remain quiet as we wait on the other officers. It doesn't take but a few minutes for them to arrive, and once they do, I call order.

I stand up so it's easier to sign while I talk. "Spike, that kitchen better be clean."

"It is, Prez," he assures me. "For a bunch of rude assholes, you're all surprisingly clean." He shrugs, then takes a bite of the PopTart in his hand. I raise a brow. "What? I'm hungry," he says around a mouthful of pastry.

All I can do is shake my head at him. While weapons and cell phones are not permitted in this room, there is no rule about food and drink. I'm fairly certain I'd have a mutiny on my hands if I instituted that as a policy.

"Thanks for that… I think." I turn to Malice to begin the reporting of each officer. "We'll start with you and an update on the prospects?"

"Jacob and Zach are doing great, and both are eager to please. I'm pretty sure I could hand them each a grenade and tell them to blow up the white house and they'd do it."

"What about Justin?" Thorn asks.

"Fucker needs to be kept busy. He's at the point where he needs to start going on runs, but I'm afraid he'd get too distracted by his damn Zippo."

"He still flicking that stupid thing open and shut twenty-four-seven?" Grim signs.

Malice nods. "How he ever gets laid is beyond me. Dude can't focus for shit and no bitch in her right mind is gonna play seconds to a lighter."

"If he can't hack it, then give him the boot," I order. "He's got a week to prove he can focus. Since we're light on jobs at the moment, make shit up for him to do. Test him… and don't be fucking nice about it."

Malice grins. "I can do that."

"Good." I face Grim and Thorn. "Any threats we need to know about, or problems within the club?"

"No threats," Grim signs, and his bored expression lets us all know just how annoyed he is by that. "Please tell me Ma…" He shakes his hands in his signature *scratch that* gesture and starts again. "Please tell me Jezebel has something for us."

"Afraid not. At least not as of last night. I'll check in with her again, but you know she'll call the second she has anything."

"I need to break something," Grim signs.

"You need to break some*one*," Spike counters.

Grim shrugs.

"Thorn, do you have anything to add?" I ask.

"No. Everything is good."

I look at Rogue. "Give us a quick financial update," I order.

Rogue opens his ledger. "Purgatory is doing well. We're still operating in the black." He lifts his head and levels his gaze on me. "But like I said last night, we need to hire more reliable staff. I think that's going to come with a price tag that will dip into our profits a bit. But it's gotta be done."

"Gimme specifics."

"Well, we need to hire a full-time bar manager so I can focus on other shit. To get someone good and trustworthy, I'd start 'em at fifty grand." When the others grumble, he signs. "Look, ya get what ya pay for. And with what goes on behind the scenes with the club, we need to make sure a manager will keep their mouth shut."

"I can get on board with that if the manager can

get creative with increasing profits." I scan the faces of the others. "All in favor?"

Six hands go up.

"Good. Rogue, how're Persuasion Ink and Sinful Wheels looking?"

"PI is in the black. The new hire we voted on last week started yesterday, and Possum seems to like him so far. As for the garage, books are looking good. We had a slight dip in profits since we had to fix that roof leak, but it won't take long to bounce back."

I shift my focus to Spike. "Brother, anything to add about the garage?"

"Nope. Everything's good."

"Abyss, anything to report on your end?"

Since he's the secretary, he gets updates from the other patched members prior to church, so if there are issues, they can be addressed without calling a full club meeting.

"Not much. Heather says the bunnies are doing well. There was a bit of drama between Gwen and Nikki, but it was handled."

Heather is married to Frenzy, a patched member of Saints Purgatory. She doesn't have to oversee the bunnies, but she seems to like it and she's damn good at keeping them from clawing each other's eyes out when shit hits the fan.

"Fort completed the monthly update on the security system, and Lock fixed the sensor on our topside garage door so we don't have to manually lift the fucker anymore."

"Thank fuck," Malice mutters. "It was getting damn old getting on and off my bike to open the thing."

"Wimp," Grim signs, and Malice flips him off.

While the clubhouse is underground, the garage where we store all our bikes, as well as any other vehicles any of us have, is camouflaged into the side of the mountain above us, and only accessible via the door that needed fixed and an elevator.

"Anything else we need to discuss?" I ask, satisfied that we've covered everything.

When no one says a word, I end church and dismiss my brothers. As they all file out of the room, I take note of Grim, who remains in his seat. Once the door slides closed behind the others, I face him.

"What's up?"

Grim narrows his eyes and rolls his neck. When he doesn't lift his hands to respond, I walk around the table and pull out the chair next to him to sit.

"I'm not a mind reader."

"No shit," he signs with clipped movements.

"Then talk to me."

After a tense minute, Grim takes a deep breath and lifts his hands. "Do you really not know?" I shake my head. "Ten years ago today we took out our first sinners."

Fuck.

"And you need to celebrate," I say matter-of-factly.

Every year since the night we burned our old church down, killing Deacon Block and Father Brine, Grim's rage takes over, and he needs to kill. Calling it a celebration doesn't make it any less the emotional outlet it is for him.

"This is the first year I haven't had a guest to celebrate with," he signs.

And by 'guest', he means a sinner who he takes down the deepest tunnel to the place he's named Hell. It's a torture chamber, plain and simple. And it's where Grim feels the most at home.

"Give me an hour, Grim. I'll find you a guest or two."

"Two?" His normally hardened expression brightens.

"Yeah, two."

Grim nods, stands, and leaves the room. I love my brother and if he needs a victim, I'll find him a victim.

So much for a day off.

CHAPTER FIVE

CECE

I've battled headaches, and my body has been numb the past few days. I can't lay around anymore and leave the boutique to suffer. Maybe I'll feel better if I get out of this damn apartment. Sitting on the edge of the bed, I give myself a pep talk when Carmella pops her head in.

"What are you doing?"

"Getting my ass out of this bed so I can go to work."

"Maybe you should stay home. You've been talking to yourself for the last five minutes." She raises her eyebrows.

"I need to get out of here, Mel. And I need to reopen the boutique." I shrug and walk toward the bathroom. "Besides, it's just grief, right?"

"That's not what I said. Don't act like that." Carmella looks at the floor.

Shit, now I feel like a bitch again.

"I know, Mel. I'm sorry, that wasn't fair." I walk back to her. "I think that if I get out of this apartment, the fresh air will do me some good."

"Alright, but Ce, you better call me if you need me. And take it easy."

"Mel, you know I will."

"Yeah right. I'll believe it when I see it," she says as she walks out the door.

After getting ready for the day, I make my way to Naughty/Nice. It feels like it's been months since I've been there when in reality, it's only been a couple of weeks.

As I unlock the shop's door, I realize I'm already feeling a little better. Getting out of the apartment was the right decision. It's weird not seeing Mom behind the counter. A wave of sadness hits me, but I push forward knowing that Mom would want me to carry on and not wallow. I start straightening shelves and dive into the mountains of inventory we've received that we never cataloged.

Not we… I.

I need to pull my head out of my ass and remember it's just me now.

Mom and I ran Naughty/Nice by ourselves but now, I can't help but wonder if that was smart. Maybe Mom would still be alive if we had help. She could have rested more, made more time for doctor's appointments, and taken care of herself.

I jot down a note to do a few job listings. Looking around the store I see just how much work has been neglected since Mom died. At ten o'clock, I unlock the door, silently praying that it's not too busy so I can get some shit taken care of.

I grab the last box of unopened merchandise before I set up the new display. As I'm working, a wave of dizziness hits me hard.

"What the fuck?" I mumble as my knees buckle and everything goes dark.

Beep, beep, beep...

What is that annoying sound? I can't place it. My eyes flutter open, and I look around. Nope, definitely not in the store anymore.

"What the hell?" Pain shoots through my hand as I try to sit up, and that's when I noticed the IV.

"Stay still." Carmella rushes forward and gently pushes me onto my pillow. "Let's wait and see what the doctor has to say."

"What the fuck happened?"

Looking around the room, I notice Mary sitting in a chair at the foot of the bed.

"I came to the store to check and see how you were doing since your mom died and found you passed out on the floor. I couldn't wake you up, so I called 911."

"Dammit! The store is un—"

"I found your keys on the floor next to you and locked up after you were loaded into the ambulance." Mary stands and walks to my bedside. "What happened? Were you attacked? You have a knot on the side of your head."

Without thinking, I rub my head and feel the knot.

"I must've hit my head when I fell. I was alone." I shake my head trying to gather my thoughts. "I got dizzy and then, lights out."

"You scared the living shit out of me." Carmella's eyes are glassy with unshed tears."I just happened to look out my office window and saw you being loaded into the ambulance. By the time I could tell Jim I was leaving, the ambulance was already gone."

"I was giving the nurse as much information as I could when Carmella came in, demanding to know where you were and what happened." Mary glances at Mel and looks back at me. "You have a very loyal bff. The nurse refused to give her any information because she isn't family and Mel came unglued."

"Yeah, you never tell me we aren't family." Mel's eyes are narrowed and her lips are pressed into a thin line. "Condescending assholes. Blood doesn't make you family. Mary was standing there. She introduced herself and told me what happened."

"Thanks for the help, Mary. I really appreciate you locking up for me and calling for the ambulance, but I'm sure you ha–"

"Stop right there. I'm not leaving until we find out what's going on. Plus, I'm a sucker for drama. This is better than a Grey's Anatomy episode." Mary laughs.

The nurse pokes her head around the curtain. "Oh good, you're awake. Let me get the doctor."

Carmella and Mary both sit in the chairs at the foot of the bed. The curtain is pushed back again, and the doctor walks in.

Oh fuck no.

"Ms. Parker, you're back," Dr. Fucktard says. "What brings you in this time?"

I stare at him for what seems like hours. I didn't want to ever see this jackass again, especially after the last encounter we had. Taking a deep breath, I hope that, maybe, he was just having a bad night the first time I came to the ER.

"Well Dr. Franklin, not really sure what happened. I got dizzy, blacked out, and woke up here."

"I found her lying on the floor of her boutique," Mary adds. "I tried to rouse her and couldn't, so I called 911."

Dr. Franklin looks at her. "And you are?" he inquires.

"I'm her friend." Mary looks at me and winks.

I don't know if she's calling me her friend because she doesn't want to get kicked out of the ER or if she really considers herself my friend. Either way, I'm glad she's here and found me when she did.

"How have you been feeling, Ms. Parker?"

"I'm still having headaches, and I'm run down." Pressing my fingers to my temple, I try and rub away the throbbing.

"Did you find a grief support group like I had suggested?

Mel stands, but I raise my hand to stop her from interrupting.

"Are you suggesting, *again,* that what I'm experiencing is grief, *Dr. Franklin*?" I sneer.

"Yes, *Ms. Parker.*" He finally lifts his eyes from his tablet to look at me. "That's exactly what I'm saying. You won't feel better until you deal with your grief head-on."

"Look, Dr. Franklin, I have tried to be nice, but now I'm out of patience." My heart rate and the beeping of the machine increase. "Something is going on, and I want to know what."

Dr. Fucktard ignores the incessant beeping so the nurse walks over to shut off the machine.

"I have other patients to see, *Ms. Parker*. I'll start your discharge paperwork as soon as I can." He disappears through the curtain, dismissing me completely.

"I'm sorry, but that doctor is an asshole," I bite out as the nurse begins to remove my IV.

"I don't know what to say," she politely comments. "I've never seen him so adamant about someone not being sick."

I absently scratch the back of my neck and the nurse's forehead wrinkles.

"How long has your neck been itchy?" she asks. "I've noticed you scratching your neck several times since you arrived."

I think about her question for a moment. "I guess it's been a while. I'm not sure when it started."

"Do you mind if I take a quick look?"

"Knock yourself out. I don't think a dry scalp would cause headaches or body aches, but there's a first time for everything."

The nurse instructs me to lean forward, and then she lifts my hair.

"How long have you had this red patch?"

"What? What red patch?"

Mel walks over and leans around me to see what the nurse is talking about.

"Girl, she's right. Kinda looks like a bullseye," Mel says.

"Could it be from me scratching?"

"I don't think so. It looks like a bite of some kind," the nurse says. "Do you recall if you were bitten by anything? A spider or tick maybe?"

"No." I shrug. "I guess it could be a spider. We live in an apartment, but it's sprayed quarterly for insects."

"You fell in that bush when we went hiking," Mel contributes.

"Let me go get Dr. Franklin and show him your neck." The nurse rushes through the curtain.

She returns with Dr. Franklin a few minutes later, and he asks to see my neck. As much as I don't want to deal with him, I know I'll get out of here faster if I'm given a proper diagnosis. I reluctantly lift up my hair, and he leans in to take a look.

"Ms. Parker, how am I supposed to effectively treat you if you don't give me all the information I need?"

"What the fu–"

Mary's phone rings, cutting her off, and she answers it. I almost forgot she was in the room, she's been so quiet. As she talks in hushed whispers to whoever is on the other end of the call, I refocus on the doctor.

"I tried to tell you it wasn't grief, but you didn't want to listen. You said, and I quote, 'I am the one with the medical degree and the head of the ER'."

I glance at Mel, who's trying not to laugh. Mary continues to glare at him and her expression is murderous.

"I'm going to order some blood tests and see if we can narrow down what that bite mark is from." Dr. Fucktard turns to the nurse. "Let's get a CBC, CMP, and Lyme Titer."

"What, no *'I'm sorry'* for the patient?" I ask.

"I'm not apologizing for doing my job," he counters. "I diagnosed you based on the information provided. I'll be back when the results come back." He walks through the curtains with his face buried in his tablet.

"What a fucking prick!"

"I'll rush these blood tests and let Dr. Franklin know as soon as the results come back," the nurse says as she scurries out of the room.

Two hours later, Dr. Fucktard returns to my ER

bay. "Your tests have come back. You have Lyme Disease."

"Seriously?"

"Yes, Ms. Parker. Luckily, I caught it before it became a serious issue."

Is this guy for fucking real??

Without discussing my care with me, he starts issuing orders to the nurse.

"I want you to start Ms. Parker on IV Cefuroxime 500mg, twice a day for three days." He types something into his tablet and continues. "She'll have to be admitted to the hospital for a few days, but then we can release her with oral antibiotics for fourteen days."

"Great, just freaking great."

"Are you going to ord—"

"Are my instructions unclear?" Dr. Fucktard snaps at the nurse.

"No, but… should we ord—"

"I'll take care of it," he says and exits through the curtain.

"Well, at least you have some answers," Carmella offers as her gaze remains glued to the spot where Dr. Fucktard was standing. "At least being admitted to the hospital you shouldn't have to deal with dickhead anymore."

Carmella was right about that. I was admitted for

three fucking days and not once did I have to deal with Dr. Fucktard again.

"Knock, knock," Carmella says as she walks through the door. I called her to come pick me up. "Look who I brought with me." Mary enters the room behind her.

Over the past couple days, Mary and Carmella have been taking turns keeping me company so I wouldn't go insane. I notice Mel carrying a bag from my favorite deli, which is fortunate for me because I miss food from the outside world. A person could starve to death on hospital food alone.

"Thought you'd like some fresh clothes to walk out of here in instead of having your ass hang out of that hospital gown." Mary tosses a duffel bag onto the mattress as I dig into my meal.

"Thanks, although I do believe I have a nice ass." I wink at her.

"Maybe that's how we get you laid!" Mel wiggles her eyebrows. "We let your ass hang out and see who takes the bait."

"Whatever, Princess." Once the last of the deli food is gone, I grab the duffel bag and head into the bathroom. "You know you're jealous. Remind me how long it's been since you've gotten laid."

"Hooker, please. I'm waiting on Prince Charming to ride in on his white horse." Mel shakes her head. "I'm just waiting on his ass to get the damn memo."

"When do men ever get the memo?" Mary quips.

Mary is officially part of our duo… no, we're a trio now. Nothing bonds people together faster than emergencies and trauma.

Mel and Mary argue as if they've been best friends their whole lives about who is going to push me out of the hospital. Both are disappointed when they're informed that an orderly has to push the wheelchair.

Once outside, I stand from the chair and inhale the fresh air. The orderly returns inside, and then Mary offers to get the car.

"Ce, I am so glad we are out of that joint. It was depressing," Mel says once we're alone. She squeezes my hand.

"Amen sister."

Intense pain invades my chest as I struggle to catch my breath. "Mel, something is wrong," I wheeze.

She grips my arm. "What? What's wrong?!"

"My chest hurts, I can't brea—"

The next thing I know, beeping sounds are invading my ears. This has to be some kind of nightmare. No way in hell am I back in the damn hospital?

I try to open my eyes, but I swear my eyelids

weigh a hundred pounds. And my chest still hurts. After I'm able to force my eyes open, my vision slowly clears, and I spot Carmella and Mary in the chairs against the wall.

"I'm getting really tired of this."

What the hell happened?

"Oh my God!" Mel rushes over. "I'm so glad you're awake."

Before I can ask any questions, Mary stands and comes forward to explain.

"I was pulling up with the car when you passed out. You weren't breathing so I started CPR while Mel ran to get a nurse." That explains the pain in my ribs. "You coded and had to be shocked to bring you back."

All I can do is stare at them. I hear Mary's words, but they aren't sinking in. Not only am I back in the ER after having been discharged from the hospital, but I also fucking died? "Please tell me you're joking. I died? Like actually died after being discharged from the hospital, before I could even get in the car?"

The beeping machines go crazy, and my head spins.

A nurse comes running in and checks my vitals.

"Let me go and get the doctor," she says when she's finished and turns to leave.

"I don't want to see Dr. Fu… Dr. Franklin."

"Oh, well that's not an issue," she assures me with a smile. "He's not on duty. Dr. DeMarco is here today."

A few minutes later a female doctor comes in and checks the monitors before focusing on me. "Hello, I'm Dr. DeMarco." She extends her hand for me to shake. "It seems we can't get rid of you."

I chuckle when she does, and I can already tell she's nothing like Dr. Fucktard.

"I've been looking over your chart and want to verify some information before we proceed." She smiles, further putting me at ease. "That is, if you are feeling up to it."

"Sure Doc."

"When you were diagnosed with Lyme Disease, did you have an EKG test done?"

"EKG?" I vaguely understand what she's talking about. "Like a heart test?"

"Yes."

"No." Panic bubbles in my gut. "Why would I need an EKG?"

"They're fairly common when someone goes as long as you did without the Lyme Disease being diagnosed," she explains. "It's done to monitor your heart rate and rhythm to make sure no abnormalities have formed. Lyme Disease can be deadly if not caught and treated in time."

I glance over at Mel and Mary. Mary is furiously typing on her phone, and Mel looks like she's going to be sick.

"Excuse me? Did you say deadly?" I ask.

"Yes, did you not realize you had been bitten by something?"

"Actually, Doctor," Mel begins. "We came in almost a week ago, and she was dismissed by your colleague. He told her that she was just grieving because her mother had just passed away the week before."

"I see." Dr. DeMarco doesn't say anything else, but her expression is tense. "While you were unconscious we ran a few more tests. After confirming with the cardiologist, we determined you have Lyme's Carditis."

"What the hell is that?"

I'm reaching my breaking point. No doubt sensing that, Mel steps up to the bed to hold my hand. Mary stands on the opposite side as she slides her cell into her pocket.

"Lyme Carditis attacks the heart when Lyme Disease is not caught or treated in a timely manner. In your case, while you were diagnosed and given the correct treatment, it was too long since you contracted the disease."

"So now what?" Mel asks.

"Ms. Parker, are you okay with continuing this conversation with your friends in the room?"

"Absolutely." I smile at Carmella and Mary. "They're family."

"I'm not going to sugarcoat it." Dr. DeMarco looks at her tablet briefly and then back at me. "Due to your heart's rhythm and the cardiac arrest you suffered outside, we are going to have to put in a temporary pacemaker and once that is placed you'll need to remain in the hospital for twenty-one days of IV antibiotics."

"Are you fucking kidding me?"

Shock doesn't even begin to cover the emotions rolling through me at the moment. Outrage, murderous intent… those are more accurate.

"I wish I was. The good news is that the pacemaker will only be temporary. The next twenty-one days will tell us if we were able to reverse the effects of the carditis." Dr. DeMarco pauses. "But, if the carditis does not heal…" She purses her lips. "We will be forced to put in a permanent one."

"Could this have been avoided if Dr. Franklin hadn't dismissed her symptoms from the onset?" Mary asks.

Dr. DeMarco shifts on her feet, clearly uncomfortable. She takes several deep breaths before carefully responding.

"In all honestly, I don't know the answer to that question because I wasn't involved in his original diagnosis." She looks me right in the eye. "But, with your diagnosis, I would've ordered an EKG before discharging you."

With those parting words, she leaves the ER bay.

"That motherfucker," Mary mutters.

Leaning back against the pillow, I try to process everything I was just told. As if the last few weeks haven't been stressful enough, I now have to come to terms with the fact that I died and was brought back to life because of the incompetence and laziness of Dr. Fucktard.

Motherfucker, indeed.

CHAPTER SIX

SOUL

"Did she seriously hang up on you?"

I stare at the screen on my cell. My sister has never hung up on me before… okay, she has, but only when she's really pissed at me. I didn't get the impression that she's pissed, and I know I haven't done anything to get on her bad side, so I'm a little concerned.

"Yeah," I respond to Thorn.

I try to call her back, three times in fact, and each time it goes to voicemail. But it goes to voicemail because that's where she's sending the call. What the fuck?

"Your worry crease is showing."

Smoothing my hand over my forehead, I glare at my SAA. "Fuck off."

"No thanks."

"You're a dick, ya know that?"

"And yet, you love me."

"Fuck knows why," I grumble.

Thorn grins. "I am incredibly lovable."

"You're a giant pain in my ass and have been for as long as I've known you." We met in the military, served together, and I trust the man with my life. But he knows how to get under my skin. Hence his road name… Thorn is, well, a thorn in everyone's side.

"Aw, c'mon, Prez," he says. "You're not still mad about Becky, are you?"

Becky, the bitch from the bar we used to frequent near the base. I called dibs and Thorn ignored it, but that wasn't the worst part. Becky flirted with me the entire night, all the way up until last call, and then went home with Thorn. He bragged about her pussy for weeks after that.

"I couldn't give two shits about Becky."

Thorn stands from the oversized chair in the common room. "Whatever you say, Prez."

He whistles as he walks away, further deepening my annoyance. It takes a lot to piss me off, but being hung up on and reminded about pussy I missed out on are two ways to make it happen.

My cell vibrates in my hand as the screen lights up indicating my sister is calling back.

"What the fuck, Ma—" I groan. "What the fuck, Jez?"

"Don't get shitty with me," she snaps. "I was busy, and you wouldn't shut up."

"Since when are you too busy to talk to me?"

"Soul, I love you, but you aren't my entire life. And neither is the club, despite your best efforts to make it so."

"So what were you doing?"

"Lucky for you, what I was doing ties into a case for the club, so I'll tell you." She takes a deep breath. "But I want it on the record that you're an ass and don't have the right to always know what I'm doing."

"Fine, noted."

"Thank you," she says sweetly… too sweetly. "I was at the hospital. There—"

"Are you okay? What happened? Did someone hurt you? I swear to God if someone hurt you, I'll fucking gut them."

"Bro, chill. I'm fine."

"Then why were you at the hospital?" I demand. She's testing my already thin patience.

"I was there with a friend."

"A friend?"

"Yes, Soul, a friend. I do have some, ya know?"

"Is this a friend like Loafer Dan was a friend?"

Jezebel growls, the sound far more menacing than

one would think she's capable of producing. "No, dipshit. Cece is actually my friend."

"Cece?"

"Yes, Cece. She and her mom own a boutique I like to shop at." She pauses. "Well, I guess it's just her now that her mom died."

"Okay." I draw the word out, not exactly sure how this will tie into a case for Saints Purgatory.

"Long story short, Cece's been feeling shitty lately, and the doctor ignored her. Fucker told her it was just grief."

"And it wasn't?"

"No, Soul," she snaps. "It wasn't!"

"Calm down, Jez." My tone is stern, and I can practically feel her bristling through the phone. "I'm just asking questions."

"Right, sorry." Jez pauses for a few minutes, and my patience kicks back in. I wait her out. "It's just… fuck, Soul. She died. Cece was released from the hospital by some ER doctor who thinks his shit doesn't stink, and she died on the goddamn sidewalk."

My stomach plummets. I don't know this Cece chick, but her death is clearly upsetting Jez, and I hate it when my twin is hurting. "I'm sorry."

"I watched her collapse, right as I was pulling the

car around for her. I did CPR, but it didn't work. She had to be shocked back to life."

"Wait. She's alive?"

"Of course, she's alive dumbass," Jez snaps.

I run a hand through my hair, no doubt disheveling it. I swear on all that's unholy, if she doesn't get to the point soon, I'm going to reach through the cell and down her throat and pull out the information myself.

So much for patience.

"Jez, get to the point," I order.

"I'm getting there," she assures me. "As I was saying… she was shocked back to life. Apparently, she has Lyme Carditis. It's a heart condition brought on by Lyme Disease, which she was finally diagnosed with before being discharged and dying."

"That sucks, Jez. And I'm sorry your friend is sick. But what does this have to do with a case?"

"Well, while the new doctor was running tests, I started digging into the original doctor," she says. "Dr. Richard Franklin is the head of the emergency department at Boulder City Memorial. He's also the most incompetent, uncaring, self-righteous doctor I've ever encountered."

"Go on."

"But even more than all that, he's lazy as hell. I managed to uncover his medical school records. The guy's smart. He knows his medicine. He just doesn't seem to give a shit about it or the patients he treats."

"So, sloth?"

My heartbeat increases as adrenaline courses through my veins. The seven deadly sins always get me fired up.

"Douchebag could fall under any of them, but yeah, for this, sloth," she confirms.

A red light flashes above the elevator door, alerting me that someone is entering the garage. I switch my call to speaker phone so I can pull up the camera. Jezebel's matte black Charger fills the screen, and I watch as she steps out and runs her fingers through her hair. For someone who says the club isn't her life, she sure goes out of her way to make it seem like it is. Black hair with purple strands and a black car with purple racing stripes. She's Saints Purgatory all the way to her soul, just like I am.

"Why didn't you tell me you were coming to the clubhouse?" I ask as I stand from the couch and move toward the elevator.

Jezebel twists her head to look over her shoulder and stares straight at the camera. Then she flips me off. "Quit spying."

"I'm not spying. The light flashed that the garage door was opened, and I was making sure it wasn't someone to be worried about."

"Soul, the garage door blends into the mountainside. The clubhouse is underground. In the middle of the fucking desert. No one is showing up here who hasn't already passed your precious security checks."

"Those security checks keep our asses safe," I gripe. "And yours when you're here."

"Yeah, yeah."

Jezebel disconnects the call, and I glare at the screen. She better stop hanging up on me. When the elevator doors open and she steps out, I tell her as much.

"Get a grip," she sasses. "The call was dropped on the elevator. You really need to work on strengthening the cell signal in there."

"I'll get right on that, *boss*."

Jezebel grins. "I like the sound of that."

"Don't get used to it."

I throw my arm around her shoulder to urge her toward the couches, but she digs in her heels.

"We're not staying," she informs me. "I'm taking you to the hospital to meet Cece."

"Why? If the doctor is our target, then we focus on him. I don't need to meet her."

"Yeah, Soul, you do." Jezebel's worry crease deepens.

"Spit it out, sis," I order softly as I rub my thumb

over her forehead. "There's something you're not telling me."

My twin, the only woman in the world I know like the back of my hand, frowns. "This isn't like the club's usual sin."

"Okay. Why not?"

"Because, it can't be."

"Why?"

"Because it's Cece."

"Jez, ya gotta give me more than that."

She huffs out a breath. "It's just… Cece is nice. She's super sweet, and after losing her mom so unexpectedly, she's had nothing but shit thrown at her." Jez crosses her arms over her chest and stares at me as if she's daring me to argue. "Yes, the doctor needs taken care of, especially after everything I've uncovered. But Cece needs taken care of too."

"You want the club to eliminate your friend?"

"What? No, of course not." She averts her gaze. "I want the club to help me take care of her, help her get back on her feet."

"You want us to treat her like a charity case," I say.

"No," she snaps and then inhales deeply. "Well, yes, I guess. But no."

"Jez, you are not making any damn sense."

"I want you to invite Cece to spend the rest of her

hospital stay here, at the clubhouse." I open my mouth to protest, but she continues. "Before you say no, think about it. You have state-of-the-art medical equipment and the space. You'd barely even notice she was here."

"No."

"Soul, I don't ask you for a lot. In fact, I pretty much never ask you for anything." She starts to tap her foot. "But I'm asking for this. Cece is a friend who has almost no one else in the world besides me and her friend, Carmella. That's it. I need you to do this."

"Jez, how will that work, her coming here?" I counter. "We're all bachelors who like our space, and then there's the bunnies. I highly doubt she'll be comfortable here."

"So?" She shrugs. "She's not a prude, Soul. Who knows? Maybe she'll snag one of the brothers and take them off the market."

"Not likely."

"Yeah, probably not. But still… please do this for me. I'll stay here to help if that makes a difference. I'm going to work on hiring some more staff for her so her boutique can reopen, but I can do that from here or just travel into the city as necessary. It's only for a few weeks."

"A few weeks?"

Jezebel purses her lips. "Uh, yeah. Didn't I mention that?"

"No, Jez, you failed to bring that up."

"Oh. Well, yeah, a few weeks. She's to remain in the hospital for twenty-one days for IV antibiotics. By the time we get her here, it'll only be twenty days, maybe even nineteen."

"My answer is still—"

"Come to the hospital and meet her first," she demands as she grabs my arm and tugs me to the elevator. "If you meet her and still want to be a dick, fine."

"You're not going to let this go, are you?"

Jez grins, knowing she's tipped the scales in her favor. "Nope," she says, popping the 'p'.

An hour and a half later, my sister is leading me through the main entrance of the hospital and then up the stairs to the third floor. We could've taken the elevator, but I'm pretty sure she's afraid I'll walk out if there are any delays.

Jezebel stops outside a door and looks at me. She pulls her lip between her teeth and her worry crease appears.

"Seriously, Jez," I groan. "What else aren't you telling me?"

"She doesn't know we're coming," she spits out quickly, as if she'd lose her nerve if she didn't.

"You've got to be kidding me."

"No. Totally serious. Cece isn't one to accept help." Jez frowns. "At least, I don't think she is." She shakes her head. "Anyway, she doesn't know we're coming. And she knows nothing about the club. So we need to tread lightly."

"Whatever. Just introduce me so we can get this over with."

Jez nods and takes a deep breath before pushing open the door and stepping inside. I enter the room behind her, fully prepared to be introduced and then leave. Saints Purgatory handles sinners, not women down on their luck.

The funny thing about thinking you're prepared for something and being certain you're going to stick to your guns is that, on rare occasions, you're simply fucking wrong.

This is one of those rare occasions.

The second my eyes land on the beautiful woman propped against the pillow on the hospital bed, my heart skips a beat, and my stomach does a cartwheel.

Fuck.

Looks like I'll be doing my twin's bidding after all.

CHAPTER SEVEN

CECE

"This cannot be happening."

I swear I've repeated that mantra a hundred times since being readmitted to the hospital. My thoughts keep wandering back to Naughty/Nice.

How in the hell am I going to pay for this hospital stay when I'm not working?

I have savings, but who knows how long that will last? And don't get me started on how far behind on my bills I already am.

I toss the television remote onto the hospital nightstand. Glancing around the room, I wonder how I'm going to keep myself from going insane over the next three weeks. A person can only watch so much daytime TV. How many reruns of Maury Povich paternity cases can one person endure? It's only day two, and I already want to claw my eyes out.

After swinging my legs over the edge of the bed, I

stand and stretch my arms above my head slowly so the IV doesn't get torn out of my arm. A sharp pain in my neck reminds me of the temporary pacemaker that was inserted yesterday.

With the IV stand in my grasp, I start toward the wardrobe door. The doctor advised me to walk twice a day around the floor, so why not start now? Yoga pants first… no one needs to see my ass hanging out.

"Knock, knock!"

I barely have time to pull up my pants before Mary rushes in.

"Hey, what're you doing here? I mean I'm glad you're here, but I figured you'd be working and I wouldn't see you until tonight." I walk back to the bed and try to get comfortable.

"I brought someone I want you to meet." She looks over her shoulder.

No sooner do the words leave her mouth than one of the hottest men I have ever seen walks into the room. My vagina even does a little happy dance. His piercing hazel eyes bore into me as he approaches my bedside.

Tall and muscular, he has a tattoo on his forearm that I can't quite make out, and his five o'clock shadow has me touching my mouth checking for drool.

"Cece, this is my brother Ma… Soul."

That explains the resemblance. I was wondering why he looked so familiar. I knew it wasn't because I'd met him before. My lady bits would remember that for sure.

"Hi, it's nice to meet you. I'm single… I mean, I'm not sick or contagious… dear God make it stop." My face is flaming hot, and I glance at Mary, silently begging her to save me from my stupid ass mouth.

Soul, the beautiful bastard, covers his laugh with a cough but continues to stare at me like I'm some sort of science experiment.

"Soul, this is Cece, the friend I was telling you about." Mary pokes Soul in his side, and finally, his gaze shifts from me to his sister.

Suddenly released from the spell he had me under, I shake my head. But the reprieve is short-lived as he quickly levels his eyes back on mine. This man sure does love eye contact. I could get lost in his stare for days.

Stop It!!! You're going to make an ass out of yourself.

Great, now I'm talking to myself.

"Pleasure to meet you, Cece."

Holy shit, his voice could melt butter. It's deep and rich, and it takes everything I have not to fan myself.

Get a grip, idiot! This is Mary's brother. Totally off-limits.

"Sorry about my word vomit. Can we start over?" He nods. "I'm Cece, and I swear I'm not usually like this. I'm going to blame my complete loss of brain function on all the crazy shit that's happened to me over the past couple weeks."

"We all have our days. Jez can tell you all sorts of fucked up stories about me."

"Jez?"

"Uh, Soul… I haven't told her that yet." Mary glares at her brother, and a silent conversation seems to take place.

"Seriously? You didn't think to do that before you dragged me down here?" He flips his hand at her in a 'get on with it' motion. "Now's as good a time as any."

"Fine." Mary huffs out a breath and then begins. "Look Ce, I wanted to tell you the truth from the beginning but… anonymity is important in my line of work. My name *is* Mary, but a handful of people know me as Jezebel… or Jez."

"Okay… I'm not really sure—" My eyes widen as her words sink in. "Wait, Jezebel as in *online shopper* Jezebel? The mystery customer from the boutique?"

Mary—no, Jezebel—starts to fidget and laces her fingers together. She takes a deep breath and continues. "Yeah, that's me. I found your shop online and as you've seen, I have a slight shopping addiction.

Once I figured out that Naughty/Nice was in Boulder City, I came in to shop." She shrugs, a sheepish look on her face. "The rest is history."

"Why didn't you just tell me you were Jezebel?" I don't understand why she kept it a secret. Why not just tell me she goes by Jez?

Unless it's classified information or something.

"Like she said, only a handful of people know her as Jez," Soul interjects, as if he can read my mind. "She tells people on a need to know basis, and you didn't need to know… until now. With my club involved, there's no getting around keeping it from you."

"Your club?"

My head spins with all their cryptic bullshit, and my heart is pounding. The machine next to the bed starts beeping incessantly. I take a deep breath to try and calm my nerves, and close my eyes. After counting to ten, I open them and see that Soul has moved closer to my side. He's looking at me closely, watching me like a predator watches their prey. It's like he's waiting for me to fall apart. Well, I have news for him… I've walked through hell and am still in one piece.

For the most part.

"Your club?" I ask, this time with more confidence.

"Yeah babe, my club." He smirks. "Seems my little sister has kept all sorts of fucking info under wraps."

"*Little* sister?" Jez scoffs. "You're only four minutes older than me, asshole. Besides, I told you I didn't tell her about the club."

"Well enlighten *me* then. Tell me about your club." It's then that I notice the leather vest he's wearing. It has a patch that says 'President' and another that says 'Soul'.

"Not a vest, a cut," he corrects, a gleam in his eyes.

Oh shit, did I say that out loud?

"Do you always blurt shit out when it comes to mind?"

Well, that answers that question.

"Normally, no. But I'm still blaming the recent shitstorm of my life." I wink at Soul in an effort to distract him from the fact that I have gone completely crazy.

"I'm the president of Saints Purgatory MC—"

"MC? You're in a biker gang?"

Oh this can't be good. My thoughts spiral out of control.

Did I win a contest in Hell or something to deserve this? The devil isn't happy I survived death so he sends Mary slash Jez and her big brother to finish the job. What could they possibly want from me? My store, my mom's life insurance? Shit! I need to warn Carmella.

My face must show my panic because the next thing I know, Jez grabs my hand and gets close to my face.

"Calm your ass down, you're my friend." Jez squeezes my hand reassuringly. "It's not a gang, it's a club. I'm sorry I didn't tell you, but it wasn't my business to tell. It's not like I'm gonna go around advertising who my brother is. Besides, the club is full of good guys, and a lot of them are ex-military. Saints Purgatory can be a bit misleading," she explains.

"Sorry, but you *are* fucking hitting me with a lot right now. How did you think I was going to react?" Tears gather in my eyes. The last thing I want to do is cry in front of some gorgeous man I just met so I bite the inside of my cheek to keep my emotions at bay.

"Look, we aren't trying to upset you, and we're not gonna fucking hurt you, so get that scared look off your face," Soul snaps. "I agree, we could've done this another way, but *someone* didn't." Soul glares at his sister as if to say *I told you so.* "Jez *does* have an idea though."

"And what exactly is *Jez's* idea?" I know I'm

acting like a brat but dammit, there's been so much going on, I'm allowed to be bitchy.

"Ce, I know how much you hate being in the hospital," Jez says. "You threatened to kill the poor nurse who had to take your vitals during the night the first time you were admitted." Jez chuckles. "I thought Carmella was gonna have to cuff you to the bed just so you'd be able to leave without a murder charge."

"In my defense, she woke me up three damn times," I pout. "And I never said I was going to 'kill her'. I said if she woke me up one more time, I was going to sodomize her with medical equipment." Was that just a couple of days ago?

"Wait… you were gonna what?" Soul looks at me.

"I kindly told her I would shove the stethoscope up her ass."

"Well, we didn't want you to add murderer to your resume. What can I say, we're awesome friends like that." Jez winks.

"Fine, you win. I'm glad I won't be in jail for murder." I dart my eyes from her to Soul and back again. "So what's this great idea?"

"Jez thinks it's a good idea for you to finish your treatment at our clubhouse. And now that I'm hearing what you're capable of, I'm inclined to agree with her. I don't have time to bail your ass out of jail."

"I wasn't going to *really* hurt the nurse," I mutter. "Um…wait, did you say stay at the clubhouse? Why in the hell would you want me to stay at the clubhouse?"

"Look, we've got the room and a brother with a medical license who can administer meds. As for why…" He hitches a thumb at his sister. "She asked."

"You have another brother?" I ask Jez.

"No." She shakes her head. "In an MC, the members refer to themselves as 'brothers'. But in this case, the men Soul is referring to are as close to blood brothers as one can get."

Finally, something I understand. Carmella is my ride or die, and she's not related to me by blood but my sister nonetheless.

Look at me using biker references.

I chuckle at myself, ignoring their strange stares that scream 'she's losing it'.

"That's generous of you, Soul," I grudgingly admit. "As much as I want to get out of here, it's not a good idea. I don't think the clubhouse would be a good place for me." I shake my head and continue. "I'm not a charity case. Thanks but no thanks."

"Ce, you're my friend, not a charity case. This is what friends do." Jez tries to assure me.

"First of all, you're being a little judgmental, don't ya think?" Soul snaps. He steps closer to me, and I find myself being swept away by his chiseled jaw and sexy smile. "Second, think about it for a minute, babe. You'd have your own room with a private bath. Jez is gonna stay too, and we'll make sure you're close to her. And the brothers will be falling all over themselves trying to make sure you're okay." He rolls his eyes. "No doubt they'll wait on you hand and foot. It's what they do around sexy women." Soul presses his lips into a thin line, as if regretting those words. "Plus, Jez will somehow make this my fault if you don't agree," he adds, piling on the guilt.

Hot damn! I swear my panties just disintegrated. If I go to the clubhouse, how will I survive twenty-one days without jumping on this man's dick? I silently remind my coochie that he's off-limits because he's Jez's brother. I swear horny slut cries.

Or maybe she's weeping. Soul does seem to make me wet.

"And we want to get your store reopened while you're recuperating," Jez adds.

Smart... trying to slide that little piece of information in while I'm clearly distracted. However, when it comes to Naughty/Nice, not even a good dicking daydream can divert my attention. That store is my life.

"No," I say more forcefully. "I appreciate it, but the boutique is my baby, and I can't be there to oversee anything. I'll deal with it after this mess is over."

Jez and Soul exchange a look. I'm not sure how I feel about the mix of *I told you so* and *this* will *happen* flying between them.

"Look, I appreciate you wanting to help me out, and I have to admit, it's tempting. Not only would you be saving me from having to eat hospital food for three more weeks and getting woken up in the middle of the night, but there's also that little murder charge you mentioned." I force a smile.

And even though I have solid reasons for saying no, I can't help but wonder if they don't have a point. It's hard for me to accept any kind of help, but it *is* a good solution and the fastest way out of this place.

Dammit!

"Ya know what? I'd love to be your houseguest." I frown. "Or is it club guest? I don't know the lingo."

Soul laughs, and the deep timbre makes my heart skip a beat. Not literally, thank God. That's all I need is for that damn machine to start beeping again.

"I'll work with setting up the arrangements!" Jez exclaims as she bounces on her feet and claps like a child who was just told they were going to Chuck E. Cheese.

"Does Carmella know about this? Is that why she agreed to leave? Do you think the hospital will go for it?" I ask. I know I am firing questions at her, but my mind is racing.

"Wait… what do you mean Mel is leaving? Where is she going?"

"Who's Mel, or Carmella?" Soul waves his hand absently. "Who the fuck is she?"

"She's my best friend," I snap, irritated at his tone. "And yes, she's leaving. She passed the bar exam and got a damn good job offer in Sacramento. Mel didn't want to leave me stranded in the hospital, but it's a once in a lifetime gig. I want her to be happy and told her to take the job."

"Oh, okay," Jez says. "Well, I figured you should be the one to tell Carmella. As for the hospital, I was hoping you'd agree to come with us so I already kinda asked." Mary tucks her chin into her chest, as if waiting for me to get mad. "They said as long as we have someone with a medical license who can administer the medications through your IV, it can be arranged.

I roll my eyes. I should've known she already knew the answer to that question. Who offers to let you come and stay with them if they don't already know it's possible?

Not that anything they've done so far has made sense.

"We're going to get the fuck outta here and get shit sorted," Soul says and pulls on his sister's arm. "I'll have Jez and Abyss set it up. Jez'll call ya to let you know when you're being sprung from this joint."

"Okay… Well, thanks." I'm blown away by everything that's happening. "Wait, who the hell is Abyss?"

"Club brother," Soul clarifies. "He's also the one with the medical license." Soul snaps his fingers as if he forgot something. "Oh, and if you value your stomach lining, don't eat anything from any club brother other than Abyss or me."

With those parting words, he walks out the door.

Jez waves goodbye and says, "I'll call you when it's all worked out. Either me or Soul will come back and get you."

Once I'm alone, I take a minute to gather my thoughts before picking up my cell and calling Carmella.

"Diva, you are *never* going to believe what just fucking happened."

CHAPTER EIGHT

SOUL

"FUCKING HELL."

I laugh as all eyes turn toward the door. I point for Grim's benefit, and we all watch as Frenzy slinks to the table and slumps in his chair. As a patched member, he knows the rules, and he just earned himself cleaning duty with Spike and the bunnies.

"We vote on the rules once a year, dipshit," I remind him and shrug. "Don't like it, don't vote in favor of it."

"I swear, they never learn, Prez," Possum says. "Maybe you should send them to Persuasion." He bounces his eyebrows. "I could teach them a lesson they won't be able to forget."

"Screw you," Spike spits out. "I may be a little slower getting where I'm supposed to be, but there's no way in fucking hell you're tattooing a possum on my ass."

"Cut the shit," Malice snaps. "You jackasses might

not have shit to do, but I do." My VP turns to me. "Let's get started."

"You heard the man," I say. "I called church for a reason and it wasn't to discuss animals or asses."

"So…" Grim signs and then rolls his fist in a circle to signal for me to get to the point.

"Jez brought us a new case," I tell them.

I slip my hand under the table to press the button that will open the door. When it slides into the wall like a reinforced pocket door, Jez is there shaking her head. She strides in and rolls the chair in the corner up next to me.

"One of these days you're just gonna invite me in like a normal person instead of making me wait in the hall like a kid waiting to be called into the principal's office."

"One more person who will never learn," Possum quips and grins at my twin. "The cloak and dagger shit is more fun, princess."

"What's the point of having a boatload of money if you can't spend it on that kinda shit?" Grim nods at the door and smirks.

Jez leans over the arm of her chair and kisses Grim on the cheek with a loud smack of her lips. His face flushes a bright red, as it always does when she shows him any sort of affection, but he doesn't react otherwise.

"You're a giant man baby," she signs. "But I love you anyway." Jez turns to include the rest of the brothers. "The rest of you are just idiots."

"Jesus, there is too much estrogen in this room," Lock gripes as he shudders.

"Focus," Malice snaps.

"What the fuck crawled up your ass?" Jez asks.

Malice doesn't respond. I make a mental note to confront him later as now isn't the time.

"Why don't you fill them in on Cece?"

Jez spends the next twenty minutes giving them all the pertinent information, as well as answering any questions they have. I watch each of my brother's faces as she reviews everything, and my cock swells with an unwelcome spark of desire at the thought of Cece being so close for any amount of time.

"What about this doctor?" Thorn asks. "Seems to me he's the case, not this Cecelia bitch."

"Her name's Cece," I snap. When Jez eyes me with suspicion, I immediately wish I could call the words back. "It's not Cecelia or bitch," I say, slightly calmer. "It's Cece."

"Okay," Thorn says with a hint of suspicion that mirrors my sister's expression. "But the question remains… What about the doctor?"

Jez slides the keyboard from under the table and,

after pressing several buttons, the screen hanging on the back wall comes to life.

"Dr. Richard Franklin," Jez begins, as several images of the prick pop up. "What I know for sure is he's a douchebag. Cece refers to him as Dr. Fucktard." Chuckles fill the room. "He's the head of the emergency department at the hospital." The images disappear and are replaced by academic records. "He's smart, graduated top of his class." She taps the keys so other official looking records are displayed. "But he's famous for taking shortcuts when treating his patients. I haven't been able to figure out how he gets away with it," she admits, a scowl gracing her face. "But I'm not gonna stop looking."

"Sloth." Grim's jaw clenches, and his entire upper body tenses.

"Yeah, sloth," I confirm.

"It's been a while since we've dealt with that sin," Rogue comments.

"And it's such a fun one to punish sinners for," Spike adds. "They're all so goddamn lazy, that it becomes their way of life. They never have a clue what they've done to deserve us showing up."

"Exactly," I agree and turn to Jez. "Is there anything else you have for us?"

She slouches in her chair and rolls her eyes. "This

is the part where you say 'Thanks, Jez, but you're no longer necessary so get out' isn't it?"

"You're catching on."

She huffs out a breath and does what she has to do to shut down the built-in computer. After shoving the keyboard back under the table, she rises to her feet and returns her chair to the corner.

"No, there's nothing else." When she narrows her eyes at me, I add, "But thank you."

Jez nods and storms out of the room when the door slides open.

After it closes again, I address the room. "Let's put it to a vote. All in favor of taking out Dr. Fuc… Dr. Franklin?" All hands go up. "All in favor of Cece staying at the clubhouse for the rest of her medical treatment?" Same result. I focus on our secretary. "Great. Abyss, you'll be working with Jez to make sure a room in the medial wing is ready. I'd also like the two of you to pick Cece up at the hospital in the morning. That way you can speak with her doctor."

Abyss scribbles some notes and then gives me a thumbs-up. "Got it, Prez."

"As for the rest of you," I begin. "I expect you to be on your best behavior. Cece isn't one of the club bunnies. She's not here for your dicks. And for fuck's sake, do *not* mention what the club does or the fact that Dr. Franklin is on our radar. As far as she's aware, we're doing this for Jez since they're friends. She's already leary about it all, and I don't wanna scare her."

"Since when do you care?" Malice asks. "She's just a job, right?"

"She's a person, and she's been through enough without us adding shit to the pile," I bark.

Malice holds his hands up in mock surrender. "Damn. Okay."

"If there's nothing else, you're dismissed."

Everyone files out of the room but Grim. Instead, he remains in his chair, his stare glued to my face as if assessing me.

"What?"

Grim shakes his head, but he smirks. "You like this chick." His brow arches in perfect sync with the last movement of his hands.

"No, I don't," I insist.

"Keep telling yourself that, Prez." Grim pushes up from his chair. "I mean, if it helps you sleep at night."

Before I can respond, he turns his back on me, making it impossible. A growl escapes, and for once, I'm glad the big man can't hear because if he could, he'd know for sure that I'm lying.

I PACE THE LENGTH OF THE GARAGE AS I WAIT FOR CECE to arrive. That's all I've done since church ended yesterday: pace and think. And conjure up images of our soon to be house guest that I have no business conjuring. So here I am, pacing and thinking, and trying to contain my annoyance at it being later than we hoped to have Cece out of that godforsaken hospital.

The delay couldn't be helped though. Abyss wanted to secure a device that would allow Cece to receive her antibiotics without the nuisance of an IV line or IV pole. His contact got greedy and dragged out the compensation negotiation. That contact is now dead, and his body is so far beneath the clubhouse that he'll never be found.

A person doesn't commit one of the seven deadly sins and survive when we're involved. It just doesn't happen.

The garage doors open, pulling me out of my thoughts, and I turn in time to see Jezebel's Charger enter. The vehicle is moving slower than normal, and I can't stop the laughter that provokes.

After the vehicle is parked in its assigned spot,

Abyss steps out of the driver's side while Jez gets out on the passenger side.

"We'd have been here twenty minutes ago if Grandpappy here hadn't insisted on driving," Jez complains.

"There was no way in hell I was gonna be the one to tell your brother that our patient was dead," Abyss counters. "Because that's what woulda happened if you drove. You're a fucking maniac."

"Do they always argue like they're married?" Cece asks as she walks around the vehicle to where I can see her.

She's no longer sporting hospital attire, which isn't exactly a good thing. Cece turned me on in that shit, but it has nothing on the way her curves are packed into the pair of leggings and sweater that hangs off one shoulder.

I'm so fucked.

"I'll take that as a yes," she says when I don't answer.

"Oh, yeah. Um…" I turn to walk to the elevator so I can adjust myself without sending her screaming for the hills. "Yeah, they argue like that all the time. Most of us do."

"That wasn't discreet, Soul," Jez calls out. "But A for effort."

"Fuck off," I bark.

I wait by the elevator for the three of them to catch up. When Cece is within feet of me, she tilts her head. Her stare reminds me of Grim's assessing gaze after church, and I don't like it.

"Are you sure about this, Soul?" Cece asks quietly. "I feel like I'm imposing."

"You're not imposing, Ce," Jez responds before I can. "Soul's just cranky in the morning."

"It's not morning," Abyss helpfully points out.

I clench my jaw and silently count to ten. Then I smile at Cece. "It's no imposition. I've just got a lot on my mind."

Her gaze lowers, and her cheeks turn a sickeningly sexy shade of crimson. With the riot of red curls piled atop her head, and her icy blue eyes, the vision she creates is way too close to those images I've been conjuring.

Yep. Well and truly fucked.

I watch her watching me, and my jeans become too tight. Short of jacking off right here and now, there is nothing I can do about it, and Cece notices. She lifts her head so fast, it's a wonder she doesn't get whiplash.

Abyss clears his throat, reminding me that we're not alone. "As fun as this is to watch, I need to get Cece's antibiotics going. I don't want her to be without them for long," he says.

"Buzzkill," Jez mumbles.

"Seriously?" Abyss chuckles. "You wanted to watch your brother eye fuck—"

"That's enough," I snarl and then take several deep breaths. "Cece, gimme your hand."

"I'm not fixing that for you." She tips her head to indicate my rock hard erection, and then her eyes grow wide. "I mean… That seems like a personal… I'm sure it's great and… Dammit!" she groans and shakes her head. "Why do you need my hand?"

Without responding, I grab her wrist and lift her hand so I can press her thumb to the scanner next to the elevator. When the doors slide open, I practically drag her inside, with Jez and Abyss right behind us.

"That's why."

"Oh." She pulls out of my grasp. "Okay. Makes… Wait." Cece lifts her eyes to mine.

"Where'd you get my fingerprint?" Her fearful eyes dart from me to Jezebel. "What have you gotten me into? What aren't you telling me?"

"Calm down," Jez coaxes. "I got your fingerprint from a database. Turns out, your parents had you fingerprinted when you were little for one of those safety program things in case you ever went missing. As for what I'm getting you into…" Jez shrugs. "The clubhouse has security in place to keep everyone who lives here safe. Your fingerprint will be required to come and go, as well as to get into any room."

"Well, not *any* room," Abyss tacks on. "There are some that are off-limits."

"Why?"

"Because club business is club business," I tell her.

"What does that even mean?" Cece practically screeches.

I face her fully, and apparently, my body has detached from my brain because I cup her cheeks. If I could control myself, there's no way in hell I'd touch her. Not when I'm already walking a fine line between sibling favor and lurid fantasy.

"There is nothing for you to worry about," I say, my tone much calmer than I actually feel. "I know we're virtually strangers, but you're safe here. Especially from us."

Cece locks eyes with me and after what feels like hours instead of seconds, she nods. "Okay."

"Good girl."

Cece's pupils dilate, and her nostrils flare at my praise. Seems I'm not the only one suffering from a case of forgive-me-father-for-I-want-to-sin.

Forcing my deviant thoughts from my mind, I spend the next twenty minutes giving Cece a tour of the clubhouse while Jez and Abyss retreat to the medical wing.

"I hope you don't expect me to remember all of this," Cece comments when we re-enter the common room.

"It's a lot to take in, I know."

"Ya think?" Her tone drips with sarcasm. "Sorry. I don't mean to sound ungrateful. I'm thrilled to not be in the hospital."

"Look, I know you don't wanna fucking be here." When she opens her mouth to protest, I rush to continue. "And that's okay. But try to relax. That's the only way you're gonna get better."

"Why do you care so—"

"Soul, baby, who is this?"

I glance down at the hand on my arm before looking at Gwen. She smiles sweetly, but her eyes spark with a possessiveness she can't hide.

"Did I ask you to touch me?" I sneer as I pluck her hand away from me.

Gwen pouts, her blood-red bottom lip poking out. As a club bunny, she's got sensual down to a science. But she needs to remember that I haven't dipped my wick in that particular honey pot in over a year and have no intention of doing so again.

Gwen glares at Cece, eyes her from the top of her

head to her toes and back again. "She won't cut it, Soul. The brothers want sex kittens, not *cat ladies.*"

"Excuse me?" Cece squares her shoulders, and her face flushes with indignation. "I don't know who you are, nor do I care, but I wouldn't push your luck, *Kitten*. I've got a boulder-sized ball of rage in me right now, and nothing would be more satisfying than throwing it your way."

"Are you gonna let her talk to me that way, Soul?" Gwen huffs.

Cece shifts her glare to me, daring me to take the bunny's side.

No worries, babe.

"Yeah, I am," I tell Gwen. Gripping her biceps, I spin her around to face her in the direction of the wing where her room is located. "Get the fuck outta here. I don't wanna see your face the rest of the day."

Gwen stomps her foot like a petulant child, but she leaves.

"Sorry 'bout that," I tell Cece. "The bunnies aren't all bad. But they're territorial."

"Bunnies?"

I scratch my chin, trying to come up with a delicate way to explain.

Delicate? Jesus, don't pussy up to impress her. Be yourself. If that's not good enough, too fucking bad.

"Whores," I clarify. "Women who hang around

the club to fuck the brothers. We've got three in house right now: Nikki, Bunny, and Gwen."

"Have you slept with all of them?" Her eyes widen, the blue irises swirling with embarrassment. "Nevermind. Not my business."

I chuckle at her. "I'm not gonna lie. I have slept with them. But not in a year or so."

"Why not?"

I tilt my head. "You really do speak whatever fucking pops in your head, don't you?"

"I thought we established this yesterday," she teases, and my cock jerks at her easy going manner. "My life is a shitstorm, which means my filters are broken, which means I have no control over what I say."

"Ah, right." I grin. "I forgot."

For a second, Cece looks like she's going to keep the banter going, but then she yawns.

Plump lips, wide mouth… the perfect place to slide my—

"I'm getting a little tired. Do you think you could take me to my room now?"

"Sure thing."

I guide her to the medical wing. When we pass the first room, Jezebel rushes to the door.

"You're just in the next suite," Jez tells her. "I'll

give Abyss some time with you to get your meds going, and then I'll pop in."

Cece nods absently. It's a stark contrast to the teasing from just a few minutes ago, but it's the reminder I need to keep my thoughts, and my dick, to myself. She's sick and overwhelmed, and I don't want to be another reason for the shitstorm to last.

I press my hand to the small of her back and urge her to the next room. She presses her thumb to the keypad when I instruct her to, and the door slides open. Cece doesn't move.

"You can go in."

She leans her head through the doorway, as if to check for hiding monsters. Then she straightens and turns toward me.

"This isn't a room, Soul," she says as she rests her hands on her hips. "It's a damn penthouse apartment!"

"Hardly," I snort. "But you're right, it's more than a room." I pull her inside the space, and the door closes behind us. "In my defense, I did tell you that you'd be comfortable. You've got the sleeping area there." I point to the left and then turn to the right. "Along that wall is the kitchenette. You also have a small living area where you can chill and watch TV if you don't wanna come out to the common room." I guide her to doors along the back wall. "Through that door is the closet, which is obnoxiously big, and through the other one is the bathroom."

Cece opens the second door and gasps. "Holy shit."

"Like I said, comfortable."

"There's a soaker tub in here."

"And a rain shower." I shrug.

"This is too much," she insists as she strides out into the main area of her suite. "I can't stay here. This in ins—"

"You're staying."

"But…"

"No buts, babe. You agreed to stay, so you're staying. It's really not that big a deal."

She opens and closes her mouth like a fish. Finally, her shoulders sag and her lips tilt into a sad smile. "Thank you."

"Don't mention it."

Cece's smile widens, morphing from sadness to something better, something more… happy content. Her eyes gleam with the emotion, and the awkwardness seems to melt away.

"So, when is Abyss going to ge—"

The door to her room slides open, and Abyss strides in. His gaze darts from me to Cece and back again.

"I can come back if this isn't a good time," he says, a shiteating grin on his face.

"I thought you wanted to get her meds going."

"I do, but it looks like—"

"Now is the perfect time," Cece says brightly. "Is it okay if I lie down while you do whatever it is you need to do?"

"Absolutely," Abyss says, and they both walk over to the bed. "I just need to get this bad boy in place, check your vitals, and then you can rest if you like."

Cece climbs onto the mattress and rolls to her back. "Sounds perfect."

"Great. First I'm going to…"

I miss everything else he says. My focus is solely on the beautiful creature lying on the fluffy comforter Jez insisted Cece needed. And my mind travels to fantasy land, pumping the brakes only to savor each vision of me doing wicked things to said creature.

My dick swells, and my jeans shrink to an uncomfortable, impossibly small size.

I'm beyond fucked.

CHAPTER NINE

CECE

"How does this work?"

I stare at the contraption Abyss is holding. It's round, about the size of a silver dollar, and very slim. If he wasn't sitting next to me, where I'm able to get a good look, I'd swear it's money.

"This is a state-of-the-art Medication Distributor IV, or MDIV for short." He smirks. "It's basically the same thing as an insulin pump. Only this little guy can hold any long-term medication, and can be controlled with the app on my cell phone."

Abyss flips the MDIV over, and I see tiny needles surrounding what appears to be a bigger needle in the center. The smaller ones remind me of hooks, and I shudder.

"Fucking needles," I mutter. I'm out of the hospital and still have to deal with fucking needles.

"Are you afraid of needles?" Soul asks from the other side of the room.

Shit, I forgot he was still here.

"No, but I've been poked and prodded more in the past couple weeks than I have in my entire life. I'm kinda over it." Shrugging, I look at Abyss. "So where do you stick it?"

"I can *stick* it wherever you want, sweetheart."

I don't miss the double entendre, and I laugh as I smack his arm. "Smartass."

"Yeah, Soul, where can Abyss *stick* it?" Jez, who seemingly came out of nowhere, smirks at her brother.

"I thought you were in your fucking room." Soul scowls, his eyebrows drawn together, and his face reddens.

If he was a cartoon character, smoke would be spiraling out of his nose. He doesn't look amused, which I don't understand because I thought the whole idea was for me to be *comfortable.*

"I figured Ce could use some backup," Jez responds. "Too much testosterone in the room."

I chuckle quietly, but when Soul's piercing gaze shifts from Abyss to me, I know there was nothing quiet about it.

"Quit fucking around. We have shit to do." Soul turns to walk out but not before he shoots a glare at Abyss.

"Alrighty then." Jez's impression of Ace Ventura is crappy, but it breaks the tension.

"Anyway," Abyss draws out, trying to get us back on the task at hand. "We can stick it wherever you want. Ideally it would be in a vein, but, as I said, this works just like an insulin pump, so it can go anywhere." Abyss explains, this time more serious. "Basically, wherever it's most comfortable for you. The only discomfort you'll experience should be the slight pinch as I attach the MDIV to your body, but after it's in place, all I'll have to do is screw this compartment piece off and swap out the cartridge every two days. You won't feel that since I'm not doing anything to the part that's attached to you."

He unscrews the compartment he mentioned to show me the four small vials it holds. Due to the MDIV's small size, I never would've guessed it could hold anything.

"This is the antibiotic." He points to the vials. "It's attached as one unit, and all I need to do when it's time to change them is pop the unit out and replace it with a new one. I'll set up everything on the app: a timer so the device knows when to distribute the medication and an alarm to alert me if you have any type of reaction. That way, when I'm not at the clubhouse, I still know what's going on and can make any necessary adjustments."

"That's pretty freaking cool." I stare at the distributor. "Where in the heck did you get something like this?"

"I know a guy," Abyss says as he grabs some cotton balls and alcohol. "Where do you want it?"

I think about it for a second. It would be nice to have it hidden but also accessible.

"Better put it in her arm," Jez says. The two of them exchange a look that I can't read.

"Cece, is that okay with you?" Abyss asks.

"Sure, works for me."

Abyss cleans an area on my arm and places the MDIV. I watch as he sets up the times and alerts in the app on his phone.

"I don't think you'll have any reactions to the antibiotics since you were already receiving them at the hospital, but I don't want to assume either, so I'll be keeping watch."

"Damn, that's more attention than I ever got from Dr. Fucktard."

Abyss chuckles.

"Thanks for setting this up for me. Your bedside manner is much better than Dr. Fucktard."

"No problem." Abyss stands and gathers his stuff. "Let me know if it bothers you at all. Otherwise, I'll check in with you later."

"Gonna warn you now, if you think about coming

in here and waking me up in the middle of the night to take my vitals, I can't be held responsible for my actions," I threaten.

"What will you do?" He arches a brow and smirks.

"I'll shove the stethoscope, or whatever else you're using to check my vitals, so far up your ass, a proctologist won't even be able to find them."

Jez explodes with laughter, and Abyss stares at me with his mouth hanging open.

"Cece doesn't like being woken up," Jez spits out through her laughter.

"No shit. She couldn't have made herself more clear." Abyss winks at me. "Don't worry, Cece, I won't be waking you up. No one will come into your room unless it's an emergency or you invite them."

"Spread the word." I smile at him innocently.

After Abyss leaves, I move my arm around to test how the MDIV feels. He was right, I don't feel it at all now that it's embedded in my skin.

"What do you want to do?" Jez asks.

"What *can* we do?"

"Basically anything we want. I need to unpack some stuff real quick, and you could probably use a minute to get situated."

I nod because she isn't wrong. Today has been a

whirlwind of activity, and I could use some alone time and a chance to freshen up.

"How about we take an hour to unwind and then meet in the huge common area?" I suggest. I'm pretty sure I can find my way back there.

"You sure?"

Nodding, I walk toward the bathroom. "Yeah, as long as I don't get lost in there," I say pointing at the massive space.

"Alright, I'll meet you in the common room in an hour." Jez waves over her head as she walks out the door. It slides shut once she's through, and I wonder, not for the first time, if there are motion sensors in place.

I step into the bathroom and glance around.

Damn, this room alone might be bigger than my whole apartment.

I swallow past the lump in my throat. My apartment isn't my apartment anymore. Now that Carmella is moving, she had all of my belongings moved over to my mom's house... Well, *my* house now.

I shake my head to clear my thoughts, not wanting to think about any of that right now. Right now, I need to unpack so I can explore my new digs. Falling apart will have to wait until later.

I grab my toiletry bag and start unpacking my

makeup and other necessities before moving back into the bedroom. The club sure didn't spare any expense to furnish these rooms. There's a large dresser and walk-in closet, both of which I barely fill with the clothes I brought.

Glancing at the clock, I notice only thirty minutes have passed, so I decide to take a quick shower to wash the hospital smell off of me. I've never used a rainshower before, but it's phenomenal. Add in the steam settings that Soul forgot to mention, and I'm rethinking ever leaving the shower. But I can't stay in it forever, so with a sigh, I grab a towel off the stocked racks and wrap it around my body.

"I'll be back," I whisper as I stroke the shower door lovingly.

Fuck, you need to get laid. A shower should not *cause an orgasmic reaction.*

Rather than trying to tame my wild curls, I pull my hair up into a high ponytail. I love my locks, but they're a bitch to control. I apply a bit of makeup... Not much, but enough to bring attention to my eyes and plump my lips. I don't know why I even bother because it's not like there's anyone to impress.

Liar! You know exactly who you want noticing you.

I shake my head and remind my lady bits that I'm not here to ride cock.

After pulling on a pair of jeans that mold to my

curves and a royal blue sweater that makes my hair look an even brighter shade of red. I swear my coochie laughs at me.

Yeah, keep telling yourself you're not out to impress.

I give myself a quick pep talk and head out the door. As I walk down the hall, I can't help but wonder if I was wrong about being able to find my way to the common room. This place is fucking massive. There are doors everywhere but not all of them are shut, and there are multiple suites just like the one I'm staying in.

At the end of the hallway, I turn to the right. The sound of music and laughter fills the air. Just as I round the corner, I run right into a brick wall.

"Fuck," I mutter. I jump back, but not before I'm grabbed by my shoulders.

"Whoa there." I lift my head toward the deep voice. "You okay?"

"Um, yeah. I think so." I rub my nose and stare at the sexy as sin biker, who's wearing a cut that looks exactly like the one Soul wears.

He winks. "You aren't so bad yourself."

"Oh shit, I said that out loud didn't I?"

"Yeah, you did," the biker says. "I'm glad you think I'm sexy as sin." He grabs my hand and kisses it. "I'm Thorn."

"Back the fuck off, brother," Soul yells. I look for

him but come up empty. "Bring her to the common room."

Thorn laughs "Ah, you must be Cece. Soul told us all about you," he divulges. "I think we are being watched." He points to cameras in the corners, all of which I hadn't noticed. "We have a security system throughout the clubhouse, which allows you to see just about anywhere, other than the bedrooms and bathrooms, of course."

"I'm... uh... yes, I'm Cece," I stutter, my mind completely focused on the fact that I'm being watched. I'm not real sure how I feel about that.

Thorn gently grabs my elbow and leads me down the hall. The farther we walk, the louder the music gets. When we reach what Thorn reminds me is the common room, I stop dead in my tracks. I know Soul gave me a tour earlier, but I'm still stunned by the massive space.

Turning in a circle, I take in several couches, two pool tables, a sound system, four or five dartboards on the wall, and a bar. And it's not a bar one would expect to find in an underground clubhouse. No, it's a full-fledged bar, and there's even a man behind it taking orders.

People are scattered everywhere. Out of the corner of my eye, I see Jez talking to a guy I haven't met yet. I take a step toward them, but Thorn takes a hold of my wrist and tugs me back to his side. I open my mouth to ask him what he wants when all of a sudden he whistles really loud. The music stops, and the room is shrouded in silence as everyone stares directly at us.

"Hey assholes, this is Cece, and she thinks I'm sexy as sin." Thorn lowers his gaze to take me in, and my cheeks heat.

"Is she drunk?" someone yells.

"Fuck you! She told me herself," Thorn shouts.

"Great, asshole's ego is big enough without adding to it," Abyss says as he steps up behind us.

"Thorn, quit being a dick." Jez hurries to my side. "Come on, I'll introduce you."

"See ya later," I call out to Thorn as she leads me away.

"He'll be lucky if Soul doesn't kick his ass," Jez mumbles.

"Why would Soul kick his ass? Oh, and why didn't you tell me I was being watched?" I tack on as an afterthought.

"What?"

"Why am I being watched? Thorn and I ran into each other in the hallway and the next thing I know, I hear Soul telling Thorn to 'back the fuck off'." I huff out a breath. "Thorn kindly pointed out all the cameras."

"Ugh, sorry. They're security features Soul insisted be installed. There aren't any cameras in the rooms, but the intercom is. Just so you can call for help or assistance," she explains. "I'm so used to it, I didn't even think to warn you."

"It just caught me off guard, is all."

We make our way to a pool table where four members are playing. Normally, I'd ask to join, but there are too many men in the room to stay focused. Not that they're my type, but I *am* human.

Damn, is it a requirement of the club to be hot as fuck and built like Henry Cavill?

"No gorgeous, it's not," a man with shaggy hair says. "The women just prefer it."

"Not again," I groan.

"Leave her alone, Spike," Jez spits out.

Jez proceeds to introduce me to the men around the table. Spike, Rogue, Possum, and Frenzy all greet me, and their stares seem to penetrate through my flesh. We chat for a minute before Jez leads me away and over to the bar.

"Can you have any alcohol?" she asks me.

I shrug. "Water is fine for now." I don't really feel like drinking anyway.

The bartender winks as he hands me a bottled water. I'm so far out of my element here, but at least everyone seems pretty nice… so far. Most of the men are big flirts. All but Frenzy, who told me he was married. He said his wife, Heather, is wandering around somewhere and that I'd meet her later.

Jez leads me to the couches, and we sit. Soul steps out of one of the rooms, and I can't help but wonder what he was doing.

"That's where the kitchen is," Jez explains as if I'd spoken out loud. "The community kitchen anyway. That's where you can go and get breakfast in the morning."

Soul looks around and smiles when he spots us. As he walks in our direction, I notice he's carrying a plate of food.

"Here, I figured you'd be hungry." He thrusts the pizza-filled plate at me. "I forgot to tell you when dinner was."

"Hey Prez, how come you didn't serve *me* dinner?" Thorn calls to Soul.

"Thorn, I swear on all that is unholy, you are trying my fucking patience today," Soul grits out from behind clenched teeth.

Of course, my stomach grumbles at this exact moment. I try to avoid eye contact with Soul as I say, "Thanks. I didn't realize how late it was getting."

"Better fucking eat then."

I inhale the sweet smell of pizza before picking up a piece and taking a small bite. Without thinking, I moan. This is one of the best homemade pizzas I've ever tasted. I look up from my plate and catch Soul staring at me with a heated gaze.

I swallow slowly and take a drink of water. "Sorry, it's just really good."

"Glad you like it."

Soul's gravelly voice has me shifting on the couch.

"Gee, thanks bro. Couldn't grab your sister a piece?" Jez's voice is like ice-cold water on my libido.

"You can walk your ass to the kitchen and get your own. You *do* remember where the kitchen is, don't you?"

"So it's like that, is it?" Jez stands. "Will you be okay out here while I go get some pizza?" She glares at Soul. "Since my brother is too much of a dick to bring me a piece."

"She'll be fine." Soul waves her off.

I nod, and Jez heads to the kitchen. I glance around the room, still not believing how big this place is.

"You get settled?" Soul asks, interrupting my thoughts, as he takes the seat Jez just vacated.

"Yeah. Thanks again for letting me stay. Everyone seems nice."

"You need anything, let me or Jez know."

I yawn and suddenly, I feel as if I was hit by a freight train. I press my fingers to my temples.

"What's wrong?"

"Just a small headache. It's been a long day."

"I knew you should've stayed in your fucking room." Soul stands and offers me his hand.

"Am I a prisoner?" I rise to my feet but ignore his hand.

He raises his eyebrows. "What are you talking about?"

"Am. I. A. Prisoner?" My tone is clipped as I snap each word.

"Why would you think you're a fucking prisoner?" Soul scowls.

"Why else would you want me to stay in my room?"

"Seriously?" he deadpans. "Because you just got out of the fucking hospital, and you need fucking rest." He rubs his hands down his face.

Regretting my outburst, I fidget with my hands. "Sorry, I shouldn't have said that. I'm tired and have a headache."

"I'll walk you back to your room."

"No, that's okay. I'll wait for Jez."

"Abyss," Soul calls out. "Let Jez know I took Cece back to her room."

Abyss simply lifts his chin in acknowledgment. I sigh at the way Soul takes charge of everything.

"What's wrong?"

"Nothing, it's just… the way you take charge." I shrug. "It's kinda hot. And I feel like I'll just be getting used to it by the time I have to leave."

Now that I say it out loud, it makes me sad. I've always felt like I have to be in control or in charge. But with Soul, I find myself wondering what it would be like to give some of that up. He does things for me, small things, like walking me back to my room, and it's nice. I've been here less than twenty-four hours, and it already feels safe and comfortable. Almost like home.

Soul glances at me with a look I can't decipher, but says nothing as rests his hand at the small of my back and guides me to my room.

When we stop in front of the door, he says, "Here we are. Use your thumbprint to open it up." He nods at the scanner on the wall. "Breakfast is at eight."

"Thanks Soul, for everything," I say softly as the door slides closed behind me.

I quickly get ready for bed and rub my temples again to ease the ache. If I didn't know any better, I'd say someone is using a jackhammer in my skull.

You overdid it.

The doctor warned me before I left the hospital to

take it easy the first couple of days. But I couldn't help it. I was tired of being cooped up in bed. I wanted to get out and explore my new place, even if it is only temporary.

I look through my bag for some pain reliever and find the Percocet. I have a couple left from the prescription Dr. Fucktard wrote for me. I've avoided taking them, other than when it's absolutely necessary. And right now, it's necessary. My head is killing me, and I need some sleep.

"Fuck it," I mumble just before popping a pill into my mouth, and then I slip into bed.

CHAPTER TEN

SOUL

"You're sayin' a whole lotta nothing, Prez, but that look…"

I glare at Asher as I flip him off. I'm fully aware of the semi-permanent scowl that's been on my face since a certain woman stepped into my world, and his pointing it out pisses me off.

"Where's Abyss?" I ask, looking around the room.

Asher shrugs. "Don't know. He wasn't here to cook this morning, so I'm guessing he's still sacked out with some no-name bitch."

I point at the pile of pancakes in the middle of the table. "Who made those?"

"I did." I whirl around to see Jez striding into the room. "Eat at your own risk." She grins.

"Fuckin' hell," I mumble and cross the room to yank open the refrigerator door.

Digging through the containers of leftovers and fresh fruit that only seems to be present when Jezebel is here. Nothing catches my eye, so I'm stuck with the pancakes that likely taste like sand.

"Ya know, you could be a little more appreciative of my efforts." Jezebel pokes out her bottom lip, but when I flip *her* off, she doubles over laughing. "You are so goddamn predictable," she says when she sobers.

"How's Cece doing?" I ask after filling a plate and sitting. I know I'm being obvious, but apparently, I don't give a shit.

"I didn't check on her." She shrugs. "Figured she'd be here."

"So no one has laid eyes on her this morning?"

"Guess not. I'm sure she's fine, Soul. She's probably just sleeping in."

I stand and dump the contents of my plate into the trash. As hungry as I am, the desire to see Cece is strong. And the worry swirling in my gut doesn't give a red scent about my appetite.

"Hey, dipshit, I worked har..."

Jezebel's words fade into the background as I make my way through the common area. My boots thud on the concrete floor in sync with the pounding of my heart against my ribcage. I'm not used to worrying about women, as they've always served a specific purpose for me, but something tells me I should get used to it where Cece is concerned.

When I reach her room, I knock, not wanting to barge in like a madman, but I get no response. I knock several more times… nothing. Taking a deep breath, I press my thumb to the scanner on the wall. The door slides open, too slow for my liking.

Get a grip, man.

As soon as I enter the room, my gaze zeroes in on the bed, where Cece is still snuggled under the blankets. I take a moment, or five, to appreciate the view. The fluffy blanket hides the parts of her that get my motor running, but there's something about the way her fiery curls are splayed out over the pillow that makes me feel… things.

Careful not to make too much noise, I walk to the side of the bed. The closer I get, the more I can see that something is wrong. Cece's face is shiny with sweat, and her skin is flushed.

I gently shake her shoulder. "Cece, babe, time to get up."

Cece doesn't so much as flinch, and the hairs on the back of my neck stand on end. This isn't good.

"Cece, c'mon," I say as I shake her a bit more forcefully. "I need you to open those pretty blues for me."

Nothing. The worry gnawing at my gut earlier intensifies. I pull out my cell and call Abyss.

"Yo, Pr—"

"Something's wrong with Cece," I bark. "Where the fuck are you?"

"She's fine, Prez," he counters. "I just checked the app and there are—"

"The app is wrong!" I switch the call to video and turn the cell so he can see her. "Tell me, *doctor,* is she supposed to be unresponsive?"

"Fuck," Abyss mutters when he sees Cece. "Get her into the shower, cool her down. I'm on my way."

With those parting words, he disconnects the call, and I stand frozen in place. I stare at Cece, Abyss's instructions flashing in my mind like the neon sign hanging on the building at Purgatory.

Get her in the shower, cool her down.

Get her in the shower, cool her down.

Get her in the—

Don't just stand here!

I toss the blankets off Cece and scoop her up. Heat radiates from her body, reminding me of a space heater cranked to the highest possible setting. I rush to the bathroom, Cece limp in my arms, and turn on the shower.

Cool water rains down from above, and without giving it a second thought, I step under the spray, clothes and all. It takes several seconds, but eventually, Cece sputters and flails to life.

"Calm down," I urge while I tighten my hold on

her so she doesn't fall to the tiled shower basin. "Cece, I need you to cal—"

"It's freezing," she screeches as she continues to struggle against me.

As her body wiggles and shimmies, my eyes lower to her nipples, which are visible through the soaked white tank she's wearing. Her shorts are plastered to her thighs, and my body reacts.

I ease her to her feet and back her against the wall, caging her in with my arms. I tell myself that it's so I can help her stay upright, but my throbbing cock doesn't see it that way. Cece stares at me with wide eyes, but her pupils are dilated. She's having a hard time being in such close proximity too.

Cece shivers, and while I'd love to think it's part of her reaction to me, I know the cold shower is the more likely culprit. I rub my hands up and down her arms, trying to warm her, even though I know the purpose of this whole thing is to break her fever.

"Wh-why a-am I i-in h-here?" Her teeth chatter with each word.

"You weren't waking up, and you were sweating from a fever," I explain. "I called Abyss, and he said to get you in the shower to cool you down."

"Fever?" Cece's face scrunches up in the most adorable way. "Is that w-why I'm so a-achy?"

"You're achy?"

Cece nods. "Every p-part of me aches, and my muscles feel like t-they're on fire."

"I'm sorry, babe." The thought of her being in any amount of pain almost brings me to my knees. "What can I do?"

"Put me b-back in bed," she snaps, but there's little heat in her tone. I have no doubt she meant there to be, but she's too tired, too weak to be even the slightest bit forceful.

"No can do." I shake my head. "Abyss said to put you in the shower and that's what I did. Now I'm keeping you here until he arrives."

Cece glares at me, but doesn't argue. Her small hands rest on my forearms, and that simple touch lights me up from the inside out.

Not now!

"I'm t-tired, Soul." She leans against my chest.

I rest my chin atop her head. "I know."

"When will Ab—"

"Jesus, I'm so sorry."

I swivel my head to see Abyss standing just outside the shower, a stricken look on his face.

"What the fuck?" I snarl. "How could you let this happen?"

"Prez, I'm sorry," he says. "I didn't get any alerts or anything to indicate there was a problem."

"I hope the pussy was worth it."

"S-Soul," Cece says quietly. "It's not h-his fault."

"Bullshit!"

"Soul, brother, it's not like that," Abyss practically pleads. "Here, let's get her changed into some dry clothes and back to bed."

He holds his arms out like he expects me to hand her over, but that shit ain't happenin'.

"I got her," I bark and lift Cece into my arms. I carry her out of the bathroom and toward the dresser. "Babe, I'm gonna need you to help a little, okay? You need to get out of these wet clothes."

"Naked? You w-wanna get me na-naked?"

I arch a brow. "Don't ask questions you don't want an honest answer to, babe." Cece's mouth falls open, and I push on her chin to close it. "But for now, let's just focus on getting you changed as quickly as possible so Abyss can make this right."

Cece stares at me for a long moment, then nods.

"Good girl." I rub my thumb over her cheek as I look at Abyss. "Make yourself fucking useful and grab a t-shirt and sweatpants for me," I order.

"On it!" Abyss rifles through the dresser and yanks out the items I asked for. "Here." He thrusts them at me.

"Help her stay on her feet while I change her."

Abyss steps up behind Cece, and when he rests

his hands on her hips, I can't stop the growl that barrels out of me. He quickly holds his hands up.

"Just stand there," I snap. "And don't let her fall."

"Got it. Hands off, don't let her fall."

"Okay, Cece, I'm gonna strip off your tank." A panicked glaze appears in her eyes, but she nods. I yank the tank over her head, forcing myself to remain locked on her stare. With hurried movements, I tug the dry t-shirt into place and smile. "There. Easy peasy."

Cece rolls her eyes. "Just h-hurry."

"I'm trying, babe." I kneel down in front of her. "This is where I need your help, okay?" She nods. "Good. Now, when I pull down the shorts, just lift one leg at a time so I can get them off and then again to pull on the sweats. Can you do that?"

"If it m-means I can lay d-down, yes."

I hate that she's still shivering, especially since her skin is still warm to the touch. Her fever might be slightly lower than when I first found her, but it's not gone.

Taking a deep breath, I hook my thumbs in the waistband of her shorts and slide them down her legs. Her scent wraps around me, and my eyes close as I inhale. A man could get used to that smell. Hell, a man could get lost in it.

"Ah, Soul?"

My eyes fly open, and I see Abyss leaning around Cece to stare at me. I shake my head, hoping like hell that it flings the memory of being this close to her cunt away.

It doesn't. Something tells me nothing could ever rid my mind of the memory of being mere inches away from heaven.

Heaven? Fuck, you're getting soft.

I reach behind me and grab the sweats before helping her to lift her legs so I can put them on her. Once the pants are loosely hanging from her hips, I stand and lift her into my arms again.

"Let's get you into bed, babe," I say as I carry her to the bed and lay her down.

Cece moans when she hits the blankets, and curls into a ball.

"Shit. I shoulda changed the damn sheets."

"You can once I'm done checking her over and figure out what caused the fever," Abyss tells me.

I sit on the edge of the mattress as he taps around his cell screen, no doubt sorting through that shit-show he calls an app.

"Well, what the hell happened?" I ask when my patience is zapped.

Instead of answering, Abyss focuses on Cece. "I'm going to check your vitals, okay?"

"Mmm," is Cece's only response.

As he works, I clench my hands so I don't reach out to comfort her. I don't comfort people, I act as judge, jury, and executioner. That's a role I'm familiar with and embrace. So why does this slip of a woman have me tied up in knots, wondering what it would be like to give someone more?

"Your temp is still a little high, as is your blood pressure," Abyss tells her. "With your symptoms, mainly the spiked fever, I'd say you have an infection. I'm going to increase the dosage of your antibiotics. I'll have to change the vials a little sooner this first time, but moving forward, I'll make sure there's enough medication to cover the increased dosage."

"Thank you," Cece mumbles.

"No problem." Abyss messes with the app again, then puts his cell into his cut. "I'm sorry I wasn't here."

"We'll discuss that in private," I tell him, not giving Cece a chance to say anything. "You can go."

"I'll be back in an hour or so to check on you," he tells her. "Get some rest."

"She will. I'll make sure of it."

"S-stop being an ass," Cece says, with a hint of censure in her tone.

"My club, my clubhouse… I'll be an ass if I want."

And now you sound like a grown man baby.

"Can you g-get Jez?"

"I'll go tell her to come here," Abyss says as he walks out of the room.

A minute or two passes with both Cece and I remaining silent. Now that we're alone, things are awkward. I don't know if it's because now I've seen her naked, sort of, or what, but I don't like it.

"Soul?"

"Yeah, babe?"

"You're g-getting the bed w-wet."

I glance down at myself and chuckle. I guess I was so focused on her that I forgot I was as soaked as she was.

"It seems I am."

"Don't."

"As soon as Jezebel gets here, I'll go change."

"At least s-stop sitting on the bed."

I hop to my feet and grin. "For someone who was unresponsive as little as thirty minutes ago, you sure are fucking bossy."

"Yep."

"Oh my God!"

I look toward the door and try not to gnash my teeth at the fact that we're not alone anymore. Jez rushes through the room and sits on the other side of Cece.

"What the hell happened?" my sister asks her.

"Fever," I snap as I cross my arms over my chest.

"Why are you wet?" Jez asks me, arching a brow.

"Had to get her in the shower to break the fever."

"You had to… I'll just bet you *had* to." She smirks, and I want to smack the look off her face. It's a good thing I don't hit women… Well, not unless I'm hired to punish a female sinner. Then all bets are off.

"Fuck off."

I stalk away from Cece, fighting everything in me that's screaming to stay. After rushing through the clubhouse to my room, I change as quick as humanly possible. I race back through the common room, ignoring my brother's questions, and press my thumb to the scanner when I reach Cece's room.

The door slides open, and I slow my steps as I make my way back to her bedside.

"That's gotta be a record, bro," Jez taunts.

"Fuck off."

"Both of you, s-shut up," Cece snaps.

"Soul, I'm sure you've got work to do. Ya know, somewhere other than here."

I glare at my twin. "Nope. I'm free today."

"Aren't you guys looking for new staff at Purgatory?" Jez counters. "I bet Rogue could use your help with that."

"If you're trying to get rid of me, give it up. I'm not going anywhere."

"And what about what Cece wants?"

I glance at the woman on the bed. "Do you want me to leave, babe?"

Cece stares at me for what feels like an hour and then shrugs. "He can s-stay."

And that's exactly what I do. I stay and watch over her as she sleeps restlessly throughout the day. I don't even leave when my stomach growls because Abyss brings me a plate of food when he stops in to check on Cece.

I stay because it's the only option. I stay, even as I internally battle myself. I know I should walk away and let my sister be the person at her side, but it's an impossibility at this point.

I stay because there isn't anywhere else my black, scarred, fucked up heart wants to be.

CHAPTER ELEVEN

CECE

"I'm telling you, something is off, Mel."

I've been at the clubhouse for a week now, and for the most part, I've been bored out of my mind. Between Carmella moving and starting the new job, this is the first chance she's had to call so we can catch up.

I've tried to stave off the mind-numbing boredom and keep busy. I'm pretty sure I have explored every nook and cranny there is in the clubhouse except for the rooms that are 'for club business', as Soul puts it. There are a lot of *those* rooms, the ones that are off-limits. Something doesn't add up for me though, and I want to know what Jez and Soul are hiding. But any time I ask questions, their answers are cryptic, or they change the subject.

On the plus side, everyone has been welcoming, and I finally got to meet Malice and Grim. Malice scares the shit out of me, what with his permanent scowl and the way he's always scanning a room. Jez assures me I've got nothing to worry about.

Grim, I found out, is deaf. I don't know ASL, so Soul gave me Grim's phone number so I could text him to communicate. He's huge and intimidating, but he has kind eyes that immediately put me at ease.

"Are you sure that it's not just your imagination?" Mel asks. "I don't think being confined in the clubhouse is good for you. You have too much time to watch TV."

"What do you mean?"

Mel sighs. "Whenever you don't have a million things going on, like you do at the store, or take any type of vacation, you watch TV and let your imagination run away."

"Okay, first off, I'm not that bad," I huff. "And secondly, what else am I supposed to think? They have *secret rooms,* Mel, rooms that are *off-limits,* and if I ask about them, they try to distract me with something else."

"Did it ever occur to you that you're just being a nosey bitch?"

"Not nosey, just curious," I correct. "What could there possibly be to hide?"

"I notice you didn't say you're not a bitch," Mel snickers.

"Whatever, Princess. Seriously though, what am I supposed to think?"

"You did say their clubhouse is underground… Could it be like an Area 51 situation, and they're a secret government agency?"

"No, that thought *never* crossed my mind." I roll my eyes. She knows that is *exactly* the first thought that popped into my head. "I mean they're a motorcycle club, and you've seen them riding around town, right? So why the secrecy?"

"Yeah, I've seen them around but that doesn't mean I know shit about them."

"Exactly! No one knows *anything* about them. Why not? Why the secrets? You don't think they're into anything illegal do you?" My mind continues to fire all kinds of conspiracy theories at me.

"Calm the fuck down. See, you *have* been watching too much TV."

"You calm down!"

"Deep breaths, Cece. You're getting all worked up over nothing. First, if they were doing anything illegal, do you really think they'd let you into their clubhouse? And second, do you think Jez would put you in a dangerous situation?"

I take a deep breath to steady my rapid heartbeat. Carmella is probably right, but there are still a lot of questions that I want answered.

"No, Jez isn't like that," I admit. "One thing I've gotten to know over the past month is that she is loyal to a fault. Not just to me, but also to the club." She has no issues going toe to toe with anyone who messes with those she considers family.

"As your BFF, that's good to know."

"Did I tell you what happened with Gwen?" I ask, bouncing to a totally random thought.

"The dick hopper? No, what?"

"Gwen was bitching about all the time Soul spends with me, which isn't much, and asked when I was leaving," I explain. "Jez told her to choke on a dick and that *no one, especially* a club slut, was going to question my presence."

"She told her to go choke on a dick? Damn, I wish I could've been there for that. Mel chuckles. "Wait, back up… Did you say that Soul doesn't spend that much time with you?"

"He doesn't."

"Then explain to me why Jez called me a week ago to tell me you're sick with a fever, and when I asked her if I needed to come back, she said it wasn't necessary because Soul refused to leave your side?"

"Soul was just making sure I was okay. He probably wanted to make sure I didn't croak in his *secret clubhouse* so he wouldn't have to dispose of a body.

Since then, I've hardly seen him, or anyone else, because they all work."

"Right, because I'm sure he has no way to dispose of a body out in the middle of nowhere," Mel says flippantly.

"Are you trying to annoy me?"

"Nope." She exaggerates the P. "Maybe he likes you. We already know you're hot for him."

"Being attracted to someone does not equate to liking them," I argue. "And I've already told you, Soul is off-limits. He's Jez's brother."

"Keep telling yourself that, Hooker. Maybe you'll actually start to believe it."

"Anyway, how's the new job?" I ask, desperately needing to change the subject.

It's not lost on me that dodging any conversation about Soul makes me a hypocrite when I'm complaining about him and Jez being cagey, but too bad. I'm serious when I say he's forbidden, which makes it ridiculous to even discuss. I don't want to risk my friendship with Jez for what could only be a one-night stand. Besides, I've seen how the men are with the club bunnies, and it makes me question if they're even capable of being faithful. Except for Frenzy, but he and Heather have been together since high school.

"Don't think I don't know what you're doing,"

she teases. "But I'll play along. I work on the fifth floor and have a small office with a great view. Right now, I'm handling smaller cases like petty theft, DUIs, that sort of thing, but I'm also helping the partners with their cases. It's been eye-opening working at such a large firm, but so far, I love it."

"I'm so happy you're living your dream. But I miss you," I admit.

"I miss you, too. Do you want me to come back and demand answers?" Mel asks. "I can come and go all lawyer on their asses."

"No, but you know you're the first person I'll call if I ever do need a lawyer."

"Oh shit." Mel laughs. "You haven't threatened or attempted to kill anyone have you?"

"You and Jez need to let shit go. It was *one* fucking time, and that nurse had it coming," I huff out.

"I'm sure the nurse feels the same way," she teases before taking a deep breath. "Seriously, if you need me to come back, I will. I don't want you somewhere you don't feel comfortable."

"No, I'm fine. You just started your job, and I won't let you jeopardize it for me. I appreciate it though."

"Girl, you're my best friend. I'd do anything for you."

"I know, but not this. I'll figure it out."

"If you're really bothered by what's going on, why don't you just talk to Jez?"

"Gee, why didn't I think of that?" I say sarcastically.

"You know what I mean. Put away the attitude, go pull her aside, and have an upfront, *adult* conversation with her."

"Are you implying that I *haven't* had an *adult* conversation with her?"

"You know what I mean. You have a tendency to be a smartass and storm off when you don't get the answers you want."

"Mel, I've tried. I'm telling you, they're hiding something."

"Sounds like you need to put on your big girl panties and talk to Jez." Mel pauses for a minute. "Do you really think it's something illegal?"

"Can't say for sure, but why all the secrecy if they have nothing to hide? Things just don't add up," I explain. "The security alone… I mean shit, I have to use my thumbprint to get into any closed door, and then there's the ones that even that won't open. Not to mention, all the whispered side conversations. Where the hell do they get the money to afford all that?"

"Maybe they won the lottery or something, and

like their privacy," she offers. "I get it though, it *does* sound a bit sketchy. But let's think about it logically. Why would they invite you into their clubhouse if things aren't on the up and up?"

"What if they're not planning on letting me go?"

"Until you talk to Jez or Soul, you're just gonna keep speculating and drive yourself crazy. I'm not saying you don't have a right to be cautious or curious," Mel says hesitantly. "But they *have* done a lot for you."

"I know." I sigh as I get out of bed to pace. "I'll let you get back to work."

"You know I love you, and I'll come home if you say the word."

"Yeah," I say, knowing she'd drop everything to come back. "But one of us has to make a living."

"Alright, but again, here if you need me. I'll talk to you later."

"Bye."

I replay my conversation with Carmella, her words stuck in my mind like gum on a shoe. She's right, I need to have a conversation with Jez or Soul.

No, not Soul. I'd probably try to climb him like a tree if I did.

Making a snap decision, I quit stalling and head to Jez's room. After knocking on the door, I think about what I'm going to say. The door opens, and Jez waves me in.

I take a deep breath, and words leave my mouth before I even step over the threshold.

"We need to talk."

CHAPTER TWELVE

SOUL

"ARE YOU SURE SHE'S WHO YOU WANT TO TAKE?"

"No, but she's better than Gwen," I snap at Thorn, but when he narrows his eyes, I sigh. "Look, Bunny isn't exactly wife material, but if her acting job in the sheets is any indication, she's our best bet."

"Just promise me you won't put her on the back of your bike, Soul. She gets any hint that you're sweet on her, she'll set her hooks and never let go."

"Seriously?" I cross my arms over my chest. "I wouldn't put that skank on the back of anything, let alone my Harley. And I'm not sweet on her. She's going to serve a purpose, that's it. Same as always."

"Good to know."

Thorn and I both whip our heads to see Bunny standing a few feet away, a smirk firmly in place.

"Bunny, look, you—"

"Chill, Soul." She laughs as she closes the

distance between us. "You were a good lay, like, way back when. I've got my sights set on someone else."

Thorn puffs out his chest. For someone who just warned me about misleading Bunny, he's sure doing a fine job of it himself.

Bunny glares at my SAA. "It's not you, dumbass. No way in hell would I fall for a biker." She darts her gaze to me. "No offense."

"Uh, none taken. But can I ask one question?"

"Shoot."

"If you don't like bikers, why the fuck are you a club bunny for Saints Purgatory?"

Bunny shrugs. "The club pays my tuition for grad school."

"Grad school?" I repeat like an idiot.

"Wow, you're as bad as the rest of them. Might want to try getting to know the woman standing on the legs y'all put your winkies in." Bunny links her arm through mine. "Now, hubby, let's get this show on the road."

Thorn's laughter follows us all the way to the elevator. When the doors slide shut, I glance down at her.

"Winkies?"

"Yep." She winks again. "My fiancé really hates me referring to other men's penises by cock. Says it gives them too much credit."

I swear I've never been as shocked as I have been in the last five minutes. And that's saying something.

"You're engaged? And he's good with… what you do?"

"He looks at it as an investment into our future. When we get married, we won't have to worry about debt. Besides, we've had an open relationship since day one, no point in fixing what isn't broken."

My nerve endings buzz, the always present need to *correct* those who sin warring with my desire to accept the people in my life for who they are.

They're not hurting anyone. Just let it go.

I tug at the neck of my long-sleeved tee and force my judgment from my mind. Bunny sure as hell isn't a saint, but really, who *is* in this world? And she's been good for my club, my brothers. Just because I don't like that she's fucking my brothers while she's engaged, doesn't mean it's the wrong thing to do. Like she said, it works for them, and that's what matters.

The drive to Boulder City Memorial is long but productive. I review the plan with Bunny as there isn't going to be room for mistakes. We need to engage Dr. Franklin, give him a story that matches Cece's circumstances, and see how things unfold.

When Jezebel came to me last night and told me that Cece is getting fed up with our secrecy, I decided it was time to take action. I understand that club business is club business. Hell, I created the rules. But for some strange reason, I hate keeping Cece in the dark about anything that pertains to her. And Dr. Franklin definitely pertains to her.

You know exactly why you hate keeping secrets from her. You fucking like her.

I called church this morning to discuss going undercover at the hospital to confirm that the good doctor is as awful as he seems. Once we confirm, we can act. And then maybe, just maybe, I can give Cece more information.

After parking the truck in the parking lot designated for the ER, Bunny and I head toward the entrance. Halfway to the door, Bunny slips her hand into her purse and pulls out a diamond ring, then slips it on her finger. I assume it's her actual engagement ring, but don't bother asking, and she doesn't offer up the information.

"How do you know we'll get the right doctor?" she asks when the entrance doors slide open.

"Don't worry about that, honey," I respond, getting into character now that we're no longer alone.

We'll be getting Dr. Fucktard. Jez made sure he was the doctor on duty. If we play things right, he's the only doctor who will be treating my 'wife'.

I step up to the reception counter with Bunny

tucked into my side. It feels wrong, her being this close, but there's no other choice. Not if we want to be believable.

"How can I help you?"

The receptionist smiles at us both.

"Bess, my wife, passed out at home. Scared the shit out of me, if I'm being honest," I say. "It was difficult to get her to come around, so we agreed that a trip to the ER was in order."

"I'm so sorry to hear that." The woman hands me a clipboard with several forms. "Have a seat and fill these out. Someone will be with you as soon as possible."

"Thank you," Bunny says, injecting exhaustion into her words. "Matthew is such a worrier."

I tense at my given name, hating the way it sounds, the way it feels. I gave up that name a long time ago, and I'd die a happy man if I never have to hear it again.

"You're welcome. I'm glad you have someone looking out for you."

Bunny—or Bess for the time being—and I sit in the far corner of the waiting room. Almost every chair is full, and the sounds and smells of sickness are in the air. We work through the forms quickly, filling the pages with lies, and then we wait.

And we wait.

And wait.

Two hours later Bess Jones is called back to an ER bay. A kind nurse takes her vitals and then tells us the doctor will be in shortly.

She fucking lied.

Dr. Franklin doesn't show his face for another forty-five minutes, and if the way he breezes in through the curtain and doesn't even lift his head up is any indication, this is going to go exactly as expected. The prick doesn't even introduce himself. Thankfully, I know what the man looks like thanks to Jez.

"So, Miss Jones, what brings you in today?" he asks, his focus on the tablet he's holding.

"It's missus," I snap.

Dr. Fucktard finally lifts his head, and gives me an assessing look. "Got it. *Mrs.* Jones."

"Well, I passed out earlier today," Bunny says as if I didn't interrupt. "And I've been really tired lately." She waves her hand dismissively. "Beyond tired really."

"Anything else?"

"She's been complaining of a headache for days," I respond. "Body aches too."

"Is this true Mrs. Jones?" he asks as he taps on the screen of the tablet a few times.

"Yes."

"Well, your vitals all look good. You don't have a fever or anything."

"That doesn't mean there's nothing wrong with her," I bark.

"No, it doesn't," he says with a frown. "But I'm the doctor, so let me do my job."

"I'm sorry, doctor…" Bunny draws out the word.

"Franklin. Dr. Franklin, head of the ER," he offers.

You sure as shit don't act like the head of the ER.

"Dr. Franklin," Bunny repeats. "You'll have to excuse my husband. Matthew tends to get a little overprotective when it comes—."

"When did your symptoms begin?"

"Um, well, about a week ago."

"Are you pregnant?" he asks, repeating one of the questions the nurse already asked.

"Does her chart say she's pregnant, doc?"

Dr. Fucktard glares at me. "No, it doesn't. But I always like to double-check. Nurses aren't always the most reliable."

Wow. I wonder if his staff knows how he feels about them.

"No, Dr. Franklin, I'm not pregnant."

"And you're sure?"

"She said she's not pregnant," I snap.

"Have there been any stressors in your life recently?"

Bunny huffs out a laugh. "Life is full of stressors."

"True. But I'm talking about something that's out of the ordinary."

"Well," Bunny begins and folds her hands in her lap. She lowers her gaze to the floor and sniffles, as if she's getting emotional. "My, uh… my brother was killed in a car accident a few weeks ago."

Before he can say anything, I add, "We also went camping shortly before his death. Bess thinks I'm crazy, but she developed this mark on her back, so I looked it up. I'm wondering if her symptoms are from a possible bite, something like Lyme Disease."

And here comes the true test. I'm handing him the diagnosis on a silver platter. Ball's in his court now.

"Based on her vitals, we can rule out Lyme Disease." The smarmy bastard smiles at Bunny. If he had any clue about the events that *one sentence* is triggering, he'd definitely not be smiling. "Mrs. Jones, what you're suffering from is actually very common and nothing to worry about."

"It's not?" Bunny says, skepticism in her tone.

"No, it's not. Grief, Mrs. Jones. All of your symptoms point to grief."

"With all due respect, I know what grief is." Bunny smiles sadly. "I've experienced it several times with the loss of my parents, as well as when my sister died."

"That's the thing about grief. It doesn't always present the same way." He shrugs. "But with the proper support, I think you'll sail past this and be just fine."

"So that's it?" I arch a brow. "You're not even going to run any tests? Shit, at the very least, shouldn't you look at her back, check out the mark for yourself?"

"Mr. Jones, there's no need to do any of that. It would be a waste of time and money." He focuses on Bunny. "Mrs. Jones, I'm going to give you a prescription for TraZodone to help you sleep. I'm also recommending a grief support group. The combination of those two things should have you feeling much better in time."

Rage. Animalistic, unfettered rage wells up in me, and I lunge at him. Grabbing his doctor's coat by the lapels, I shove him against the wall and get in his face.

"My wife says it's not grief, *doc,* so it's not grief," I snarl. "Do whatever fucking tests you have to do to find a diagnosis that actually makes some goddamn sense."

I know this isn't part of the plan, but I can't seem to stop myself. The thought of Cece sitting in an ER bay just like this one, listening to this asshat dismiss her concerns, has me seeing red. So fuck the plan.

Dr. Fucktard—an apt name if I ever heard one—glares at me. He tries to push me away, but I don't budge. I'm bigger, and meaner than I look. And we're just scratching the surface of what I'm capable of. In time, he'll look back at this moment and wish he hadn't pissed off the pussycat with the pretty 'wife'.

"Listen, pal," he says. "I've got a medical degree and have successfully been treating patients for some time now. I think I know what I'm talking about more than you. And definitely more than some website you looked at."

"Bullshit!"

A hand settles on my forearm, and I turn to see Bunny standing next to me, confusion written in the creases at the corner of her eyes.

"Honey, calm down," she says softly.

I blink several times, but it does nothing to cool the burning fury zipping from one brain cell to the next.

"Listen to your wife," Dr. Fucktard orders.

Orders?! He thinks he can fucking order me around?

I yank my arm away from Bunny, but don't let go of the pompous douche in front of me. "I'm not some uneducated child you can order around," I growl. "Run some damn tests, or get me another mother fucking doctor!"

A nurse pokes her head in through the curtain. "Dr. Franklin, would you like me to call security?"

"Yes!"

Dr. Fucktard and I shout at the same time.

"He's gonna need someone in his corner if he doesn't help my wife," I bark at the nurse, and she scurries away.

Bunny returns to the gurney and sits. And Dr. Fuck-a-dickin'-douchbag continues to struggle, but I hold him in place. I have no clue how much time passes, but the curtains part and it isn't security who enters. It's another doctor, who looks eerily similar to the dead man walking.

"Who the fuck are you?" I grit.

"I'd be happy to answer any of your questions, once you release Dr. Franklin," New Guy says.

"I have this under con—"

New Guy holds a hand up to silence Dr. Franklin. "Clearly, you have no control. So please, be quiet," he snaps.

I dart my glare from one man to the other. After a tense moment, I back away and watch with satisfaction as Dr. Franklin straightens his jacket and tie.

Stabbing a finger in the air at New Guy, I say, "You better be here to help my wife."

"Mr…" He takes the tablet from Dr. Fucktard's hand and glances at it for a second. "… Jones, I'm here for several reasons. Yes, one of those reasons is to help your wife. But I'm also here as the President of this hospital to make sure my staff is safe. You seem to have caused quite a scene."

"And I'll continue to do so if yo—" I press my lips together, trying to reign myself in. He's right, I've caused a scene, and that wasn't the purpose of this little undercover mission. But I don't seem to be able to control my mouth or actions where Cece is concerned. "Look, I'm sorry. But your doctor here," I say, pointing to Dr. Franklin. "He's not doing his fucking job."

New Guy stares at me for a moment longer and then walks to the gurney and sticks his hand out for Bunny to shake. "Mrs. Jones, I'm Dr. Richard Franklin Sr. I apologize if you feel you've received less than the best care."

Dr. Richard Franklin Sr.? So he's douchebag's daddy? This just keeps getting better.

"So you're his father?" I ask, narrowing my eyes and not allowing Bunny a chance to respond. "How convenient."

"Yes, I am. But first and foremost, I'm in charge of this hospital and my loyalty is with the patients. So please, let me help get this sorted out."

"I don't fucking think so." I reach for Bunny's hand, and she links her fingers with mine. "C'mon,

Bess, we're outta here. I'll take you somewhere else."

"Okay, honey," she says sweetly.

Ignoring the elder Dr. Franklin's pleading for us to stay, we march through the waiting room and out the door. As soon as we're in the parking lot, Bunny slips her hand from mine.

"That was… not what I was expecting, Soul," she says. "And I'm guessing you weren't either."

"Fuck no it's not what I was expecting. I have no clue how this was missed," I growl.

As soon as we reach the truck, I grab my cell from the center console and call Jez.

"Hey, bro," she says by way of greeting. "How'd it go wi—"

"His goddamn dad runs the hospital, Jez," I bark.

"What?"

"Dr. Fucktard isn't the only Dr. Fucktard at Boulder City Memorial. Turns out, dear old daddy runs the damn place."

"Oh shit."

"Oh shit is right. How did you miss this?"

"Seriously?" she snaps. "I don't miss shit, Soul. The fact that we're just now learning this information tells me that it was buried. The question is why."

I take several deep breaths. Jez is right. She never misses things. *Ever*.

"Find everything you can on father and son," I order.

"I'm on it."

"And clear the security feed at the hospital from our visit. I clocked seven cameras that would have caught us."

"Consider it done."

"Thanks."

I lower the phone to disconnect the call, but Jez's shout has me lifting it back to my ear.

"What?"

"Aren't you even going to ask about our patient?"

Cece. Our patient.

Abyss's patient.

But our house guest.

"How's she doing today?" I try to inject annoyance into my tone, but even I can hear the concern lacing my question.

"She's good." The smile in Jez's words has me clenching my teeth. "We talked. I only told her what you said I could."

"Good."

"But, I, uh… well, I al—"

"Spit it the fuck out, Jezebel."

"I also told her that you'd talk to her when you got back. Bye, Soul. Love you."

The call disconnects, and I glare at the phone. Fucking sisters.

Bunny's chuckle fills the cab of the truck.

"What?" I snap.

"Oh, nothing," she says.

"Dammit, Bunny. Just say whatever it is that's on your mind. I'm not in the mood for games."

"You asked for it." She grins as wide as the Cheshire Cat. "You are so fucked."

Yes. Yes, I am.

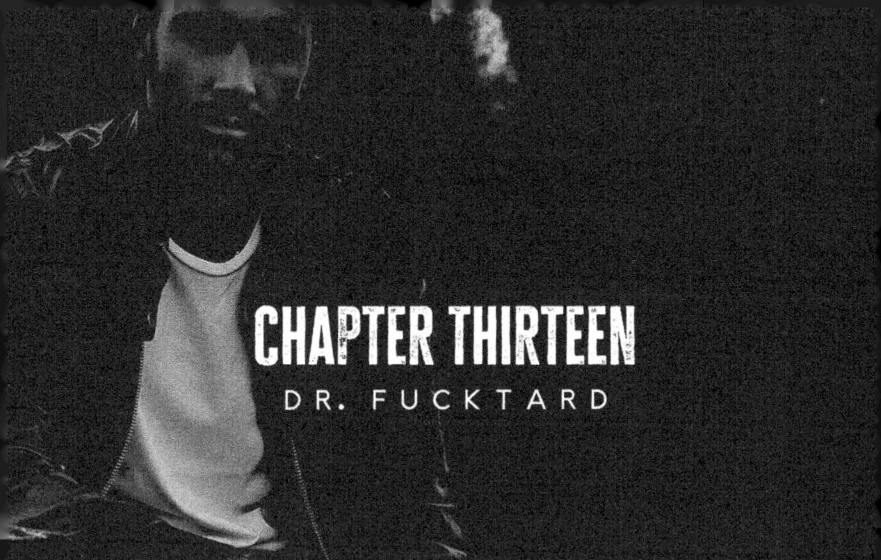

CHAPTER THIRTEEN

DR. FUCKTARD

"How many times am I going to have to rescue you, Ricky?"

I swear blood trickles out of my ears at my father's use of my childhood nickname. He paces the length of his office, his arms stiff at his side, and the creases of frustration on his face barely visible because of all the botox injections he receives. He's as vain as he is an unrelenting perfectionist. It's a wonder he hasn't made me stand at attention and salute him with his personal version of Heil Hitler.

"I'm not a damsel in distress, Father," I say with a dismissive wave of my hand. "I was handling it."

"Handling it?" he scoffs. "You were shoved against the wall by a thug who couldn't beat an ape in a game of Go Fish."

"I was handling it," I repeat.

He snatches up the tablet on the edge of his desk

and taps the screen until he finds what he's looking for. He thrusts the device at me and when I make no move to take it, he lifts my hand and forces me to.

"Then explain this, Ricky," he orders. "Explain this woman's chart and make me understand why you were refusing to do more tests."

I glance at the screen and see he's pulled up Miss —correction, *missus*—Jones' visit summary. Rolling my eyes, I toss the tablet onto one of the two leather chairs in front of the desk.

"She's *sad,* Father. Sad and depressed because her brother died," I explain, even though it galls me to do so. "I prescribed a mild sleep aid to help her sleep and told her to get help."

"She came here for help!" he shouts.

"And I gave it to her," I argue. "What more was there to do?"

"You're not this stupid, Ricky. Hell, you graduated top of your class at medical school so there's documented proof of your intelligence."

I pinch the bridge of my nose. "Where are you going with this?"

"Does the name Cece Parker ring any bells?"

"Jesus, you're never gonna let that go, are you?"

"Why should I let it go," he snaps. "It's only the millionth time I've had to doctor hospital records to cover up your laziness. If you wouldn't have dismissed her, run a few—"

"You *are* a doctor."

My eyes water from the pain when he backhands me because the insignia ring he insists on wearing hits my cheekbone.

"Don't you dare speak to me that way," he grits out. "I'm not only your father, I'm also your boss. Or are you forgetting who signs your paychecks?"

"How could I forget?" I mutter.

"I blame your insolence on your mother. She coddled you as a child, never expected more from you than to color pretty pictures she could show her church friends." Father tips his head back. "May she rest in peace." When he returns his stare to me, his eyes blaze with disappointment. "I never should have started fixing things for you when you were a teenager. Maybe you'd have a sliver of accountability and work ethic if I hadn't."

This is the same lecture he always spouts. It's as if he forgets one very important fact. I cross my arms over my chest and smirk.

"If you don't want to clean up after me, don't." I shrug. "It makes no difference to me. But…"

Father narrows his eyes. He knows what's coming, and it infuriates him that he also knows I'm right.

"But," I repeat. "You will always step in and *clean up my mess,* as you put it. Because if you don't, you know how it will reflect on you." I mock shudder. "And heaven forbid you look bad."

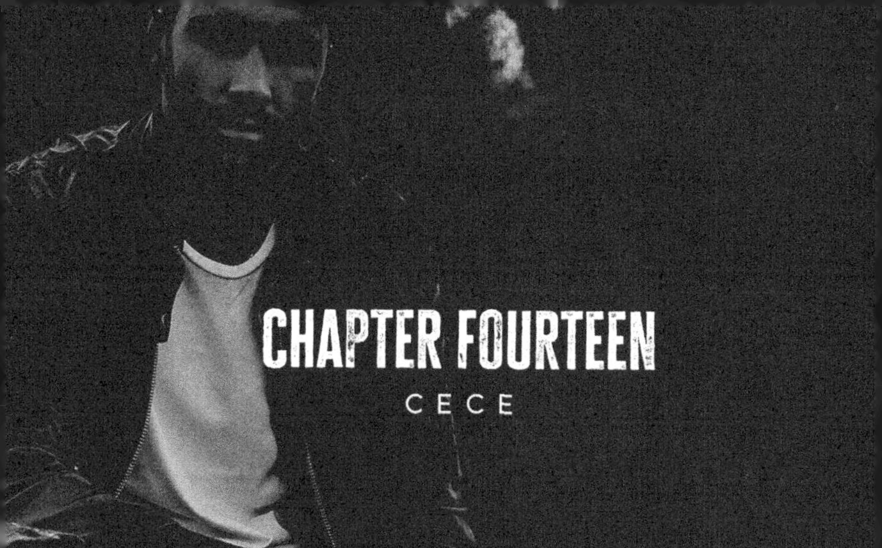

CHAPTER FOURTEEN

CECE

"Who was that?" I ask Jez as she makes her way back over to the couch with a couple of beers.

After our talk, Jez and I decided to spend some time in the common room. Jez didn't tell me much more than she already has, but she did explain club business. She also told me that, even though Saints Purgatory brothers aren't saints by any means, they do help people. And what they do requires privacy, sort of like HIPAA.

That makes sense, and I feel a little better about all the secrecy. I certainly wouldn't want shit about me being aired for everyone to hear. . But it doesn't explain everything. Jez told me to talk to Soul if I want to know more, that's my plan… as soon as I see him. He's been MIA today.

"Soul." Jez pockets her cell and sits next to me.

"Oh, he's not here?"

"No. He went out." She stares at me for a long minute before continuing. "Is there something you need from Soul?"

"Um… no, not really. You did tell me to talk to him about my concerns though." I fidget and start picking at the invisible lint on my shirt.

"Uh huh, okay."

"What?"

"Nothing." She shrugs. "So how do you like the clubhouse and the guys?"

"Everyone is pretty cool, and this clubhouse is awesome, but I miss Naughty / Nice."

"I know, but you only have two weeks of treatments left, and then you'll be able to go home."

A knot forms in my chest at the thought. As much as I want to go home, I *don't* want to go home. Without my mom there, and Carmella in another state, it'll be lonely. Squaring my shoulders, I push my feelings down and look around the room. Brothers are slowly trickling in from work, so the crowd isn't too big yet.

"Hey ladies," Thorn yells from where he and Malice are playing a game of pool. "You wanna play?"

Swallowing past the lump in my throat at the scowl Malice directs at me, I shake my head. Jez glances over her shoulder and shoots him a murderous glare.

"Don't pay any attention to him." She stands and pulls me along with her, despite my objection. "That's just his permanent expression. He doesn't know how to turn it off."

Thorn hands us cues, and we break into teams: Jez and me against Thorn and Malice. I lose track of time, so caught up in the fun of something normal. Just as I take my current shot, movement catches my attention out of the corner of my eye.

"Whoop!" Jez reaches up to high five me, and it takes me a second to realize I sank the ball.

"What the fuck?" Malice mutters, but he's looking at me with a little more appreciation than when we first came over.

"I love pool." I duck my head and peak through my lashes, embarrassed that I'm still kind of scared of him.

"Fucking pool shark is what you are," Malice grumbles with what sounds a lot like admiration.

"Damn right, and don't forget it." I wink at him.

Before lining up my next shot, I glance across the room and see Soul walking, with Bunny—at least I think that's her name—right behind him. He stops to turn and face her. I watch closely as he leans in and kisses her cheek. Heat climbs up my neck, and my heart hammers against my ribs as jealousy swirls in my gut.

"So, Cece, do you still think I'm sexy?" Thorns bobs his brows.

That's just the distraction I need to break my focus on Soul. I laugh at Thorn, but still miss my shot.

"Sure, Thorn. You're still sexy." I smirk at him. "But you suck at pool."

Thorn reaches for me, and I dodge him to run behind Malice, who crosses his arms and glares at Thorn.

"Oh come on, brother. She has it coming," Thorn pleads.

Lucky for me, Malice isn't budging, so I peek around him and stick my tongue out.

"That's it, you're mine!" Thorn dashes around Malice, and I let out a high-pitched screech as I try to dodge him again.

"What the fuck is going on here?" Soul bellows from across the room.

Thorn and I freeze. I didn't even realize Soul was still in the room. I figured he would take Bunny back to his room and fuck her into next year.

You wish he was fucking you.

I want to deny my thoughts but unfortunately,

Soul doused the distraction that Thorn was providing.

"Nothing, Prez," Thorn replies. "Just seeing if our little Cece is still attracted to me."

"She's not *our little Cece,*" Soul spits out as stalks toward us.

I peer around Malice, who hasn't so much as relaxed his stance.

"Oh boy," Jez mutters under her breath.

"I fucking told *all* of you, hands off." Soul's tone is menacing as he pushes into Thorn's space.

"What did you just say?" I stomp around Malice, who I swear smirks like he's enjoying the show, and glare at Soul.

"I was just messing around, Prez." Thorn shrugs. "She's like a little sister."

"I asked you a question," I snap.

"I was reminding them that you're hands off."

"And what the hell is that supposed to mean?" I demand.

"It means that no one in this fucking club, or anyone else for that matter, is going to touch you. You're here to heal, not to fuck my brothers."

Or anyone else? What the—

"Ce, let's just go ba—"

I shake off Jez's attempt to pull me away.

"This is bullshit!" I cry. "It's okay for you to fuck

dick hopper, but I'm not *allowed* to fuck your brothers?" I shout. I chose to leave out the whole 'anyone else' thing because, honestly, I don't even know how to address *that*.

I realize my mistake when Soul's face turns a bright shade of reddish purple. He grabs my elbow and drags me toward the hallway. He's not hurting me, but his grip is firm.

"Soul, maybe you shou—"

Soul spins around, his hold on me still tight, and shoots an icy glare at Malice. Malice holds up his hands in surrender.

"Nevermind, Prez," he says and backs away.

If Malice won't even help, you are screwed. Fuck this!

I yank out of Soul's grip, and he slowly turns to face me. His eyebrows are drawn in, and add that to the fact that his face still looks like a bruised tomato, and I know I should be frightened. But for whatever reason, I'm not. Soul doesn't scare me. "What the hell is your problem?"

"What's my *problem?*" he counters. "You don't come into *my* club and fucking yell at me. I'm the goddamn president, and you'll show me respect." His chest heaves, like he's run a marathon. "I let Jez bring you here to heal, not to flirt with or distract my brothers."

"Fuck you Soul!" I shout as I push into his space.

"You don't get to come at me like that. First of all, I wasn't flirting, we were playing pool, not that it's any of your business. Second, I'm a grown-ass adult, and so are your brothers. If I consent, it will happen."

"The fuck it will." Soul crowds me until I stumble backward.

When I hit the wall, Soul cages me in with his arms and leans into my face. We stare each other down, neither of us willing to break eye contact. My chest is now heaving in sync with his, and I wonder if Soul feels it, feels the electricity zapping the air around us.

"You will not tell me who I can and can't sleep with," I scoff at Soul. "Not when you're sleeping with Bunny."

"That's exactly what I'm telling you," he growls. "And I'm not fucking her *or* anyone else."

"Quit being so damn dramatic and kiss already," Jez teases as she walks past us toward her room.

I keep my gaze locked on Soul as if his eyes will reveal what he's thinking, but all I get is a stare that's as intense as my own. His hazel irises seem to smolder like embers in a fire. My breath hitches, and I lower my eyes to the floor.

Say something, anything.

I don't know if my thoughts are for me, or if they're a silent prayer for Soul to speak. Not that it matters. After a moment, I lift my head and peek at him through my lashes. His breathing is ragged, and he's still staring at my face like he's searching for the missing half of a two-piece puzzle.

God, I want this man.

CHAPTER FIFTEEN

SOUL

"Quit being so dramatic and kiss already."

I stifle the groan that claws its way up my throat and ignore my sister. Even if I wanted to pay her any attention, I couldn't. Looking away from Cece is impossible, not to mention, unthinkable. The absolute uncertainty in Cece's gaze draws me in like a moth to a flame.

When she looks at the floor, my fingers itch to touch her, to tip her chin up so she can't ignore what's brewing between us. But I don't. Instead, I wait. And for a brief second, I wonder if she'll ever look at me again, and then… bam.

Cece lifts her head and her lids are hooded.

"God, I want this man."

My nostrils flare. "What?"

Her eyes widen, and the cutest pink flush kisses her cheeks. "Huh?"

"What did you say?" I ask.

I can see the moment she realizes she said her thoughts out loud… again. The flush deepens, and her hand flies to her mouth.

"Did you mean it?"

A second passes. Then another, and another. Cece slowly nods, and that's all it takes. I grab her wrist and pin it to the wall above her head, then fuse my lips to hers.

Cece stiffens, but when I flatten her hand and link my fingers with hers, she relaxes. I swallow her moans, and coax her mouth apart with my tongue. She leans into me, but I use my body to keep her tight to the wall. I know she likes control, but she's in my house now.

I move my hand from beside her head and grip her waist. My fingers dig into her flesh, and my cock begs to be freed. Needing my skin on hers, I slide my hand under her shirt and trail my fingertips up her side. Her skin ripples in response.

Cece grinds against me as our tongues swirl and intertwine like they were designed for each other, only each other. Releasing her hand, I cup her thigh and lift her leg so my denim-covered dick thrusts against her center.

She whimpers and digs her nails into my chest so

hard I'm sure she's broken skin, even through my shirt. I nip at her lip and suck it between my teeth as I bend so I can pick her up and guide her legs around me.

Before I can get her off the floor, hurried footsteps invade my ears, and they're followed by the squeak of a shoe on the polished concrete and a string of curses.

"I'm, um…"

I break the kiss and slowly turn my head to see Abyss standing several feet away with his cell phone screen pointing in our direction.

"Did you need something?" I growl.

His Adam's apple bobs as he swallows. "I, uh… The app alerted me that Cece's heart rate was climbing. After what happened last time, I wanted…" He shakes his head and grins. "I guess she's just fine."

Cece pushes against me and moves around me to face Abyss. "We weren't… It isn't what it… shit."

She whirls on her heel and races away toward her room. I swivel my head to watch her go, and my eyes drop to her ass. There's a reason the cliché 'I hate to see her leave but love to watch her go' exists. Cece is that reason.

What I wouldn't give to sink my teeth into that perfect peach.

I shift to adjust my cock and roll my eyes when Abyss laughs behind me. Keeping my focus on the woman who literally got away, I see her slap her thumb against the scanner when she reaches the door to her room. When the door doesn't open, she stomps her foot in frustration.

Her lips move as she mutters to herself, and she tries again. It takes her five tries before the door slides open and then shuts once she's over the threshold.

"That was painful to watch," Abyss says.

I look to my left, where he's now standing, and glare at him. He shoves his hands in his pockets and rocks on the balls of his feet.

"So, I guess there was nothing wrong with her heart," he comments casually, like he didn't just douse the fire Cece and I were happily letting consume us. "But it looked like she was having fun," he tacks on.

With a growl and steely determination, I fight the urge to rearrange his face as I push past him. I storm to the elevator, and only once I'm in the garage, do I slow my steps. My Harley is parked in my spot to the right, and as I swing my leg over to straddle her, the intercom comes to life.

"Where are you going?"

I stop and look at a camera in one of the corners.

Using ASL, since I know she can see but not hear me, I sign, "None of your fucking business, Jez."

"Don't you have a run tonight?"

"The guys can handle it."

"Since when do you back out on a run?"

"Since you opened your goddamned mouth." My movements are sharp, concise.

Her sigh washes over me like acid.

"Don't do that."

"Do what?" she snaps.

"Sigh like I've hurt your feelings. It's annoying."

"And you're an idiot."

"Seriously, Jez, leave me alone."

"No. I get that you're pissed that I goaded you into doing something you shouldn't have needed your *little* twin sister to goad you to do in the first place. But you—"

I slice my hand through the air before signing again. "Mary! Shut the fuck up."

She hates being called Mary, and she knows I know she hates it. So when I call her that, she also knows I'm past the point of being reasoned with.

"Fine. Have it your way. Just…" She sighs again. "Just be careful, Soul. I worry about you riding around when you're like this."

I drop my head and shuffle my feet.

Dammit.

I lift my head to stare at the camera again. "I'll be careful."

"Love ya bro."

"Back at ya… Jez."

"WASN'T EXPECTING TO SEE YOU TONIGHT."

I down the shot Rogue sets in front of me and slam the empty glass on the bar.

"Wasn't planning on being here."

"What's got your panties in a bunch?"

I glare at him.

"Okay, fine," he huffs. "What's got your boxer briefs twisting around your balls?"

"You hire a manager yet?" I ask, desperately wanting to avoid his questions.

Rogue's head swivels to the left, and I follow his stare. Standing at the opposite end of the bar is a hipster-looking man, who's laughing at something a female customer said.

"Waylen started a few days ago," Rogue explains. "I told you that though. Where's your head at, Prez? It's not like you to forget shit."

"What about a new bartender?"

Rogue heaves a sigh and points to his right. "Skye started last night. I told you that, too."

I glance at Skye. She's making drinks and interacting with customers like a pro. And the men sitting at her end of the bar have numerous empty glasses in front of them, so I know they like her. The better looking the staff, the better business is. It might seem shallow, but it's true.

"So, I'll ask again," Rogue says, pulling my attention back to him. "Why are you here and what the hell is causing that worry crease?"

"Get me a beer, will ya?" I growl.

"Answer my question first."

We stare at each other for a minute, both of us waiting for the other to back down. Unfortunately, I'm too fucking in my head to fight him any longer, so he wins.

"I kissed Cece," I blurt.

Rogue reaches beneath the bar and brings up a frosted glass. He fills it with… hell, I don't even know. It's beer, so I don't care. Only after he sets the glass in front of me does he speak.

"And?" He arches a brow.

"And what? I kissed her. Isn't that enough?"

"Soul, you've tongue-fucked dozens of chicks, and probably in more holes than I care to hear about.

So forgive me if it isn't all that surprising that you kissed the hot girl who's invaded the clubhouse."

"She hasn't invaded the—"

"You know what I mean," he snaps. "Why is this bothering you so much?"

I groan and lift the beer to my lips in an effort to stall. After swallowing down half of it, I search my brain for a way to explain my frustration to him. I've got nothing… at least nothing that makes any damn sense.

"I like her," I admit.

"You say that like it's a bad thing."

"It *is* a bad thing," I insist. "She's my sister's friend, and a guest of the club."

"Again… and?"

"And she's off-limits."

"Why? Did Jez tell you she is?"

"No."

"Did God send you a message declaring that Cece is forbidden fruit?"

"Fuck you, asshole."

"Look, all I'm saying is that it seems you're the only one who's struggling with this."

"Because she's not there to be fucked and dismissed," I argue. "Cece's been through a lot lately, and the last thing she needs is to be sucked into the darkness that is me."

"Are you planning on fucking and dismissing her?"

"I'm not *planning* anything," I snarl.

"But?"

"Why the sudden interest in my love life?"

"Love life?" Rogue grins. "And here I thought we were just talking about sex."

"You know what I mean."

He nods. "Yeah, I do. As for the interest… you're the president of a one-percenter MC, and nothing fucking rattles you. Fucking. Nothing… Until now. And it's rattling you so much that you're not out on the damn run with the others like you should be."

Before I can respond, someone bangs a fist on the bar and rams into my shoulder. I turn to see who the fuck it is and am met with a solid wall of pissed off enforcer.

"Forget something, Prez." Grim's eyes are hard, his movements agitated. I lift my hands to remind him who he's talking to, but he doesn't give me a chance. "I get that you're all up in your fucking head, but if one kiss is gonna send you off the deep end, maybe you should appoint one of the brothers acting president. Because we need a goddamn president."

I stand and square my shoulders. "First of all, remember who the fuck I am. And—"

Grim shoves my hands down. "I haven't

forgotten shit." He pauses and taps my head. "What's going on up there?"

If it were anyone else, I'd wrap my fingers around their neck and squeeze the life out of them. And I'd fucking enjoy it. But it's not anyone else. And I can't exactly refute his argument. The second I laid eyes on Cece, my world spun on its axis, and it hasn't slowed down since.

I plop back down on my stool. "Shit."

Grim arches a brow. "Gonna fine yourself fifty bucks for not signing? I'm in the room, or did you forget that too?"

"Okay, brother, you've made your point."

"Have I?"

"I fucking like her," I admit. "I barely know a damn thing about her, and yet my head is fucked up for the girl. And she's sweet. Nice. Too good for a man like me."

"Prez, you're an idiot," Rogue says, and unlike me, he remembers that Grim is present. "Cece lives with you. Let me repeat that a little slower so it has a chance to sink in. Cece. Lives. With. You." He smirks. "You're in the perfect position to get to know her. Take advantage of that. As for being too good for you… maybe. But that doesn't mean she can't handle this life. You said it yourself, you barely know her. Fix that."

I glance at Grim. "Anything to add?" I ask.

"Yeah. Man up and claim her if you wanna explore her. Because if you don't, another brother will."

"It's not that easy."

"It is," Grim counters. "Now get the fuck up so we can go kill a lustful man." He cracks his knuckles and then continues. "I'll even let you get in a hit or two."

I throw my head back and laugh, feeling a bit lighter. If I can't sit here and drink my problem away, becoming a sinner to purge a sinner is the next best thing.

I follow Grim out of Purgatory, and see the others waiting on their bikes, ready to go. Straddling my Harley, I know that nothing has been solved. I still have no clue what to do about Cece. On the one hand, I wanna see if there's anything between us, but on the other, I don't want to shatter her already fragile world.

She's light.

I'm dark.

She's good.

I'm bad.

She's sweet.

I'm an asshole.

She's… too good for me.

And damn if I'm not gonna say fuck it and go for what I want. Because too good or not, Cece's a craving, a desperate and burning *need* I can't ignore.

I grab Grim's arm before he can walk to his bike. He arches a brow, confusion in his eyes.

"You're gonna give me more than a hit or two, brother. I'm finishing this one."

CHAPTER SIXTEEN

CECE

"LET'S DO SHOTS!"

The music in the common room is beyond loud, so I have to yell for Justin to hear me. He's behind the bar tonight, although that's not unusual because he is most nights.

Several hours have passed since Soul kissed the life force right out of me, and I've been doing everything I can to forget about it. I even strummed my clit like a damn guitar, and while I got release in the moment, I'm still turned on by the memory and in desperate need of an outlet. The kiss wasn't just hot, it was the best I've ever had. But what does it mean? Does Soul want me as much as I want him, or am I just a convenient lay?

I was beyond embarrassed when Abyss interrupted our make-out session in the hall and instead of facing Soul like a grown adult, I ran away like a coward. If Carmella were around, she would've handed me my ass for being such a chicken shit.

Damn, I miss her.

After I gathered my wits, I came out of my room to look for Soul to discuss what was happening between us, but he was nowhere to be found. Jez said he and a few of the brothers went on a run, which of course is club business. And once again, I'm in the dark about what really goes on around here.

So, I'm choosing to drink to forget, and I'm taking any willing participants along for the ride.

"I'll bring the bottle and some glasses," Justin shouts.

"Are you sure you want to do shots?" Jez shoots me a pointed look.

"Absofuckinglutely!" I wave the bunnies over, inviting them to join the rest of us. "Make sure you grab enough glasses, Justin. Everyone is doing shots tonight."

The bunnies give off a wary vibe as they approach our table. Gwen is at the helm, and she's glaring at me, while Bunny and Nikki hang back a little bit. The bunnies always keep their distance when I'm around, but I'm not having it. I'm letting loose and want everyone to have a good time.

"What do you want?" Gwen sneers.

She's clearly not my biggest fan, but I'm not hers either so we're even. Besides, I'll be going home soon enough, and she can have Soul all to herself once again. At least that's what I keep telling myself.

"We're doing shots," I say as Justin sets down a bottle of tequila and glasses. "Justin, you have to do shots too."

"Um… probably not a good idea, Cece." Justin's eyes dart around the table. "I'm on bar duty."

"I don't think one shot will kill you, Prospect." Possum starts pouring the liquor. "Cece wants everyone to drink, so we all drink."

"What are we drinking to?" Bunny asks.

I raise my glass. "To new friends."

Fruity drinks and margaritas are more my speed, but the warmth of the tequila as it goes down my throat is exactly what I need right now. It's going to hit me faster than I'm used to, which is perfect.

Possum pours everyone another shot while Justin scurries from the table as fast as he can. I look at Jez, who just shrugs. I guess Justin doesn't drink on the job. Sucks for him because everyone seems to be having a good time, if their laughter is anything to go by.

Why, then, do I have a strange feeling in my gut that has nothing to do with the alcohol? Drinking was supposed to make me forget, but it's not working like I'd hoped. Instead, my brain keeps going back to the fact that Soul is on a run. I don't have a clue what happens on these runs, which makes me nervous. I shift my attention to Heather, who's at ease and laughing at Animal, who's threatening her with a strip tease.

"Come on! Frenzy isn't here to kick my ass." Animal slowly lifts his shirt, exposing his chiseled abs. "I can finally show you what you're missing out on."

"He might not be here, but I don't need him to do my dirty work. I can kick your ass and then watch him kick it again when he gets back." Heather winks at him.

"You're no fun," Animal complains.

"Who wants to dance?" I ask, and then down another shot before hopping up from my chair.

All the females jump up, and we make our way to the middle of the room.

"Put on something more upbeat," I yell to Jez, who's already connecting her phone to the sound system. "I wanna dance my ass off!" Maybe then I can get rid of my pent-up energy.

Highway to Hell by AC/DC cuts off, and *All the Single Ladies* by Beyoncé pumps through the speakers. With my hands raised above my head, I shake my hips to the beat, really letting my body feel the music. When a pair of hands grip my waist, I turn with a shriek and see Possum grinning at me.

"You're a pretty good dancer," he says, leaning close to my ear so I can hear him.

I look Possum up and down as he moves with me. "You're not so bad yourself," I admit.

"Possum, I wouldn't do that if I were you," Fort shouts, but I don't see him in the fray of people.

I glance over and notice Fort, Lock, and Asher still sitting around the table, watching the rest of us have fun.

"They're just dancing, Fort" Jez rolls her eyes. "It's not like she's been claimed."

"Claimed?" I repeat, confused and more than a little buzzed.

When the music stops, I head back to the table to get something to drink, and Possum steps up next to me.

"Don't worry about it." Possum hands me another shot. "We're just having fun, and Fort's jealous."

"Your funeral, brother," Lock mumbles.

I swallow the liquor and pour myself another as I try to follow their conversation.

Possum snickers. "No one is being buried tonight, brother. Well except for… Nevermind."

"What's he talking about?" I ask Lock.

"Nothing. He's talking out his ass." Lock shoots Possum a dark glare that seems to hold a warning.

"Here, take another shot." Jez passes out another round.

"To sexy men who leave us wanting more!" I raise my glass to toast and then slam back the booze.

"Cheers!"

"Wait a minute." Animal raises his hand like a second-grader in school. "Who left you hanging, darlin'?"

"No one of importance," I say and gulp down another shot. "Wait, is someone being buried tonight?" I dart my eyes from Possum to Jez and back again. "I feel like I'm missing something."

My brain might not be firing on all cylinders, but I swear Possum mentioned burying a body.

Right? Shit, I'm hammered.

I haven't been this drunk since Carmella was accepted into law school and we celebrated by drinking our weight in alcohol. We were miserable the next day, but it felt damn good while we were doing it.

"It's nothing, darlin'. Like Lock said, just talking out of my ass." Possum grabs my hand and drags me back to the makeshift dance floor. "Let's dance some more."

While we dance, Possum talks. I learn that he isn't around a lot at night because of the tattoo shop, Persuasion Ink. He explains that customers tend to come later in the evening, and some designs can take hours to finish. Possum is wild, and a lot fun to be around.

Time passes in a blur as we dance and drink the hours away. I manage to forget all about Soul and that kiss and the orgasm he left me on the edge of.

No, you haven't. You're drinking, yes, but you're not forgetting a fucking thing.

"What're you trying to forget?" Possum asks while twirling me around.

"Uh… what are we talking about?"

"You said you're drinking but not forgetting a thing. What are you trying to forget?"

"Damn it, I really need to quit doing that. It's nothing." I shrug. "I've, uh, had too much to drink and am thinking about my mom."

"I heard about that," he admits. "I'm sorry."

"Thanks, but I'm okay."

I paste a smile on my face and hope like hell that Possum doesn't see through my lie. I look over and see Lock and Fort still sitting at the table.

"Hey ladies," I shout. "I think there are some

party poopers over there that need to have some fun." I point at the brothers.

Gwen pulls Lock out of his chair, and Bunny grabs Fort. The four of them start to dance,while Jez spins Heather around. Possum dips me down low and leans in as if to whisper in my ear, but before he can say anything, the music suddenly stops.

"What the fuck is going on?" Soul's angry gaze lands on my upside down one, and he narrows his eyes when Possum slowly pulls me upright.

"Nothing, Prez," Possum says quickly. "Just blowing off some steam." He nods at me. "Cece is quite the dancer."

"I had a good partner," I add as I playfully smack Possum's chest.

I sway on my feet at the small movement. Shit. I've had more to drink than I thought. Possum steadies me with a hand at my waist so I stay upright.

Blowing out a deep breath, I finally turn to face Soul head on and gasp. He's got blood all over him and not just a few spots either. There's a smeared streak of crimson on his cheek, and his shirt is covered. His jeans also have splatter marks all over them. I glance around the room and find that no one else seems bothered by Soul's appearance.

What the hell happened to him?

My pussy throbs, and I squeeze my thighs together.

And why the fuck does the sight of him covered in blood have me so turned on?

CHAPTER SEVENTEEN

SOUL

I HAD A GOOD PARTNER.

Red. I see Red. And it's not Cece's hair.

I had a good partner.

When I walked into the clubhouse, the only thing I wanted to do was take a shower and fall into bed. I'm exhausted. Sinning does that to a man.

With my fists clenched at my sides, I stalk across the room, stopping only when I'm a foot away from Cece. Possum remains at her side, his hand hovering at her waist like he's waiting to catch her if she falls.

"Back off, *brother,*" I snarl at him, while my stare remains fixed on the heat in Cece's ice-blue eyes.

"Soul, nothing is goi—"

"Back. Off."

Cece's eyes narrow with a mixture of lust and anger. She takes a step toward me and when she kicks my booted feet, she wobbles. Rather than steady her so she can give me a piece of her mind, I lift her up and toss her over my shoulder.

I shift to look at Jezebel, whose grin is bordering on obnoxious. "Sign so the—"

"Put me down!" Cece pounds my back and kicks her legs. "Fucking pu—"

The crack of my palm on her ass shuts her up. "Not happenin', babe." I focus on Jez. "Sign for me so the big guy doesn't miss a word of what I'm about to say," I demand.

Like the smart ass that she is, my twin lifts her hands. "Ready."

Turning in a circle and ignoring Cece's continued attack, I glare at every single person in the room. "I will only say this once, so listen the fuck up." I point to the woman on my shoulder. "Cece is mine. Got it? M-I-N-E, mine."

"I am *not* yo—"

"Babe," I growl. "Not now."

"Don't you ba—"

Cece bites my back through my shirt when I smack her ass again.

"Does anyone have any fucking questions?" I ask, turning in another circle. When all I receive in response is blank stares and snickers, I start toward the hallway. "We'll be in my room. Do *not* interrupt us unless someone is dead or dying. Understood?"

A chorus of 'understoods' is my only response.

"Mine!" I shout for good measure.

As I carry Cece through the hall, it occurs to me that I have no clue what I'm doing. I saw her dancing with Possum when we returned from our run, and my brain short-circuited. All I could do was invade their space and get her away from him.

And claim her.

"Where the hell are you taking me?" Cece grumbles against my back.

"My room."

"Well why didn't you jus' say so?" she slurs. "And what took you so long?"

Cece's drunk, pissed, and not thinking straight. Not two minutes ago, she was demanding to be put down and acting like a hellcat. Now she almost sounds… excited?

When I reach my door, I scan my thumbprint. Carrying Cece inside, I stalk to the bed and toss her onto the mattress.

"Stay there," I demand before turning on my heel and going to the panel on the wall to shut down the intercom and security features of the room. The last thing I need is my nosy brothers spying on us, or worse yet, my sister.

Once I assure myself that we're one hundred percent alone, I take a deep breath and return to the bed. Cece is trying to scramble to her knees, but the heels of her shoes keep getting caught on the blanket. I cross my arms and watch her for a minute. She's completely unguarded and oblivious to the way her ass sticks in the air every time she falls.

"Need help?" I ask, every ounce of the anger and jealousy I experienced now gone.

Cece freezes, almost as if she forgot she isn't alone. She slowly swivels her head to look at me over her shoulder, and her eyes widen.

"Where do you did you come from?" She wrinkles her nose, like she knows she got the words wrong but doesn't know how to fix them. "No wait. You… where'd you—"

"I just carried your ass in here," I remind her.

She struggles for another minute and finally, she's on her knees. On all fours, actually. And my dick jumps at the sight. It would be so easy to plow into her at that angle.

"Uh, I…" She relaxes her elbows and rests her cheek against the bedding. "I think I'm gonna—"

Cece gags, and I rush to lift her into my arms and carry her to the bathroom. I manage to get her in front of the toilet just as her body heaves. She wraps her arms around the porcelain bowl and vomits.

"That's it, babe." I hold her hair away from her face and rub circles over her back. "Get it all out."

I don't know how much she drank, but if the number of times her body convulses is any indication, it was a fucking lot. I'm surprised she was standing at all when I arrived.

When she finally relaxes, I quickly get a washcloth and run it under cold water before pressing it against her forehead. She tries to push me away, but gives in when her attempts don't work

"Relax, Cece. I've got you."

I settle against the side of the soaking tub and pull her between my legs. She's so exhausted, she doesn't even fight it. She just sits there, with her head leaning on my chest and her arms limp at her sides.

My legs start to tingle after a while, but I don't want to move her. Not yet. It feels good with her in my arms. It feels right, like she belongs there. A little more time passes, and soft snores escape from her lips.

I maneuver to my feet, lifting her up as I stand, and carry her back to the bed. Wanting her to be comfortable, I grab a t-shirt from my dresser and then get her out of her clothes so I can slip it over her head. When I notice she's not wearing any panties, I groan and make a mental note to tell her that's not acceptable… unless she's with me.

Once I'm confident that she's comfortable, I strip out of my blood-stained clothes and take a quick shower. That's what I wanted to do when I got to the clubhouse, before I was distracted by a feisty redhead.

After I'm clean, I stride back into the bedroom. Cece is still sleeping soundly, but she's sprawled out across the mattress. One arm is flung above her head, while the other is almost straight out at her side. She's managed to kick the covers off her body, and her legs are spread.

She looks like a damn human sacrifice.

Or a sexual sacrifice.

I adjust my now aching cock. Gently, so I don't wake her, I shift her around so she's on one side of the bed. And then I crawl in beside her, naked and horny. Not that I'll act on it… but I want to. Desperately.

This is gonna be a long fucking night.

"WHAT THE FUCK?!"

I bolt upright, yanked from my dreams by a furious shout. It takes one point two seconds to realize the question came from Cece, who's kneeling on the edge of the bed and glaring at me like I'm a monster.

"What the fuck happened?" she demands. "Why am I in bed with you? And why does my head feel like a damn boulder was thrown at it?"

I rub the sleep from my eyes. "That would be the alcohol you drank last night."

"I didn't drink that much."

I huff out a laugh. "The ten solid minutes of vomiting you did say otherwise."

Her eyes widen, and her cheeks flame with what I assume is embarrassment. "I didn't."

"You did." I shrug. "It's fine. Happens to the best of us."

"But not…" She shakes her head and then groans. "Fuck, that hurts."

I throw the sheet off me, swing my legs over the edge of the bed, and get up to get her some Tylenol. When she gasps, I smirk.

Oh yeah, I'm naked.

"Did… Is… Why are…" Cece groans. "Did we do anything last night?"

I don't respond until I return with a glass of water and two Tylenol. "Here, take these."

She takes the pills and washes them down, draining the glass. After she hands it back to me, I set it on the nightstand.

"I gotta admit," I begin. "It's a little unsettling

that you're so upset about the prospect of us fucking."

I didn't think it was possible for her to turn a darker shade of red, but her cheeks flush a bright crimson.

"I'm not…" She lowers her gaze and fidgets with her hands. "I'm sorry."

"To answer your question, no, we didn't do anything last night." As much fun as it would've been to mess with her, I don't like that she's uncomfortable. That's the opposite of what I want from her. "You puked and then fell asleep. Yes, I changed you so you'd be more comfortable, but nothing happened."

"Nothing happened?"

"Nope. And call me crazy, but I want you fully aware of what's going on when I'm fucking you." I grin. "Enthusiastic participation would go a long way too."

Cece lifts her head, but her gaze snags on my erection and lingers. She stares for a minute, but then she seemingly pulls herself together and looks at my face.

"Can you put some damn clothes on?" she snaps. "I can't concentrate."

I wrap my hand around my dick and stroke it. "Why not, Cece?"

Her gaze drops as her tongue darts out, and she slides it across her bottom lip. I reach out and trace my thumb in its path. When her mouth forms an 'O', I push the digit in and let it rest on her tongue.

"Why can't you concentrate, Cece?" I tug on my cock as she swirls her tongue around my thumb instead of answering me. "Sweet Jesus," I moan. "I wanna fuck your mouth so bad."

I might as well have dumped a bucket full of ice water over her head because she pulls away from me so fast that she lands on her butt in the middle of the bed. We stare at each other for a few seconds, and her eyes blaze with lust.

"Scared?" I taunt. I know I shouldn't, but I can't help myself. She wants this, *wants me,* just as bad as I want her.

"I'm not scared," she says in a shaky voice. "I just… put some damn clothes on."

Smirking, I release my cock and go to my dresser. After pulling on a pair of gym shorts, I move to sit on the edge of the mattress.

"One of these days, Cece, I will have you," I vow.

The mattress shifts as she crawls toward the headboard. With her back against it, she draws her knees up to her chest. I watch all of this, and stifle a groan when her pussy peeks out from beneath the t-shirt she's wearing… *my* t-shirt.

"When you're in the clubhouse, you will wear panties," I snap, remembering that she was dancing and flirting with my brothers while practically bare. "Unless I'm with you," I clarify. "Then feel free to leave them off."

"Excuse me?"

"You heard me."

The anger from last night is returning in full force now that I'm fighting a case of blue balls.

"Yeah, I did. And that's the problem." She glares at me. "You don't get to tell me what I can and can't wear."

"My clubhouse, my rules."

"You've told me that before," she counters. "I didn't like it then, and I don't like—" Her face scrunches up. "Wait a second. Did you tell the entire club last night that I was yours?"

"And if I did?"

"I'm not a piece of property, Soul!" she shouts. "I'm a person. A human being with thoughts and feelings and, oh yeah, a brain to make my own decisions."

I shift to my knees and crawl toward her. "You're mine, Cece. I will not have my brothers making passes at you because they want a hot piece of ass," I snarl. "Possum was dangerously close to losing his life last night. Is that what you want?"

"What? No, of course not." She sucks in a deep breath. "But I'm a grown-ass woman, and if I want to flirt, I'll flirt. It's not like I belong to—"

"You do belong to me," I bellow. "I claimed you. You are mine." When her eyes widen, I smirk. "Don't you dare pretend that you don't fucking want me. Don't pretend that what I'm feeling is all one-sided because I can see it in your eyes every goddamn time I look at you that it's not."

"And what exactly is it that you're feeling, Soul? Because fuck knows you haven't clued me in."

"I like you, dammit! Is that what you want to hear? I fucking like you." I lean in so I'm inches from her face. "I can't get you outta my head, which makes no goddamn sense because I barely know you. But I want to know you. I wanna know every single fucking thing about you. I wanna learn every inch of your body, possess every part of you until it's impossible to tell where you end and I begin. I. Fucking. Like. You."

"Oh."

"Oh? Oh?" I bark out a humorless laugh. "You're the girl who can't keep her damn mouth shut and spews every thought that comes to her mind, but I tell you I like you and all you can say is 'oh'?"

"Well, I..." Cece bites her lip for a moment and

then straightens like she's about to say something important. "I don't know what to say."

"How about 'I like you too, Soul' or 'I wanna fuck you too' or better yet, *anything* other than 'oh'!"

My chest is heaving, my head is spinning, and my heart is pounding like I just ran a marathon. I stare at her, silently willing her to say something, but when she doesn't, I get off the bed and start toward the door.

"Forget it," I snap. "There are plenty of ot—"

"Tell me about the tattoo on your back," she blurts, causing me to freeze.

I take a deep breath and close my eyes. The Saints Purgatory MC logo, along with our motto, is forever emblazoned on my body with black and purple ink. The tattoo covers my entire back, and it's the one I'm most proud of.

I've got others: Jesus entwined with thorny vines on the cross graces my forearm and the Yin Yang symbol covers my left calf. There's more, but those are the ones that matter, the ones I have a deep connection to.

"Please, Soul," Cece prods when I remain silent.

Slowly, I turn to face her. She's in the same spot against the headboard, but the anger that was written on her face a minute ago is gone. Instead, I stare into the blue depths of curiosity.

"You've seen the image all over the clubhouse," I begin as I walk back to join her on the bed. "It's the club's logo."

"It's on your cut, too," she says.

"It is."

"Why did you choose purple? I mean, it's everywhere." She smiles, and for the first time since, well, I don't know when, the smile reaches her eyes. "I gotta admit, purple is kind of the last color I'd associate with a motorcycle club."

I chuckle. "Yeah, I get that."

I take a few deep breaths and then sigh. I don't even know where to start in my explanation. Hell, I probably shouldn't tell her anything. But I'm going to. Because there's something between us, something big. I don't understand it, can't explain it, but it's there, like giant rays of fucking sunshine demanding entry to my dark world.

Yeah, I'm going to tell her. Because if my gut is right, if these feelings are real, Cece is going to be the club queen someday, and she should know what she's reigning over.

"Jez and I grew up in the Catholic church." I swallow as memories assault me. I hate my story, but it's the reason I'm the man I am, so I can't hide it from her. "Grim and Malice too. The four of us grew up together. Purple is a significant color to Catholics.

It symbolizes sorrow and suffering, but also wealth and power."

"How does that tie into the club?"

"Saints Purgatory MC was born out of suffering. A lot of fucking suffering." I look at her expecting to see questions in her eyes, but all I see is acceptance and even… understanding. "When we were teenagers, we vowed to make those who caused the suffering pay for their sins. It took some time, what with me and Malice going into the military, but we did it. We made the sinners pay, and then we created the club."

"But… why? If you did what you vowed to do, why the club?"

"See evil, hear evil, become evil, purge evil." Chills race over my spine, as they do every time I recite our motto.

"That's on your back."

"It's the club motto," I explain. "The sinners from our childhood were only the tip of the iceberg. There are bad people, evil fucking people, in every corner of the world. Saints Purgatory MC exists to take out the sinners, to make the world a better place."

"Take out?"

And this is where she runs screaming from the room, never to be seen again.

"Kill, Cece. We kill sinners."

She sucks in a breath, and I brace myself for the running and screaming. But it doesn't come. I chance a look at her, and she's focused on my eyes as if searching for the evil in *me*. It's there, hovering just beyond the good parts of me, and I can only hope she sees it for what it is: necessary.

"Do the people you kill deserve it?" she asks quietly.

"Define 'deserve'."

"Do they hurt other people? Do they cause harm? Are we talking child molesters and murderers or stealing food to feed their family and jaywalking?"

"Last night it was a child molester," I tell her. "And yes, murderers too. Pretty much anyone who commits one of the seven deadly sins to a degree that it hurts others."

"So that's why you were covered in blood?" I nod, and she seems to consider things for a moment. Then she shrugs. "Okay."

"Okay?"

"What were you expecting?"

"Honestly?"

"Of course, honestly," she says but doesn't give me a chance to answer before continuing. "Soul, you say you like me. You say you want to get to know me. Well, that works both ways. You can only expect from me what you're willing to give. So yeah, I want you to be honest. Always be honest."

"I thought you'd leave," I admit.

"Why? Because you think I can't handle what you do, what the club does?"

"Most chicks can't, babe."

"And I'm not most chicks, *babe*." She grins. "I'm stronger than I look, Soul. And while I might not agree with how you handle sinners, as you call them, that doesn't mean I don't understand."

"You don't hate me? Think I'm evil?"

"No. I think..." Cece sighs as she picks up my hand and threads her fingers through mine. "I think you're kind of wonderful," she says softly. "In an uber-hot vigilante sort of way."

I throw my head back and laugh. "You do realize you said that out loud, right?"

"Yeah. I meant to."

"Uber-hot vigilante?"

Cece nods with a grin.

"I should put that on a patch for my cut."

"You're insane."

"Maybe." I shrug. "But apparently you like my brand of insane, so I'm good with it."

CHAPTER EIGHTEEN

CECE

"We're taking your Harley?"

Now I understand why he insisted I wear a pair of Jez's boots and one of her leather jackets. He even told me to pull my hair back in a braid. It seemed like a strange request, but I didn't bother to ask why. It's a beautiful day, so I should've known he'd want to ride, but for some reason, it didn't occur to me that we'd ride his Harley to the hospital.

I thought we'd be taking one of the cars, especially since Soul ordered Asher to come to the garage with us. I'm going home today, and all my stuff is packed and sitting behind one of the club's shared vehicles.

Excitement buzzes through me when Soul swings his leg over the seat and holds out his hand. "Get on."

"What about my stuff?"

"Asher's gonna take it to your place. You got a

spare key?"

Opening my purse, I dig until I find my keys and pull off the extra one.

Soul takes the key from my hand and gives it to Asher. "Bring that key back to me, Prospect."

"No problem, Prez." Asher loads the car up and glances at me. "Anywhere special you want me to put this Ce?"

"Just set it in the hallway." I smile at him. "Thanks, Asher."

Asher shoots me a toothy grin and gets in the car. Once he's out of the garage, I turn back to Soul.

"I've never been on a motorcycle." My voice shakes with nerves. "What if I fall off?"

"You're not gonna fall off." Soul gets off the bike and steps into my space. "We'll start slow, I promise. And I'll only speed up once you're comfortable."

"How the hell are you going to know when I'm comfortable?"

"Trust me, I'll know." He winks. "Step on this peg and swing your leg around. There's one on the other side too." He explains. "Keep your feet on those and avoid these pipes." He points to indicate what he's referring to. "They get hot, and I don't want you to burn yourself."

I look down to where he's pointing and make a mental note to keep my legs as far away from them as possible. I'm going to the hospital to get my pacemaker out, not to be treated for burns.

Soul helps me get seated on the bike and then hands me a helmet. When I struggle to get the chin strap secured, he takes over for me. After he's satisfied that I'm as protected as I can be, he puts his own on and throws his leg over the seat.

Two seconds later, the engine roars to life, and I'm straddling the biggest vibrator known to man. I squirm at the sensation, and Soul glances over his shoulder and smirks.

Yep, he definitely knows what this is doing to me.

If this is how it feels sitting still, I can't wait to see what happens once Soul takes off. As if he can sense my thoughts, Soul grabs my hands and wraps them around his waist.

"Scoot closer and hold on tight, babe," Soul yells over the engine.

I wiggle my ass up in the seat, making sure my feet stay on the pegs, and that I avoid the pipes he warned me about. I intertwine my fingers and once I'm plastered against his back, he taps my hand and slowly takes off.

I'm shaking like a leaf when we pull out of the garage, and dirt kicks up around us as we hit the sandy earth. I didn't pay attention to the camouflage of the mountainside when I first came to the clubhouse. I was too busy looking around for the *actual* clubhouse, not knowing it was buried underground. It slowly starts to creep behind us as Soul accelerates. I inhale a deep breath and my muscles begin to uncoil. Instead of sitting like I've got a rod up my ass, I lean further into Soul's back. I still have a death grip around his waist, but my mouth tips into a grin at how freeing it is to be behind him.

It feels like I'm flying. Isn't that what people say about riding motorcycles?

Soul must sense me relaxing, because the bike picks up speed, causing me to clench my legs as tight to him as I can. My pussy tingles, and the rat bastard knows what it's doing to me because his abs ripple and his shoulders shake with laughter.

Two can play that game.

I reach down and massage his crotch. Soul stiffens and shakes his head. Probably not the safest thing I've ever done, but fucker deserves it. He revs the engine again, and I growl into the back of his cut. The man doesn't even have to touch my pussy, and I'll orgasm.

Yeah, he's gonna pay for this.

The urge to raise my hands in the air and scream is strong, but I resist because I don't want to startle Soul. He looks over his shoulder, and my smile grows. He gives a curt nod and turns back to watch the… road? Path? Shit, I have no idea what it is beyond being just the desert. It's not exactly like they can pave a road to the clubhouse if they want to stay incognito.

My mind wanders as I think about the time since Soul *claimed* me. We spent almost every night together, talking, watching TV, and we even made out like horny teenagers. But that's it. We still haven't had sex. I feel like a tightly wound spring, one more turn and I'm going to snap.

But I'm going home today, and that means no more sleepovers. Or so I thought. That was the topic of our one and only argument. Well, the one and only since we became a… couple?

"Soul, the pacemaker gets removed on Monday."

"I know. Doesn't mean you gotta leave."

"That's exactly what it means," I argue. "Abyss gave me a clean bill of health. I'm healed, and it's time for me to get back to my life."

"What the fuck does that mean? I told you, you're mine. M-I-N-E, mine.*"*

"Put your club down, caveman," I snap. "I need to get back to Naughty/Nice. It's all I have left of my mom, and it's important to me."

Soul's shoulders sag, and he pulls me into his chest.

"I'm a selfish bastard. I want you here."

"So if I leave, we aren't together anymore?"

"What?" He pushes me away so he can look me in the eyes. "Fuck no! It just means I don't have easy access to this hot body and delicious, sassy mouth anymore."

"You can always come stay at my place."

"We'll figure it out."

We never did figure anything out.

A little over an hour later, we roll into the hospital lot, and Soul parks as far away from other vehicles as he can. I guess he doesn't want his baby getting scratched. After we both get off the Harley, I glance at the building. My libido is completely forgotten as shudders barrel through my body.

Bad memories assault me, and it becomes almost impossible to breathe. Soul rips the helmet off my head and hangs it on the handlebar. Then he grabs my face and stares into my eyes. "Deep breaths, babe. Breathe with me." He inhales through his mouth and exhales through his nose. "In and out, in and out."

I mimic Soul, and after several long seconds, I'm about to breathe a little easier. It doesn't diminish the trepidation coursing through me though. I hang my head in defeat.

How in the hell am I supposed to walk in there when just looking at the place has me freaking out for no fucking reason?

"You're freaking out because you lived through a goddamn nightmare," Soul says because once again,

I've spoken my thoughts out loud. He engulfs me in his arms, and I savor the calming effect he has on me. "But as long as I'm here with you, nothing bad is gonna fucking happen." He shakes his head. "I knew we should've waited for Abyss to remove the pacemaker."

Abyss had to leave on a run, and I didn't want to wait another four days. I need to get back to Naughty/Nice, and I can't do that if I'm sitting around the clubhouse. Sure, I could've gone back with the pacemaker still in place, but I want to move on. I *need* to bury the negative memories deep down where I can't see them every day.

I straighten my shoulders and look Soul in the eye."I'm fine. Let's do this. Besides, I don't even have to see Dr. Fucktard."

Soul laughs. "I'll never get tired of you calling him that."

We walk through the parking lot side by side, and when we reach the entrance, Soul grabs my hand to lead me through the sliding doors. He walks straight to the reception desk and tells the woman that we're here to see Dr. Chang. After she gives us directions to the outpatient wing, we head to the elevators, where Soul jabs the up arrow.

I smile at him as he squeezes my hand, but then the air around me seems to shift and the hairs on the back of my neck stand on end. When I glance over my shoulder to find the source of my unease, my entire body goes numb.

"What are you doing here?" Dr. Fucktard sneers.

I open my mouth to respond, but then realize his glare is aimed at Soul, not me.

Why is he talking to Soul?

"None of your fucking business," Soul growls. "You need to turn around and walk the other way before we have another *conversation*."

Another conversation? When the hell did they talk?

Dr. Fucktard peers around Soul to see me standing there.

"Is this your sister?" he asks, clearly dismissing me as he returns his focus on Soul.

"No, I'm not his sister," I spit out. "You know who I am. I'd like to think you remember the people you almost kill."

"Oh, I *do* remember. I remember you not telling me *everything* so I could properly diagnose you."

"The fuck you say?" Soul steps into the doctor's space, and I grip his arm to pull him back, but he doesn't budge as anger vibrates through his body.

Dr. Fucktard steps back and looks down at our joined hands. His eyebrows hitch up, and his gaze darts back and forth between us. After a brief, and incredibly tense, moment, he narrows his eyes and his face reddens to an almost purple color. It's on the tip of my tongue to tell him he should have that checked out, but I manage to keep my mouth shut.

Thankfully the elevator pings, and when the door slides open, I pull Soul in with me. But not before he throws Dr. Fucktard one more dirty look.

"What the hell was that?" I demand after the door closes.

"Nothing."

"No, not nothing. When did you talk to him?"

"A couple weeks ago. It's not a big deal," he says dismissively.

"Why didn't you tell me?"

"Wasn't anything to tell you."

When the door opens, we step off the elevator and run into Dr. DeMarco, which effectively ends our conversation.

"Oh, Ms… Parker, right?" Dr. DeMarco sticks out her hand, and I shake it.

"Right. I'm surprised you remember me."

"It's not easy to forget someone almost dying in front of the hospital." Her brows furrow, and she shudders as if chilled.

"So you're the doc who saved her?" Soul asks.

"Oh, I'm so sorry, Dr. DeMarco. This is my boyfriend, Soul."

I immediately want to call back the words. Soul

and I haven't discussed what we are or put a label on *us*, and now I've shoved my foot so far in my mouth it might be stuck there forever.

Dr. DeMarco and Soul shake hands.

"Her man, not boy," Soul corrects with a laugh in his tone.

So he is my boyfriend? Well, man. He's my man. I like the sound of that.

"Pleasure to meet you, Soul," she says before looking back at me. "What brings you back to the hospital?"

"I'm getting the temporary pacemaker removed," I explain and then smack myself in the head. "Shit, I forgot to have Abyss remove the MDIV. I finished the antibiotics yesterday."

"What's an MDIV?"

"I'm sure someone here can remove it."

Dr. DeMarco and Soul speak at the same time.

As Soul explains what the MDIV is to her, she practically dances in place.

"That sounds interesting, and very much like the kind of medical equipment I'd like to have access to," she says with an almost child-like giddiness. When Soul doesn't react to her statement in any way, she asks me, "What time is your appointment?"

"Nine thirty."

She checks her watch. "It's only eight fifty-five.

Maybe I can take a look, see if I can remove it?"

Her eyes are hopeful, and she's grinning from ear to ear. There is no mistaking her resemblance to a kid in a candy store I glance up at Soul, and he nods.

"Sure," I tell her with a shrug.

"Great, let me find a surgical room that isn't being used."

Dr. DeMarco scurries away and speaks to a nurse sitting behind a desk about halfway down the hall. Her face lights up when the woman points to a room with an open door.

Dr. DeMarco waves us over, and when we reach her, she says, "Follow me."

She turns on the lights as we enter the room and tells me to hop up on the hospital bed.

"Where's the device?" she asks. I slip off the leather jacket Jez loaned me and hand it to Soul. The doctor's eyes focus on my arm, where the MDIV is attached. "You weren't kidding. This looks just like an insulin pump." She leans in to inspect it. "Where did you get it?"

"A friend of ours is working with a pharmaceutical and medical equipment company to get it patented. It hasn't been released to the public yet," Soul explains. I have no idea if he's telling the truth or not because that's more information than I was given. "You're gonna have to keep this quiet, Doc."

"This could help a lot of people, especially children that need constant treatments for various diseases," she mutters and when he glares at her, she continues. "I won't say anything, of course. But, will you let me know when the patent goes through? I'd love to take this to the board and get it stocked in the hospital."

"I think we can do that."

Okay, so maybe he was telling the truth.

"It would be per—" She shakes her head. "Nevermind they won't listen."

"Who won't listen?" I ask.

"The board." Dr. DeMarco sighs. "Dr. Franklin isn't as forward-thinking as some of us are."

"Which Dr. Franklin?" Soul asks.

Which Dr. Franklin? There's more than one fucktard?

"Senior," she clarifies. "Dr. Franklin Jr is just a lazy piec—"

"You looking to move up in the world, Doc?"

What the hell is happening here?

"Who isn't?" Dr. DeMarco shrugs. "But I don't want to move up for the money like some people. I want to actually start making a difference and see new procedures and devices like this come into our small town. It would be nice to do more advanced treatments versus having to send patients to Las Vegas. A lot of people can't afford to do that."

Soul rubs his chin as if deep in thought but doesn't say anything.

Dr. DeMarco washes her hands before sliding on surgical gloves, and then steps toward me and asks me to stretch out my arm. The device is easily removed, with only a few drops of blood trickling from where the needles punctured my skin. Her eyes light up as she inspects the underside portion of the MDIV. After she disinfects and bandages my arm, I hop off the table.

"Yes, this would definitely be good for patients." She wraps the device in some paper towels and hands it to Soul. "I'll just give this back to you since we never had this conversation."

Soul grins. "Thanks, Doc. I'll remember this."

A knock on the door has us all shifting our attention. Dr. DeMarco crosses the room and answers it.

"We're ready for Ms. Parker," the nurse says.

"Thank you again for everything, Dr. DeMarco." I shake her hand again. "I'm glad I could help. Don't take this the wrong way, but I hope I don't see you back here anytime soon."

Soul laughs. "We're gonna do our best to make sure you don't."

"If you'll follow me please," the nurse says impatiently.

Four hours later, Soul and I walk out of the hospital, and I breathe a sigh of relief.

I made it, and nothing bad happened. Well, sort of. I could've done without running into Dr. Fucktard.

We walk across the lot and spot Animal standing by Soul's Harley.

"What are you doing here?" Soul demands, instantly tensing as if something is wrong.

"Abyss called. Said he forgot to tell you to take Cece home in a cage."

"Cage?" I ask as I search the parking lot for anything resembling a cage.

"Car or anything other than a motorcycle," Soul explains. "We call them cages because we feel caged when we're in them."

Oh, that makes sense but still doesn't explain why *I* need to ride in a *cage.* Animal must sense my confusion because he rolls his eyes and starts to explain.

"He said, and I quote, Cece needs to be in a cage since she was given sedatives, and even though she wasn't knocked out completely, she could still have drugs in her system that could affect her ability to ride safely." His imitation of Abyss is eerily accurate.

"That was sweet of him to think of me, especially since I'm no longer his patient."

Tears of gratitude, and sadness if I'm being honest, well in my eyes. I hate that I'm not going to be around the brothers all the time anymore. It feels as if I'm losing my family all over again. I shake my head to clear my thoughts and look up at Soul. He's studying my face, but thankfully, he doesn't call me out on my emotions. Instead, he throws his keys at Animal.

"Thanks, brother. I don't have to tell you what'll happen if there's even a single scratch on her when I get back to the clubhouse, yeah?"

"I know, I know. Disembowelment, tearing off of limbs, death… all the good stuff," Animal jokes.

"Scratch her and find out fucker."

"Alright, alright." I push Animal toward the bike. "Get out of here before he kills you with all these witnesses around."

Soul laughs and pulls me against his chest. "We're gonna go grab lunch since she couldn't eat before her procedure, and then I'll drop her at home before I head back."

Animal nods but grabs my wrist and tugs me gently into his arms for a hug. "Don't be a stranger."

He doesn't even flinch when Soul growls and yanks me away from his brother. "Get you're own fucking woman."

"Yeah, yeah," Animal grumbles. "See ya at the clubhouse, Prez."

I wave at Animal as he gets on the bike and takes off. Soul unlocks the SUV and opens the door for me.

Before getting in, I cup his cheeks and urge his head down so I can place a gentle kiss on his lips.

Soul fists his hand in my hair and pulls me closer. He nibbles on my bottom lip, coaxing my mouth open. When I grant him entry, he slips his tongue inside and swirls it with mine. I groan and press my breasts against his chest, needing to be as close as possible.

Soul cups my ass and lifts me off the ground. Without thinking, I wrap my legs around his waist and his hard cock rubs against my core. My panties dampen at the friction. I growl in frustration as I try to grind in an effort to increase the pressure, but Soul only chuckles and sets me in the passenger seat. The man has a nasty habit of leaving me panting and wanting more.

"As much as I want to devour you, I don't think the parking lot of the hospital is the best place to tear off your clothes and feast."

"Probably right," I huff and clench my knees together.

Soul adjusts himself as he struts around the hood to the driver's side like he's fucking king of the world, and my mouth waters at the sight.

"Since neither of us is getting a happy ending, the least you can do is take me to get some tacos." I wink with a grin.

CHAPTER NINETEEN

SOUL

"DID YOU NEED SOMETHING, OR ARE YOU JUST GONNA hover?"

Jez's fingers fly over the keyboard, and several new windows pop up on the computer screen in front of her. I try to make sense of what I'm seeing, but it all appears to be geek speak. In other words, Jez is the only person in the clubhouse who could possibly understand it.

"I'm not hovering," I snap, annoyed that she's calling me out.

"Soul, I love you, but you're absolutely fucking hovering." She shrugs. "It's what you do when you're all up in your head. And you've been in your damn head since you got back from taking Cece home yesterday."

I shove my hands in my pockets. "I have no id—"

Jez spins her computer chair around and stomps

on my foot with her heel. "Lie to me all you want, but don't lie to yourself."

"What makes you think I'm lying to myself?"

My sister stands and presses her thumb to my forehead. "This right here."

I groan. "Seriously? My worry crease?"

She grins. "It's a good thing you don't play poker."

"Never understood the point in throwing money away on a game."

Jez arches a brow. "That's your story, huh?"

"It's true," I insist.

"It's not. You don't play poker because you suck. And you suck because you can't control your damn forehead."

Throwing my hands in the air, I spin around and stomp to the door. "I can't win with you," I say over my shoulder.

"Love you t—"

Thankfully the door slides closed behind me, and I don't have to listen to her gloat. Fucking sisters. I went to Jez for advice, but when her snarky side appeared, my plan went to shit. I swear, she brings out the worst in me.

And the best.

As I make my way through the clubhouse, I check my cell. I sent Cece a text this morning, and she still hasn't responded. Why isn't she responding?

Maybe she wants nothing to do with you now that she's gone.

Bullshit. I refuse to let my mind wander with ridiculous negativity. Cece wants me. All I have to do to remember that is conjure up any memory of our kisses or the way she practically suctions her body to mine like an octopus when we're on my bike.

So if I leave, we aren't together anymore?

That was her question, not mine. So why the fuck would I worry that she's ghosting me or doesn't want to be with me now that we're not existing under the same roof? Shit, she even called me her boyfriend at the hospital yesterday. She wouldn't have done that if she was planning to walk out of my life the second she walked out of the clubhouse… right?

"Hey, baby."

Gwen seems to appear out of nowhere to block my path, which proves how hard I was failing at not letting my mind wander.

"I don't have time for you, Gwen."

She rests one hand on her hip and flattens the other on my chest. "Maybe you should make time," she purrs. "You know I can make you forget that cunt if you'd just gi—"

"Her name is Cece," I snarl as I grip her wrist and shove her away from me.

Gwen stumbles on her impossibly high heels, but before she topples over, Jez is there. My twin does what I can only fantasize about. She slams the club bunny against the wall with her hand around her throat. Gwen claws at Jez, but my sister only tightens her grip in response.

"Please, Soul, let me take out the trash," Jez grits out with her eyes locked on Gwen.

"Make her stop," Gwen pleads, her voice wheezy. "C'mon, baby. You know you—"

I smack my hand on the wall next to her head. "I'm not your baby. Never have been and sure as fuck never will be."

Gwen opens her mouth to argue, but Jez uses her free hand to bitch slap her.

"My brother might hold back because you're a chick, but I've got a vagina just like you, so I don't have the same restrictions." Jez tilts her head. "Well, not *just* like you. My vagina isn't a garbage dump for cum."

"Get her outta here," I order Jez but then lock eyes with Gwen. "I don't want to see you ever again. If I do, I'll forget that society dictates I not lay my hands on you."

"But, baby, I want your hands on me."

"Jesus, you don't give up, do you?" Jez grumbles as she wraps her hand in Gwen's hair and starts to drag her down the hall.

I laugh as I watch Gwen struggle and fail miserably to get away from my sister. Jez might be a woman, but she can take care of a bitch just as well as any of the brothers.

"Hey Jez," I call out just before they turn the corner into the common room.

"Yeah?" she asks as she looks over her shoulder.

"Did you need something?"

"What?"

"You were working, and then you were just there." I shrug. "Thought maybe you came out of your hole because you needed something."

"Oh." She scrunches up her nose. "I don't even remember why I came out." Jez shrugs. "But it definitely couldn't have been for anything more fun than this," she says as she yanks Gwen's hair again.

Shaking my head, I chuckle and continue down the hall toward the sanctuary. Church starts soon, and I refuse to be the last brother in the room. That's only happened to me one time, and that was back when we first started Saints Purgatory.

I scan my thumb and the door slides open. I'm

surprised to see Malice and Grim already in their seats. Malice is frantically signing something, but I can't make out what because Grim is blocking my view. Based on the way my enforcer's shoulders stiffen, it can't be anything good.

"What's wrong?" I ask as I take my place at the head of the table.

Malice lifts his chin at Grim.

"Nothing," Grim says. It's not often he uses his voice, but when he does, I know it's because he's too angry to use ASL.

I narrow my eyes. "Don't bullshit a bullshitter."

Grim shakes his head and Malice sighs before lifting his hands. "Dude's pissed because I got the girl."

Grim shoots up from his chair so fast it crashes to the floor. "She only chose you because you're not deaf!" His hands fly and his jaw tics. "Bitch said she wanted the man attached to the cock inside her to be able to hear her screams."

Malice smirks and grabs his crotch. "Fucking pussy was tight, too. And she was definitely a screamer."

"Fifty bucks," I snap.

"You've gotta be kidding me!" Malice counters as he jumps to his feet.

I shrug. "You know the rules. And you're up to a hundred."

Grim finally smiles. "Keep going, VP," he taunts and his movements are slower, more controlled. "See if you can get it up to a few hundred."

Malice plops back into his chair and shakes his head. "Fuck you both."

"Hundred and fifty," I say.

The door slides open and the rest of the brothers file into the room. Since they all arrived together, I take pity on them and don't assign any of them cleaning duty.

"Sit the fuck down and let's get this shit started," Malice grumbles, but lucky for him, he follows the rules and his fine doesn't increase.

"You weren't signing again, were you?" Rogue asks Malice with a laugh. "Whaddya owe me today?"

"Buck fifty."

"If you'd keep your dick in your pants, you wouldn't—"

Malice slices his hand through the air, and Grim's only reaction is to chuckle, although he does lower his hands and sit.

"We're gonna skip updates today," I begin. "But, one thing you all need to know is Gwen is no longer welcome at the clubhouse. Jez escorted off the property." I turn my attention to Lock and Fort. "The two of you need to deactivate Gwen's credentials in the security system. You've got one hour, as protocol dictates. Time starts as soon as church ends."

"Done," our security and tech experts say in unison.

"What'd the bitch do this time?" Rogue asks.

My muscles tense as I remember her words in the hall. "She called my woman a cunt," I growl. "And in case any of you were wondering, the only name Cece will be addressed by is Cece. Or Queen if you prefer."

"Queen?" Thorn asks with an arched brow. "You making her your old lady?"

"Did you doubt that when I claimed her?"

"Not even for a second."

"Smart man." I glance around the table. "Anyone got a problem with that?"

"Uh, Prez," Frenzy begins. "Take it from a man who's been down that road… Women don't take kindly to not having a say in their future."

"Oh, Cece has a say." I smirk. "And she's gonna say yes when the time comes."

I have no idea if that's the direction Cece and I are headed, but I damn sure intend to find out. Once I have my mind set on something, I don't waver or drag my feet. And I've made up my mind on Cece. I want her, and I will have her.

"When you say 'off the property'," Malice asks. "How far off the property are we talkin'?"

"Knowing Jez, only as far as outside the garage door." I face Grim. "When we're finished, I need you to head up and make sure Gwen finds her way to the road. After that, I don't give a shit where she goes."

"I should just kill her." The glint in Grim's eyes at the thought is concerning, and also why he makes the best enforcer the club could possibly have.

"She stays alive," I order. "Unless she does something to warrant death. Then I'll leave the decision to you."

Grim nods with a smirk. Something tells me one of the prospects is going to be burying a body later tonight because there is no way Gwen isn't going to give Grim a reason to justify purging her sinning soul.

"You know you just gave him the green light," Animal says.

"See evil, hear evil, become evil, purge evil." I briefly lock eyes with each brother as I recite the club motto. "If Grim sees or hears evil, he becomes evil to purge evil. I trust him to do the right thing, as I do with all of you."

"Understood, Prez," Animal says, somewhat chagrined.

"Moving on," I say. "Dr. Franklin's purge. We need a plan."

"We've been waiting on you, Prez," Malice counters. "But with Cece here, you never wanted to move forward."

"And she's gone now," I remind him, anger infusing my words.

"Well, are we purging junior only, or Daddy too?" Rogue asks.

"Junior only. Fucktard senior hasn't quite crossed the line yet. But Jez is watching, and she's got orders to let us know if that changes."

"That makes it easier then," Thorn says. "We know his work schedule, where he lives, his habits. Hell, we even know he prefers his coffee black. Give us a deadline, and consider him purged."

I shake my head. "Not this time. I want in on this one. And he needs to suffer."

"What do you have in mind?" Grim's face couldn't possibly get any brighter with excitement.

"Here's what I—" I glare at the door when there's a loud bang. "That prospect is a—"

The emergency light above the table flashes red. Every single person who enters the clubhouse is instructed to never press the button to activate that light unless someone is breaching the property or death is imminent. I nod at Grim, who reaches under the table and grabs the one and only weapon permitted in the sanctuary.

He stands and crosses to the door. Once he's in position, I push the button and the door slides open. Grim immediately levels the gun at the intruder, and Jez lifts the laptop in her hand in front of her face.

Grim's shoulders sag as he lowers the weapon. When my sister glares at him, he shrugs. He won't apologize for doing what he's trained to do, and she knows it.

Jezebel pushes past Grim and stomps to the table where she sets her laptop down so she can sign.

"Maybe use the cameras you insisted on to see who's at the door instead of assuming it's trouble," she snaps.

"What the fuck do you want?" I bark. "Is Gwen refusing to leave? Is there death and destruction going on out there?" I ask, nodding toward the hall.

"What? No."

Grim steps up behind Jezebel and passes the gun to me. Then he taps her on the shoulder and she spins to face him.

"Then why the emergency alert?" he asks and his eyes slide down her body and then back up to her face. "Are you hurt?"

"No. I'm fine. But I need Abyss to look at something." Jezebel slides her laptop across the table and walks around to the other side to stand behind Abyss's chair. "Do those medical records look normal to you?" she asks him.

"What is this about, Jezebel?" I demand.

She holds a finger up. "Gimme a sec."

"You've got to be kidding me," I snap. "You know the goddamn rules. As soon as I'm outta church, I'm helping you pa—"

"Prez," Abyss says, shock written in his expression. "You should be thanking her, not threatening to kick her to the curb."

I roll my eyes. I swear on all that's unholy, I have no control when these fuckers put their mind to something.

"Well?" I arch a brow at Abyss. "What the fuck are you looking at?"

"Two sets of medical records."

I stiffen. "What? Whose medical records are they?"

Jez looks at me with sad eyes. "They're Mrs. Parker's."

"Mrs. Parker? As in Cece's mom?" Jez nods. "Why would there be two sets of records?"

"I've done the deep dive into Dr. Fucktard's father, like you asked, and things appeared on the up and up, but I couldn't let it go." She shrugs. "So I kept digging. I found a second set of login credentials that Senior only uses when he logs into the hospital system to look at his son's patient's records."

"Okay."

"We already suspected that Dr. Franklin Sr. was covering for Dr. Franklin Jr., right?" I nod. "So I paid specific attention to any records they both accessed. Cece's was one of them."

"We figured you'd find that," I remind her.

"I know. But I never expected to find them both in Mrs. Parker's file."

I focus on Abyss. "Can you dumb this down for me? I'm not understanding why there would be two sets of records or why this is such an emergency."

"At first glance, each of these files wouldn't raise any red flags." Abyss stands and brings the laptop to the end of the table to show me what he's talking about. He points to the screen. "This one here lists the night her mom died as the only visit to the hospital. There's also an autopsy report attached to it, listing the cause of death as a brain aneurysm."

"Yeah okay. Cece told me that's how her mom died."

"Okay, now look here," he instructs and points to the other file.

"Wait." I skim the record. "There's a second

hospital visit listed." I read through the report. "And this autopsy lists the cause of death as a brain tumor," I say. "Why are they different?"

"That's what I wanted to know," Jezebel says. "The first one you looked at is the *official* file. And the second one is the *original* file."

I let her words roll around in my brain, and when they sink in, my blood runs cold.

This can't be right.

I dismiss the thought immediately. It's right. Jez wouldn't be here if it weren't.

"Would someone please explain for the rest of the class?" Rogue barks.

"Cece's mom didn't have to die," Abyss says quietly. "According to the file, Mrs. Parker sought out treatment for persistent headaches. The treating physician on that visit was Junior, and he didn't run any tests. The brain tumor causing the headaches was operable and could've been removed. The surgery would've been extensive and not without risk, but the chance of survival was high."

Grim slams both fists on the table, and all eyes turn to him. He raises his hands as his expression turns murderous. "Are you telling me that Junior fucked up, and Senior covered it up?" Abyss, Jez, and I all nod. "So Cece didn't have to lose her mom?"

Again, we nod to confirm his thoughts. "So our queen-to-be hurts when she doesn't have to?"

Grim is a tough man, a hardened man who sees and understands far more than anyone gives him credit for. Despite that, or maybe because of it, he's a fucking softy when it comes to the people he cares about, to the people he considers family. And he considers Cece family because she matters to me.

"Yes," I confirm, emotion clogging my throat at how easily he accepts others while the world around him so callously rejects him.

"They both die." Grim crosses his arms over his chest and glares around the table as if to dare any of the brothers to argue.

"I think it's time for a vote," I say. "All in favor of purging both Junior and Senior?"

All hands go up, including my sister's. She doesn't get a say in this, but we all appreciate the sentiment.

We spend the next hour planning the purge. And only when I'm sure we're all on the same page and have the plan committed to memory do I adjourn church. The brothers file out, but Jez remains behind.

"I'm sorry I inter—"

"Don't," I snap. When tears gather in her eyes, I regret my tone. I pull her into my arms and rest my chin on the top of her head. "I'm sorry. I'm not mad at you. You did the right thing by triggering the emergency light."

Jezebel nods even as she sniffles. I push her slightly away from me so I can see her face, and when I see the tears freely flowing down her cheeks, my heart cracks. I hate it when my twin is hurting.

All of your women are in pain.

"What is it?" I ask softly.

"Cece lost her mom, Soul. She lost her, and she didn't have to."

"I know."

"It's not fair."

"No, it's not."

"We have to tell her."

"We?"

She nods. "Yeah, we. I'm not sitting this one out, Soul. Don't you dare even think about asking me to."

"Then I suggest you pull yourself together because she's going to need us to be strong for her."

Jezebel squares her shoulders as she swipes her cheeks. "Done."

I chuckle. Her eyes are red, and her cheeks are blotchy, but I don't call her out on it.

"When do you want to leave?" she asks.

"We ride out in ten. I'll meet you in the garage."

Again, she nods, but rather than linger, she strides

to the door and exits the sanctuary. I flop down in my chair and rest my chin in my hands.

How the hell am I supposed to tell all of this to Cece? How *can* I tell her *without* causing her a world of pain? I only ever want to bring Cece pleasure and happiness.

But pleasure and happiness will have to wait.

CHAPTER TWENTY

CECE

"Time to unpack."

Great, now I'm talking to myself.

After Soul dropped me off yesterday, I had plans to go to the boutique. But I was so tired and decided to open a bottle of wine and binge-watch some *New Girl* on Netflix instead.

Stretching my arms over my head, I slowly stand up from the couch. I didn't even make it to my bed last night. I grab my suitcase from the hallway and roll it down to my old room. The past hits me in my face as I push open the door. Pictures of Carmella and me are hanging on my corkboard next to my dresser. The bed is made with the same yellow comforter I had in high school.

I drop the suitcase on the bed and start putting things back in their correct drawer. Carmella must have aired out the house and cleaned before she left for her new job because the house doesn't smell musty.

As I'm working, an envelope on my nightstand catches my eye. I pick it up and see my name on it, so I slide out the piece of paper inside.

Cece,

I knew once you came back home you wouldn't feel up to cleaning. I washed all your sheets and blankets so you wouldn't have to worry about it and cleaned up as best I could before I left. I unpacked everything you had left at the apartment so if you can't find something just call or text me and I will let you know where I put it. I'll miss you but I'm only a phone call away.

Love ya Hooker,

Mel

God, I love that girl.

I grab what I need to take a quick shower and make a mental note to go to the grocery store. That's the one thing Carmella didn't do, but I'm glad she didn't. The food would've spoiled by now. After turning on the water, I step under the hot spray and let the water massage my aching muscles.

Forty-five minutes later, I walk out of the bathroom feeling somewhat refreshed and glance down the hallway. My heart lurches as I force my feet to carry me in the opposite direction from my room. Taking a deep breath, I grip the door knob in front of me and slowly push the door open.

I glance around the room as I'm frozen in place in the hall. My feet are heavy and won't budge, as if concrete blocks are weighing them down. Mom's room was left untouched. I still haven't been able to really process her death but standing in the doorway of her bedroom is like a giant slap to the face.

She's never coming back.

Tears run down my cheeks as I close the door. I slump against the wall and slide to the carpet.

I'm not sure how long I've been sitting here, but it's been long enough for my feet to fall asleep. I wobble and ache as I push myself up off the floor. I walk back to my room and grab my shoes and purse. I can't put off the inevitable any longer, and I need to get out of this house for a while. Too many memories are flooding my mind, and I have shit to get done. The pity party will have to wait.

After grabbing my keys off the hook, I open the door that leads to the garage. Ah, there she is… My black 1987 IROC Z28 Camaro. She's my pride and joy next to Naughty/Nice. The Camaro was my dad's car but after he passed away, my mom gave it to me. Dad would only drive it on special occasions, so it's in prime condition. Mom told me it was always the plan to be mine, and I'm thankful to have a piece of my dad with me.

I climb inside and rub my hand over the dashboard. "Did you miss me, baby?"

The car purrs to life when I turn the key, and I slowly back out of the garage to head to Naughty/Nice. As I drive, all I can think about is everything that's going to need done. I might even have to bring in a cleaning service to help me clean since it's been shut up for so long, and I don't want to wait much longer to reopen. Inventory needs done, and I have to catch up on online orders. This is going to be a giant cluster fuck figuring all this out.

There aren't any available parking spaces in front of Naughty/Nice, which is odd, so I park at the side of the building. I walk around the corner to the front door and gasp when I see someone coming out of my *closed* store with bags.

What the ever-loving fuck?

I race toward the entrance, my shoes clopping on the sidewalk like a damn horse running in the Kentucky Derby. The open sign hanging in the door seems to mock me, but I force my eyes to shift to what's beyond the glass. Anger surges through my system even as my feet become glued to the pavement.

People are milling around the boutique, flitting from rack to rack and lining up at the cash register. My brain refuses to process what I'm seeing, and question after question piles up like building blocks in my frontal lobe. But one question flashes, demanding to be answered.

Carmella is the only person, other than me, who has a key to Naughty/Nice, and she's in another state. So, how the fuck is my store open?

Every muscle in my body is coiled tight with adrenaline, but I push through it and yank open the door to the boutique.

"What the fuck is going on in here?" I demand, ready to fight whoever tries to leave before I get answers.

A woman slowly steps toward me with her hands raised in front of her. Her eyes are wide and her cheeks pink. "Are you Cece?"

"Of course I'm Cece," I snap as I march right up to her, stopping only when I'm inches from her face. "Who the hell are you, and why are you in my fucking store?"

Like falling dominoes, silence slowly settles over the room until the only sound is the *thud, thud, thud* of my heartbeat. The hairs on the back of my neck stand on end, and I scan the store as if searching for a threat. All eyes are focused on me, confusion and apprehension written on everyone's faces.

"Someone better start talking before I have you all arrested for breaking and entering... and theft." I pull my cell phone out of my pocket and hold it up so they know I'm serious.

The woman in front of me giggles nervously as she takes a step back.

"It's okay everyone," she says. "Please continue shopping. There's just a little mix-up." She extends her arm toward me. "This is Cece Parker, the owner of Naughty/Nice." No-name grabs my hand and starts to drag me toward the back of the store.

I'm too shocked at the action to even try and stop her, but manage to come to my senses after a few feet.

"Hold up." I pull my hand out of her grasp. "What the hell is going on?"

"Please Cece, come with me to the office," she pleads with an apologetic smile. "I swear I can explain, but I don't want you to lose customers hashing this out on the sales floor."

I shake my head and raise my eyebrows. "By all means, let's not lose any customers. We can go to *my* office, but if I don't like what you have to say we *will* have a problem."

Again, she lifts her hands up in surrender. I stomp past her toward the office, refusing to be led around like *I'm* the person who doesn't belong. When I find the office door already open, I shoot a glare over my shoulder. No-name hangs her head, and her cheeks redden even more.

Keeping the door open, I motion for her to sit down while I lean against my desk. "Start talking."

"First, I just want to say it's a pleasure to finally meet you."

"I'm not trying to be a bitch, but you've got about ten seconds to tell me what the hell is going on?" When she only stares at me, I shrug. "Okay, yeah, I'm being a bitch. But it's my store and you, or anyone else for that matter, shouldn't be here. So…" My body pulses with rage.

"It's not what you think," she insists. "I'm Trista, the new manager."

"The new—" I press my lips into a thin line as my body stiffens. Fisting my hands at my sides, I try again. "I didn't hire a new manager."

Trista nods frantically. "I know. Um, I was hired by Soul and Jezebel."

More secrets?

"What are you talking about?"

"Soul and Jez hired me to be your new manager." Trista's voice is shaky with what I hope is fear. "They said you were out on medical leave and that the store needed to remain open. So they hired me, Holly, and Laura."

"Who the hell are Holly and Laura?"

"They're part-time employees. Laura is here with me today, and Holly works tomorrow."

I pinch the bridge of my nose. "So you're telling me that Soul and Jez hired you to *run my store*?" I ask, my words dripping with sarcasm.

"Yes, they really did." Trista nods, reminding me of a bobblehead. "Can I show you the contract?"

"Contract?"

"They had us all sign a contract." She rises slowly and points to the desk. "May I?"

"Go ahead."

I watch her closely as she walks around the desk and opens the top drawer. She hands me a piece of paper, and I take a moment to read it. It basically says that Trista, Holly, and Laura were hired on a temporary basis, and upon my return, their employment can be terminated if I decide not to keep them on. Everyone signed it, agreeing to the terms. *Everyone but me*. Hell, Soul even threw in a hefty bonus for all three of them, to be paid for by the MC, if I choose to let them go.

"I have keys to the store, and Jez showed me how to work your point of sale system, and Rogue comes to get the deposits every other day so we don't have to deal with that."

Shock and rage don't even begin to describe what I'm feeling right now.

They knew!

Soul, Jez, Rogue… all of them fucking knew, and no one said a damn thing to me. I take a deep breath to steady myself, but it doesn't help.

"No one told me any of this," I say unnecessarily. I'm sure Trista's already figured out that I knew nothing.

She shrugs. "Maybe they didn't want to bother you while you were—"

I silence her with a look. "How long have you been working here?"

"Just over three weeks now."

The sharp knife of betrayal twists in my gut. Bile rises up my throat, and I grab the desk for support as I try to breathe through it. I told them at the hospital I didn't want them to hire anyone. They blatantly ignored my wishes.

There's only one reason they'd do this… to take my store.

I continue to focus on my breathing as my mind races to come up with a game plan. If the club thinks they're going to steal my store out from under me, they don't know me very well. I'm capable of more than they're giving me credit for.

You're being irrational. What would they want with Naughty/Nice?

That's the thing about irrational thoughts… Just because you recognize them for what they are doesn't mean they're easy to ignore. Shit, I even have a signed contract leaving the final decision to me regarding the new employees. But I still can't make sense of any of it.

"I'm gonna call Soul and get some answers." I level my gaze at Trista. "Until I do, you don't leave."

"Understood." She hugs the wall as she walks around the desk, toward the door, and keeps her eyes on me the entire time. "I'm just gonna go and help Laura. I'll shut the door so you have some privacy."

I flop into my chair, and pinch the bridge of my nose in an effort to ease the stress headache forming behind my eyes.

Think. Think. Think. Why would Soul and Jez do this?

I need answers, and sitting here sulking isn't getting me any. But the person I want to strangle can, so I grab my cell from my purse and tap his contact info. The asshole answers on the second ring.

"Where are you?" Soul's voice is gruff, which only fuels my anger.

"What the fuck were you thinking?" I shout.

"What are you talking about?"

"I specifically told you *not* to hire anyone to work in *my* store."

"Shit," he mumbles. "You're at Naughty / Nice?"

"Ding, ding, ding. We have a winner, folks."

"We were only trying to help," he says with a sigh. "Life was fucking you over and knocking you down." He takes a deep breath. "I came to talk to you about something, and we can discuss this too."

"Where are you?"

"Jez and I are sitting in your driveway. We need to talk to you about something. But it should be face to face."

"You can forget it," I snap. "I want you to leave. Both of you." I sniffle back the threatening tears. So much for staying strong.

"Babe, listen," Soul cajoles. "I know you probably have a million thoughts running through your head but I promise, it isn't what you think." He pauses. "Come home so we can talk or let us come to the store."

Yeah, so they can tell me more lies.

"Dammit, woman. I didn't want to do this over the phone." He takes a deep breath, as if waiting for me to give him permission to come to Naughty / Nice. When I remain stubbornly silent, he continues. "Jez told the club how much the store means to you and that, with your mom gone, the store might be okay for a while, but she didn't want it to just be *okay*. Jez loves you, and she wanted to make sure you didn't have any stress when you came back to work. I agreed with her."

Dammit.

"It still doesn't explain why neither of you told me," I huff out.

"I'm sorry we didn't tell you, but I'm *not* sorry we did it," he admits. "You had the weight of the world on your shoulders, I wanted to take the weight of the world *off* your shoulders."

"It wasn't your call to make, Soul." The anger hasn't disappeared, but my heart thaws at his words.

There's a knock on the door right before it swings open, and Laura smiles sheepishly. "Sorry to bother you, but we're getting ready to close, and Trista said you might want to clear out the register yourself."

"Thanks. I'll be right there," I say. Once the door closes, I refocus on my phone call. "Soul, I have to go."

"When will you be home?"

"I think I need some time alone." I sigh. "Just go back to the clubhouse. I'll talk to you later."

I hang up before he can respond and take a minute to compose myself.

I will not cry.

Several minutes later, I emerge from my office and take the time to *really* look at the store. The shelves are stocked, and Laura is running around straightening up displays from the onslaught of customers earlier. Trista is studying the computer by the register. Everything appears to be in good shape.

Trista and Laura are doing what I normally do, which leaves me feeling useless.

"Can I help?" I ask, stepping behind the counter.

"Actually yes. I had this order come through, and I can't make sense of it." Trista points to the screen.

I scan the order and chuckle. "That's an order from Jez. It took me a while to figure it out too. She wants one of every color of thong in size small, as well as one of each of the matching bras."

"Are you sure? That's a lot of panties and bras."

"I'm sure. She puts in an order like this every six months."

"Oh good." Trista says with a sigh of what sounds like relief. "I thought I was losing my mind."

"Nope." I take a deep breath. "I'm sorry I bitched at you earlier. It isn't your fault I had no idea any of this was going on."

"Hey, I get it. If this were my store and someone did that to me, I'd be furious. I'm just glad you didn't punch me." She laughs.

"Hi, I'm Laura."

Trista and I gasp as we whirl around to face Laura.

"Laura, I told you to quit doing that shit," Trista snaps, shaking her head.

I reach out and shake Laura's hand. "I'm Cece. Nice to meet you." I glance at Trista. "Now, what shit?"

"She's so quiet, and you never hear her coming until she speaks," Trista explains. "She scares the shit out of me all the time."

"Maybe we can put a bell around her neck," I tease.

They look at each other and burst out laughing. I join in, feeling good for the first time today.

"Listen, I'm gonna be honest with you," I say when the laughter dies down. "I don't know how I feel about this situation, and I'm gonna need some time to wrap my mind around all of it."

"Trista told me you didn't know about us or the store being open," Laura says. "But if I may, we all love working here. I know you have a lot to process, but we'd really like to stay if you decide to keep on employees." She flashes a bright smile. "Rogue always mentions you when he stops to pick up the deposit. It sounds like the club really cares about you."

Trista nods in agreement. "I can go over the new

inventory we received while you were out, and anything else you want to know, whenever you're ready. But for the most part, things have gone smoothly. Whenever we didn't know something, we called Jez, Soul, or Rogue." She leans against the counter and tilts her head as if she's trying to remember if there's anything else. "Oh, and some guy named Lock installed cameras and fingerprint locks on the safe. You and Rogue are the only two who can access the money. Soul thought that would make you feel a little better about strangers being here."

At least he got that right.

I look around and, sure enough, there are cameras everywhere. I'm sure someone at the club is watching, and because I'm feeling childish, I stick my tongue out and flip off the camera situated above the register.

"I'm gonna like working for you," Trista says with a wink.

And as much as I hate to admit it, I think I'm gonna like working with them.

"Alright ladies, let's lock up and call it a night. I think we've had enough excitement for one day."

CHAPTER TWENTY-ONE

SOUL

THREE HOURS.

That's how long I've been sitting on Cece's porch steps waiting for her to come home. I know she told me to leave, and I did, but I couldn't stay away. Jez told me coming back was a bad idea, and I'm beginning to wonder if she was right. As it stands, I've already had a run-in with one neighbor.

I chuckle at the memory of the spunky old lady's determination to protect Cece.

"Who the hell are you?"

The unmistakable ch-chunk of a shotgun being racked punctuates the words, and I whirl around to see a pint-sized grandma in a worn pale yellow housecoat.

"I asked you a question, boy," she says as she raises the gun a little higher in her arthritic hands.

I lift my own hands up to show her I mean no harm. "I'm a friend of Cece's, ma'am," I tell her in a tone I hope conveys that I'm one of the good guys, despite how I look.

Normally I love the fear that enters people's eyes when they see my cut, but right now I'm wishing I'd have left the damn thing at the clubhouse. It'd be a hell of a thing to die of a gunshot wound at the hands of a woman who's no bigger than a minute.

"How come I've never seen you before?" she asks, the wrinkles on her face becoming more pronounced as she narrows her eyes.

"I was here earlier, with my sister. We came by to talk to Cece, but she was at work. We left, but I decided to come back and wait for Cece to get home."

She stares at me as if trying to determine if I'm telling the truth. I don't know what the fuck I'll do if she deems me a liar. After several tense minutes, she lowers the barrel, but not enough that I'm out of danger. Sure, my head won't be blown off, but my nuts will be, and I'm not too sure which would be worse.

"Miss Cece has only lived here since yesterday," the woman states. "Come to think of it, she was dropped off by a young man." She takes a step closer. "Was that you?"

"Yes, ma'am, it was," I confirm. "I know that this is where Cece's mother lived before her death, and—"

"Barb Parker was a good woman. She'd come next door to check on me every few days." She shakes her head sadly. "Such a shame she died like she did."

"Yes, ma'am, it is." I smile. "Whaddya say you put that shotgun down, and then you can ask me all the ques-

tions you want until you feel better about me being here?"

"What's your name, boy?" she asks. "And none of that road name crap." When my brows shoot up, she shrugs. "I may be old and shriveled, but I'm not stupid. I've seen an episode or two of that biker show."

I can't stop my lips from tilting into a wider grin. "Name's Matt. Matt Hodges." Saying my given name doesn't sit right with me, but I'm not a fucking idiot. I'd like to keep my cock and balls, thank you very much. "But my friends call me Soul."

"Soul, huh?" I nod. "Well, Matt, *if I lower this shotgun, what's to stop you from pulling out that gun I saw poking out of your pants and killing me?"*

This lady doesn't miss a damn thing. Deciding that honesty is the best policy, and recognizing that it could be a huge mistake, I say, "Nothing, ma'am. But if I wanted to kill you, you'd be on the ground in a pool of blood already."

I expect her to become outraged, to let fear seep into her bones, but she shocks me when she throws her head back and howls with laughter.

She lowers the shotgun to her side. "I like you, Soul. You're just what Miss Cece needs in her life."

"If you could tell her that, I'd sure appreciate it. She's pretty upset with me right now."

"She'll get over it," she says with conviction. "Women

aren't that complicated, boy. Be honest with her like you were with me, and she'll come around."

Headlights cut through the dark, pulling me back to the present. I clock the vehicle's movement, and when it pulls into the driveway, my pulse kicks up. I don't know if her neighbor was right or not, but I'm about to find out.

Cece steps out of the driver's side and marches toward me, a scowl on her face. When she stops in front of me, she squares her shoulders and clenches her fists at her sides.

"I told you to go home," she snaps.

My dick springs to life at the heat in her glare. I know she's pissed off, but she's never looked more beautiful. Her hair is piled on top of her head in a messy bun, and curly wisps are blowing in the night breeze. The jeans she's wearing are tight, showing off her curves, and the blue sweater matches the color of her eyes when she's turned on.

I want to grab her by the waist and haul her inside to have my wicked way with her, but instead, I stand and shove my hands in my pockets.

"I went home," I tell her, my tone gravelly, and shrug. "You weren't there so I came back."

Cece's shoulders sag. "Soul, please. I can't do this right now." She pushes past me toward the front door. "Go home. We can talk in a few days."

I follow her, and stand to the side as she unlocks the door. "I survived a death threat to see you. I'm pretty sure I can survive your anger too."

Her gaze whips to mine. "Death threat? Who threatened you?"

Under the glow of the porch light, there's no mistaking the worry in her expression.

I tip my head toward the house next door. "Your neighbor lady."

"Mrs. Stims?"

"Didn't catch her name." I shrug. "I was too focused on the racked weapon pointing at my crotch."

Cece groans. "Yep, that's Mrs. Stims." She shakes her head and chuckles. "She's an itty bitty thing, but she acts like she's ten feet tall and could take on fifty grown men."

"She means well… I think."

"Tell that to my junior prom date," she scoffs. "She ran the poor kid off before we could even take pictures, and I ended up crying on my dad's shoulder because I missed the dance."

"I don't scare that easily."

Cece locks eyes with me for a moment and then sighs. "Fine. You might as well come in since you're here. But you've got ten minutes to make me feel better about you all lying to me and then you leave."

Ten minutes?

I lower my eyes. Down, down, down until I've caressed every inch of her with my gaze.

I can work with ten minutes.

When I refocus on her face, her cheeks are flushed and her tongue darts out to sweep across her bottom lip.

"If you still want me to go after ten minutes, I'll go."

"I… That'd…" She clears her throat. "Thank you."

Cece pushes the door open and steps inside. I walk in behind her, making sure to crowd her space as I kick the wooden barrier shut. When it slams closed, she flinches. I lean forward and graze her earlobe with my lips.

"Anything for you, babe."

She whimpers, but scurries away like a scared kitten. Grinning to myself, I watch as she sets her purse on a narrow table behind the couch before moving through the living room to the kitchen. She stops in front of the counter and, gripping the edge of the sink, stares out the window above it.

"Nine and a half minutes left," she calls over her shoulder, her tone husky.

So this is how she's gonna play it?

I stride across the room and stand near the island.

The distance between us isn't more than several feet, but it might as well be as wide as the ocean. She's so damn close, and yet it's almost as if she's the farthest away she's ever been.

"I'm sorry you had to find out about the new staff the way you did," I say, desperate to break the tense silence. "That wasn't my int—"

Cece whirls around and takes a few steps toward me, the flush of lust tainted with the heat of rage. "Apologies don't mean shit," she snaps. "Actions do, Soul. And you lied to me. The whole fucking club lied to me."

"Don't be mad at the brothers. They were just following orders."

"And that's part of the problem," she insists, her voice rising. "They blindly followed your orders without giving my feelings and what I wanted a second thought." She takes another two steps forward. "Naughty/Nice is *my* baby, Soul. Mine! You and Jez had no right to do what you did."

My brain is screaming at me to close the distance between us and scoop her in my arms, but I resist. For me to have any chance of staying past my allotted time, she needs to come to me on her own.

"You're right."

Another step forward. "And what's worse, I specifically told you I didn't want you to hire anyone," she says, repeating her argument from our phone call.

"You're right."

"I get that you have some antiquated notion that you're the man so what you say goes, but that's not gonna fly with me." She takes the last three steps toward me and stabs a finger into my chest. "I'm a grown-ass adult who can make her own decisions. I've lived my life this long without you there to take care of me, and I can keep doing it."

Unable to hold back, I brush my knuckles over her cheek. "You're right," I say again because one of these times she's going to hear the words and they're going to sink in.

"I'm not some naive little girl who needs a big strong man to protect me. I'm not the damsel in distress you're treating me like."

I nod. "You're right, Cece."

"And even more tha—" She presses her lips together and shakes her head before continuing. "What?"

"You're right."

"I'm right?"

I chuckle at her confusion. "Yeah, babe. You're right."

"Oh, well…" She lowers her arm. "Good. I'm glad you're seeing things fr—"

I fuse my lips to hers, needing her to shut the hell up. She's taken up half of my time to prove her point, and now it's my turn. Breaking the kiss, I rest my hands on her shoulders.

"What was that for?" she asks.

"Because I've only got about four minutes left, and I'm going to make the most of them," I tell her. "Everything you said is true. I had no right to do what I did behind your back. I should've respected your wishes, and I'm sorry I didn't. But I'm not sorry for doing what I thought was the right thing to help you."

She opens her mouth to argue, but says nothing when I shake my head.

"You had your chance to talk, and I listened. Now you listen." She narrows her eyes, but nods. "I've already told you I like you. And I'll keep telling you. I fucking like you, Cece. I care about you."

I rub my hands down her arms and shift them to her hips to slowly urge her backward toward the counter. "And when I care about someone, I'll do anything to help them, to make their life easier. I don't know how to do anything different. Ask any of the brothers, and they'll tell you that I will stop at nothing for those important to me."

Her body jolts when she hits the granite countertop.

"I can be your biggest supporter, cheering you on as you make your life exactly what you want it to be. But I won't do it from the sidelines." I cup her cheeks and lean in close. "You want to be a businesswoman and open a chain of boutiques? Great, I'll support you and help you do it. You wanna run for president and be the most important woman in the country? Fucking awesome. I'll stand by your side and be the best first man I can be. But if you expect me to stand on the periphery of your life and twiddle my damn thumbs when you struggle or need help, you're gonna be fucking disappointed. If you expect me to sit back and watch as someone tries to assassinate you, you're dead wrong. I'm not that guy. Never have been and never will be." My chest heaves with the determination to make her understand. "I know you think you're alone in this world, but you're not. You don't have to be strong all the time, babe. There's no shame in leaning on me or Jezebel or the club. There's no shame in letting people in."

Her lips part on a sharp inhale. "I can't, Soul. I let them in, and I get hurt. People die, people move away, people leave."

My heart breaks at the sadness in her words, reminding me that I have one. It's black and dark and seemingly in a perpetual state of purgatory, but it still beats. And it beats for her, only for her.

When the hell did that happen? When did she become more than a job, more important than purging the most evil sinners in the world?

Second by second, minute by minute, hour by hour, day by day… Cece burrowed into my soul and set up camp. I'm certain that wasn't her intention, but I have no desire to evict her. Not now, and probably not ever.

I run my thumb over her bottom lip. "I'm not going anywhere."

She tries to avert her eyes, but I hold her face in my hands, forcing her to remain with me, present in the moment. She stares at me, her baby blues bouncing back and forth as if she can't focus, and finally, *finally*, she huffs out a breath.

"I'm still mad," she pouts.

"I know."

"I appreciate that you were trying to help, but my store, my decisions."

"Okay."

"Promise me, Soul. Promise you won't do anything like that again."

For a split second, I wonder if she heard a word I said. She's asking me to do the impossible.

"I can't, babe." I shrug. "I can't promise that I'll never cross a line again, that I'll never step in when I think you're drowning." She opens her mouth, and I silence her with my thumb. "But I can promise that I'll talk to you about it first. I promise that I won't go behind your back."

Cece rolls her eyes. "That's the best I'm gonna get, isn't it?"

"Yep."

"Fine." She pulls her arms between us to cross them over her chest. "Your ten minutes are past up."

I ease her arms down to her sides and pin her to the counter with my body pressed against hers. Her nostrils flare, and her pupils dilate. I lean close to her ear and whisper, "Do you still want me to leave?"

Cece's breath hitches, and I'm ninety-nine percent sure her hips bucked of their own volition.

"I'll go if that's what you want," I tell her just before dragging my tongue down her neck.

I pull the shoulder of her sweater aside, ripping the fabric, and nibble at her collarbone.

"I…" She nods, and I stiffen, bracing myself for her to tell me to disappear. "Don't go."

Don't go.

Don't go.

Don't go.

Those two words play on a loop, over and over as if I need to hear them again and again for it to sink in that Cece's not kicking me out.

Don't go.

Don't go.

Don—

"Soul."

"Hmm?" I pull away and look her in the eyes.

"Why'd you stop?"

That's a damn good fucking question.

I lift Cece like I did the night I came back to the clubhouse to find her drunk. Only this time, she laughs rather than yells at me.

"Bedroom?" I growl as I carry her toward the hallway I saw when we came inside.

"Last door on the right."

I run the short length of the hallway to barrel through the doorway. After setting Cece on her feet, I remove my cut and hang it over a chair in the corner. I start to take off my shirt, and notice her standing exactly where I deposited her, not moving a muscle.

"Babe, you've got about ten seconds to get naked."

She arches a brow. "And if I don't?"

I yank my tee over my head and toss it on the floor. Her eyes settle on my abs. I stalk toward her and tilt her head up.

"Naked or I put my shirt back on."

I've never seen a woman strip so fast in my entire life. And I've been to strip clubs. This is nothing like that, but in the best possible way.

When she's bare before me, she lifts her arms to cover her tits, but I grab her wrists.

"Don't ever hide yourself from me," I order.

With her wrists still in my hands, I take a step back and leisurely explore her body. Her skin pinkens under my scrutiny, but I don't let that deter me.

"You are the sexist creature I've ever laid eyes on." I walk around and stare at her ass. "And that peach." I groan as I use my free hand to squeeze one rounded globe. "Fucking hell, babe. I could come just looking at you."

I flatten my front to her back, grinding my denim-covered cock against her ass cheeks. She mewls as she shoves back into me.

"I wanna feel you," she says, her tone desperate, pleading.

Without letting her go, I make quick work of the button and zipper before pushing my jeans over my hips and down to my ankles. I toe off my boots before I kick my feet free of the denim and thank all that's unholy that I'm free-balling it.

I reach around her and cup a tit, massaging the mound while I let my thick cock slap against her ass. Using my body to move her forward, I pinch her nipple and then move to the other one and do the same.

Cece's head falls back against my chest when I pin her to the wall. She tries to reach back and touch me, but I grasp her hands with one of mine and hold them above her head.

"No touching," I growl against her ear.

I spread her legs apart with my foot, making room to do what I want to her. I use my free hand and release her hair from the confines of the ponytail holder, loving the way it cascades in a curly mass down her back. I ease it over her shoulder and trail my tongue toward her spine.

"I'm gonna let go of your hands," I say. "But you better not lower them, or I'll stop."

Cece frantically nods, and I grin. Fuck, I need her. Her taste, her smell, her body and soul… all of her.

I lick a zig-zagging path down her spine as I run my fingertips over her flesh, savoring the way she shivers beneath my touch. When I reach the top of her ass, I slide a finger between her cheeks to tease her puckered hole. I don't try to penetrate or do anything beyond a feather-light ghosting of my skin against hers.

As I reach my knees, I spin around and slide between her legs to rest my back against the wall. My head isn't quite at pussy level, but that's about to change.

I run my finger through her slit and find her wet.

Using her own arousal, I tease her clit with fast little circles. I don't let up until her legs start to quiver, and then I pull my hand away.

Cece groans, causing me to chuckle.

"You're not getting off that easy, babe." I guide her legs over my shoulders, one at a time. "Keep your arms up and brace yourself against the wall," I command and she slaps the wall. "Good girl. Now sit."

"What?"

"Sit on my face," I growl. I pull her down until her pussy is lined up with my mouth. I hum against her core as I hold her weight with my hands on her ass. "So fucking sweet."

Licking her slit, I tease her opening. She tries to stand, but I keep her in place. I kneed her ass cheeks, slipping a digit between them every few seconds. As I worship her pussy, eat it like a starving man, my cock throbs.

Cece rides my face, grinds her hips to demand more from my mouth. And I give her what she wants. I lap at her clit, flicking it over the sensitive ball of nerves until she's a quaking mass of need. I want to taste her release, inhale it until it's a part of me, but I want to feel it surrounding me more.

Ignoring her whimper of displeasure, I pull my face away and lower her right onto my dick. I lift my hips up, thrusting into her cunt until I'm balls deep. Her walls clamp down, but she rocks her hips. The drag of her pussy, back and forth, back and forth, brings me so close to losing it, I have to take back control and slow things down.

Cece wraps her arms around my neck and manages to wedge her feet between me and the wall to circle my waist with her legs. I slide out of her so I can stand and carry her to the bed. She remains attached to me like a spider monkey as I crawl onto the mattress.

As soon as she's on her back, I thrust into her. I fuse my mouth to hers, kissing her savagely. Her tongue shoves its way inside to twirl with mine. And the entire time we're kissing, my hips are flying.

I fuck her. It's raw, rough, and she matches my energy. We're two primal beings chasing a release that's hovering just out of reach. My spine is tingling, but my brain won't let me fly over the edge without her.

Reaching between us, I press my thumb to her clit and rub slow circles. "Come for me," I demand just before biting down on her collarbone.

The combination of pleasure and pain has her back arching off the mattress. Cece bucks her hips, and my balls draw tight. When her pussy spasms, clamps down and refuses to let my dick go, I soothe the spot I bit with my tongue.

Cece digs her nails into my thighs and screams her release. Her orgasm seems to go on forever, and just as her body begins to relax, I stiffen. My cock pulses inside of her, and I throw my head back on a roar. She traces her fingertips over my flesh as I come, the light sensation intensifying my pleasure.

When I'm spent, my arms begin to shake, and I collapse on top of her. She grunts under my weight, so I roll over, dragging her with me. Cece curls into my side and slips a leg over mine.

Running my fingers through her sweat-dampened hair, I lay there, silent and… happy. So goddamn happy it should be illegal.

"Really?"

I tuck my chin to my chest so I can look at her. "Really what?" I ask.

"You're so happy it should be illegal?"

"Shit. I've turned into you." I chuckle. "I didn't realize I said that out loud."

She laughs softly and runs her hand over my chest. "Me too."

I open my mouth to say something, but close it just as fast. There's nothing to say. The moment is good, *we're* good, and the last thing I want to do is ruin it. So I hold her. And only when her breathing evens out do I allow myself to fully relax and seek out sleep.

The next thing I know, Cece is detangling herself from me and scrambling off the bed. She grabs my t-shirt off the floor and pulls it on as she races out of the room. Sunlight streams through the windows, and I stretch before getting up and tugging on my jeans.

I stroll out into the living room, but freeze when I see her with her cell phone to her ear and a bitter look on her face.

"Who is it?" I ask, stepping up to her from behind and wrapping my arms around her waist.

She puts the call on speaker.

"... greatly appreciate the opportunity to meet with you."

My blood boils at the voice on the other end of the line. Cece turns in my arms and flattens a hand on my chest.

"I'm not sure what there is to talk about," she says.

"There's a lot to talk about, Miss Parker. I understand you didn't receive the best care at our emergency department, and I can't sit back and ignore that."

"Mr…" She shakes her head as if trying to recall something. "What did you say your name was again?"

"I'm the Hospital Director."

"His name is Dr. Richard Franklin Sr.," I say.

Cece's eyes widen. "Senior?"

He sighs. "Yes, ma'am. I'm Dr. Franklin Sr. The ER doc that treated you is my son."

Cece laughs bitterly. "How convenient."

"I understand how this looks, Miss Parker," he says. "But I'm simply trying to resolve your dissatisfaction with our facility."

"My dissatisfaction?!" she cries. "I almost died! Scratch that… I *did* die because of your son's incompetence!"

"Yes, I understand that. And I would like the opportunity to discuss your care face to face."

My heart is in my throat as I wait for Cece to respond. I can't stop her from agreeing to meet with him, but I also can't let her go into a room with that man before she knows the truth about what happened to her mother.

"I don't know what good it'll do," she finally says. "Goodbye."

She disconnects the call and tosses her phone onto the counter. When she looks at me, there are tears in her eyes.

"Can you believe that man?" she snaps and

presses her fingers to her temples. "Shit. I just wanna forget about that damn place."

Fuck. Fuck. Fuck. I have to tell her.

I grab her hand and tug her toward me. When she rests her forehead against my pecs, I take a deep breath.

"Do you remember me saying that I came to talk to you about something yesterday?"

"Yeah," she mumbles.

I blow out a breath. "Actually, Jez and I came initially. We needed to tell you something about Dr. Fucktard."

She stiffens. "What about him?"

"There's no easy way to say this, but… He treated your mom."

Cece shoves away from me, her eyes wide. "What do you mean he treated my mom?"

Ten minutes later and all the details of her mother's care at Boulder City Memorial are out in the open. Well, almost all of them. There's only one thing left that Cece doesn't know, but the moment I said her mother didn't have to die, the air in the room crackled.

I wait for her to move, to react in any way so I can tell her the final piece of information, but she stands there, staring at me but not really seeing me. It's as if her feet have been superglued to the floor and a giant weight dropped on her. Zero expression, zero movement.

Absolutely nothing.

The wheels are turning, the smoke is billowing, but there's no life there.

It's terrifying to witness.

I take a step toward her and, when she doesn't retreat, I take another and another until I'm inches from the ghost she's instantly become.

"Cece, babe, say something."

CHAPTER TWENTY-TWO

CECE

"AAAAAAAHHHHHHHH!"

What the hell is that noise? Who the hell is screaming? Is that Me?

There's an agony in the scream that I understand. It matches the pain deep in my soul, the pain that is all-consuming. My knees buckle, and when they hit the floor, realization dawns.

The scream is mine.

The last thread holding my life together snaps like a twig being stepped on. My heart shatters like a mirror splintering into a million pieces. My spirit and mind are broken. I have nothing left.

"No, no, no," I chant, shaking my head. "You're wrong. Why? Why are you doing this to me?"

Peeking up at Soul, I see nothing but sympathy. He reaches for me, but I snap, "Don't... don't touch me."

I curl in on myself with my knees pulled tight to

my chest and rock back and forth. Sobs wrack my body, and tears pour down my cheeks to soak my shirt.

"Fuck Cece, you're killing me." Soul crouches down and brushes my hair out of my face. "Let me hold you."

I shake my head and scoot further away from him. My efforts are feeble because Soul's arms slide under my body, and he lifts me off the floor. I pummel his chest in a weak attempt to get away from him, but it's no use. He only squeezes me tighter. I sag in defeat as he carries me to the couch and sits while keeping me in his lap.

"It's not true. Tell me it's not true," I plead.

Soul rubs my back in a soothing motion. There's a small part of me that wants to accept the comfort he's offering, that wants to give in to it. But I can't. Because giving in to it means letting myself feel the anguish. And I don't want to feel it. I want to remain numb.

I scramble off his lap to put some distance between us. He doesn't try to stop me but his gaze never leaves my face. His brows are drawn in creating lines between them, and his mouth is turned down in a grimace.

If I don't do something, I'm going to go insane. I stand and pace back and forth in front of the couch.

They're wrong. Jez got the information wrong. No, no, no.

"Cece." Soul's hushed tone knocks me out of my trance. "There's no mistake. Jez confirmed the records with Abyss."

"No!" Abyss is wrong then." I stop and glare at him. "Why do you want to destroy me? I can't think. You need to leave, now!"

"Fuck this." Soul stands and grabs my arm to crush me to his chest. "If I could've kept this from you, I would've. I *never* want to see you in pain, and I sure as shit don't want to be the cause of it. But we both know if I'd have kept this from you and you found out, it would've destroyed you. Destroyed *us*."

My mind wants to deny what he's saying, but he's absolutely right. If I found out another way and knew he withheld this from me, it would've destroyed any future we might have. That doesn't mean I'm any more willing to accept what he told me.

"It doesn't make any sense. They told me she died from a brain aneurysm."

"I know," he spits out, as if he's as angered by the lies as I am. "According to Abyss, a brain tumor can present the same symptoms as a brain aneurysm." Soul takes a deep breath before continuing. "The problem is, your mom saw Dr. Franklin, and he di—"

My head snaps up, almost clipping Soul in the chin. I back up and look into his eyes. "What the fuck are you talking about? My mom never saw Dr. Franklin."

"Let's sit down, and I'll tell you everything I know, or what we could piece together anyway."

"I don't want to sit down. You can sit down."

As if sensing I'm about to explode, he sits back down on the couch and watches me like a spectator at the zoo watches the caged animals. I clench my fists at my side and nod for him to continue.

"Did you know your mom had been experiencing severe headaches?"

"Yeah, she told me she had an appointment with her doctor scheduled."

"Apparently she went to the ER one night when one of the headaches got too bad for her to deal with."

"No, she didn't." I search my memory. "She'd have told me."

"Babe, she went. The dates on the records coincide with the dates you and Carmella went camping."

My body seizes, and with lightning-quick reflexes, Soul scoops me up before I collapse again. For the first time since he told me my mother should still be alive, my eyes are dry. I don't want to hear anymore, but I have to know what happened.

"Tell me the rest."

"Ce, I think we should stop for a while and give you time to process what I've already told you," he says gently.

"If you stop, my soul will be shredded all over again when you finish telling me. Please… please don't do that to me," I beg.

Sighing, he begins. "Your mom went to the ER one night when Dr. Franklin Jr. was working and, according to the records, she'd had a persistent headache for a couple days. Over-the-counter pain reliever wasn't helping. Dr. Franklin prescribed a strong dose of ibuprofen and told her to follow up with her primary doctor. It was documented by the nurse that she'd been suffering from these headaches for over a month, but Dr. Franklin didn't run any tests to see what could be causing them."

"Just like me," I whisper.

"Yeah, babe. Just like you." He smiles, but there's nothing good in his smile, nothing happy. "Want me to keep going?

Want? No. Need? Unfortunately.

"I need to hear it all."

"Okay," he says. "So, like I said, Dr. Franklin gave her a stronger medication, but Abyss thinks the tumor must have grown because the headaches she described were becoming more frequent and more severe. Abyss spoke with a neurologist he knows, and *he* said the tumor was operable. There's no way of knowing whether or not she would've survived the surgery, but the prognosis was good that she'd still be alive," Soul says, delivering the final blow.

I know he said earlier that she didn't have to die… That's what sent me into a tailspin in the first place. But hearing it all together, hearing it *again…*

My mom could still be alive. He killed her. Dr. Fucktard killed her.

And just like that, my world goes dark.

"CECE, WAKE UP!"

I swat at the hand tapping my face. Groaning, I try to open my eyes, but my lids are heavy. When I finally manage to get them open, Soul's face hovers above me.

"What happened?"

"You scared the shit out of me," he snaps, but his tone conveys worry, not anger. "You fainted."

"Did you smack me?"

"Not hard. I was trying to wake your ass up."

I push to sit up, but Soul holds me down by my shoulders. "Wait a minute. You've had a big shock, and Abyss said you need to take it easy."

I scan the room, but we're the only two here. "Abyss?"

"I called him when you fainted," he says sheepishly. "He said your mind shut down because it was overwhelmed."

"Oh." I roll my eyes. "I'm getting really tired of fainting."

There's nothing else to say because he's right. This is all… too much. My muscles are stiff, and I ache like I have the flu. Chattering teeth is the only warning I get before my body convulses with chills. Soul grabs the blanket from the back of the couch and drapes it across my body, but I can't quit shaking.

When nothing he tries warms me, he carries me into the bathroom and sets me on the toilet seat.

"You're going into shock," he explains as he nods at the tub. "We'll both fit."

The jacuzzi tub is big enough for two people, but all I can think about when I look at it is that Mom loved soaking amid the jets. Tears fall from my eyes, and Soul wipes them away with his thumb.

"I got you," he says.

Soul turns on the faucet so the tub begins to fill with hot water. I stand, and the blanket falls away from my shoulders. My movements are robotic as I start to take the t-shirt of his off, but he brushes my hands to the side.

"No, let me."

Soul keeps his gaze locked with mine as he slowly raises the shirt over my head and drops it on the floor. Next, he takes his jeans off and tosses them with the shirt.

Soul lifts me up and over the edge of the tub to immerse me in the warm water. I moan as the heat engulfs my body. Soul sinks behind me, and after he turns on the jets, he begins to massage the tight muscles in my shoulders. There's nothing sexual about any of it. He's simply taking care of me, treating me like fine china.

"Tell me about your mom," he says after a few minutes.

"She was the best." I lean against his chest, and he wraps his arms around my waist. "Mom always made me feel like I was the center of her universe. She came to every school activity, cooked dinner most nights, except for those rare occasions we ate out. Besides Carmella, she was my best friend."

A tear slips down my cheek, and I don't even bother swiping it away. I haven't talked about my mom since the funeral, and even though it's hard, it's cathartic.

I have no idea how long we remain in the tub, but when the water cools off, Soul gets out. After drying himself off, he helps me up and tucks a towel around my body.

He's taking care of me exactly like he said he would.

Soul dresses us both, and feeling more human, I walk out of mom's bathroom and don't allow myself to look around her bedroom as I rush to the hallway.

"Why don't you lay down for a bit?" Soul suggests once we're in the living room. "I can fix us something to eat while you rest."

"You don't have to cook anything."

"Babe, you need to eat."

"Fine." I wave my hand dismissively. "But I probably won't be able to rest."

"It doesn't hurt to try," he says. "Would you rather lay out here or in your bed?"

"I'll just stay out here."

Soul disappears down the hallway and comes back carrying a pillow and blanket from my bed. He tosses the pillow onto the end of the couch, then waits for me to lie down before covering me and tucking me in like a parent would a child. My heart swells with an emotion I'm not quite ready to identify, and butterflies flutter around in my stomach.

"Try to rest." He leans over and kisses my forehead. "I'll go see what I can make us to eat."

I'm more exhausted than I thought, because the next thing I know, Soul is shaking me awake.

"Food's ready, babe."

My mouth waters at the aroma coming from the kitchen. I rub the sleep from my eyes and stand to follow him to the table. A chicken casserole and salad await us, and we waste no time digging in. I guess I'm able to eat after all.

"I've got this," he says when I stand to carry my empty plate to the sink. "Go sit, and I'll be right there."

After turning on the TV, I flip through the channels until I find something that doesn't require too much brain power. But rather than watch the program, I let the events of the day rush forward.

Mom didn't have to die. Jez and Soul gave me the information as soon as they found out, and Soul is taking care of me.

Despite his efforts, I'm still overwhelmed by it all, and emotions continue to threaten to break free. Anger, hurt, sadness, gratitude, and so much more. My stomach swirls with trepidation.

Soul eventually sits next to me and pulls me onto his lap. He caresses the back of my neck with his fingers, and I lean into him, soaking up the strength and heat radiating from his body.

"Tell me a happy memory about your mom," he urges.

"Ok." I tap a finger on my chin, trying to think of just one. There are so many. I snap my fingers when one hits and chuckle. "I used to hate cleaning, and Mom always had her hands full trying to get me to help. I'd pout or come up with an excuse to get out of whatever chore she wanted me to do. She never yelled, but she would give me that signature 'mom look', and I knew my ass better get going." I smile as an image of that look fills my mind. "When I was fifteen, I was extremely difficult. The look wasn't as effective. So Mom would turn on the stereo and blast *Ice Ice Baby.* Then she'd proceed to walk around the house dusting and shaking her ass. Suffice it to say, I was shocked. I mean, she was my *mom.* Anyway, it worked. From that point forward, I'd help clean or do my assigned chores while we both shook our asses and sang horribly with Vanilla Ice. It became our weekly ritual. We both took turns selecting the playlist and would clean the house."

"Sounds like fun."

"I was a brat."

"Babe, every teenager is a brat. I'm pretty sure there's a picture of fucking teenagers next to the word brat in the dictionary."

"What about you?"

"What about me?"

"What was your family like?"

Soul stiffens, making me think I'm not going to get a reply. So when he speaks, I'm a little shocked.

"I had a typical childhood. It was me, Mom, Dad, and Jez. But sometimes, I would fantasize about making myself an only child. Jez was a fucking brat," he says with fondness. "Honestly, though, Jez and I have always been two peas in a pod. She's the other half of me. Followed me and my friends around, but I never had the urge to tell her to get lost."

"That's nice you had that growing up."

"I used to threaten the other boys at school away from her. One day, she came home from school, and she was skipping and humming. But she wouldn't tell me why. Come to find out, a boy at school kissed her."

"And I bet you just loved knowing that."

"I tried to get her to tell me who so I could beat the shit out of him, but she wouldn't tell me. To this day, the little shit won't say who it was."

"Alpha to the core, even when you were a kid," I tease.

"Guess so." He shrugs. "Tell me about your dad. You never mention him."

A memory of officers knocking on our door one stormy night surfaces. I shiver, but refuse to let myself be swept into the past, much preferring the present.

"Dad was killed in a car accident on his way home from work. It was storming really bad that night, and we were worried because we hadn't heard from him." I fidget with my hands. "Eventually, there was a knock on the door, and when Mom answered it, our lives drastically changed." I take a deep breath. "Dad was awesome. I was his little princess, and he spoiled me rotten. He always told me I could be anything, do anything, to never let anyone hold me back."

I don't even realize I'm crying until Soul swipes the tears from my cheeks.

"We don't have to talk about it."

"It's okay," I assure him. "I want to." I close my eyes, and the memory assaults me. Soul's grip on my body is the only thing keeping me tethered to the here and now. "Mom and I were both devastated. Mom lost her childhood sweetheart, and I lost my father during those difficult teenage years. I'd like to say I was the golden child and was there for my mom but unfortunately, I turned into the spawn of Satan. I lashed out at her, even though none of it was her fault. She was grieving, I was grieving, but the one thing she never did was push me away. If anything, she tried to get me to talk about my feelings. I was so torn up. I didn't want to face the pain, so I didn't. Instead, I turned into a bitch, pushing her and everyone else away. Fortunately for me and Mom, Carmella got sick of my behavior and called me out. Mom always treated Carmella like a daughter, and Carmella was *not* fond of my new personality and basically threatened to kick my ass if I didn't *knock my shit off*."

"I can't wait to meet her. She sounds like she's a handful." Soul chuckles.

"You have no idea." I smile fondly, remembering all of our youthful shenanigans. "Even though my parents are gone, I still have them with me in a way. Dad left me his '87 IROC Z28 Camaro, so I'll always have a piece of him, and I have Naughty/Nice, which is a part of my mom."

"An '87 IROC Z28? So that's the car I saw you in last night." Soul whistles. "Fuck, I'm definitely taking that for a spin."

"The hell you will, that's my baby!" I smack his chest. "Never get between a woman and her baby."

Soul tickles my side. "I'd never dream of it, babe."

We spend the rest of the day wrapped in each other's arms, sharing happy stories of our childhood. It doesn't escape my notice that I do most of the talking, but being in Soul's embrace gives me back the strength I thought I lost.

"Let's go to bed, babe," he says hours later, when the sun is no longer high in the sky, and the darkness of night has settled over the world like a weighted blanket.

I lead Soul to my room, and pull him under the covers with me. He settles close, almost as if he can't bear to be anywhere but fused together. Neither of us speaks, but it isn't long before sleep drags us under, relieving us of the emotionally charged day.

CHAPTER TWENTY-THREE

SOUL

SAND KICKS UP AROUND ME AS I FLY ACROSS THE DESERT. I spent the night at Cece's, as I have every night since I shattered the world as she knew it, and even though I should've been at Sinful Wheels two hours ago, I decided to run to the clubhouse to check on everything there.

Today is the day I do my monthly rounds on all the club businesses to make sure things are running smoothly. I know I'm given weekly updates in church, but it isn't quite the same as seeing for myself. Besides, when the cat's away, the mice will play. I've gotta make sure the mice aren't fucking playing.

An hour later I'm parking in the back lot at Sinful Wheels. The employee entrance door flies open, and Spike strolls out.

"Long time, no see, Prez."

"Don't start," I snap as I push past him.

We both go inside, and I see Abyss and Frenzy hard at work on a custom job they were hired to do. Asher's voice carries through from the front, so I assume he's dealing with a customer. Even here, prospects get the shit work.

"He lives," Frenzy teases.

I smack him upside the head as I look over his shoulder at the Harley they're restoring. "Shut the fuck up."

"Whaddya think, Prez?" Abyss asks as he stretches his arms over his head. "She's looking good, huh?"

"She better be, considering who it's for."

The custom job is for the mayor, who likes to let loose on the weekends... His words, not mine. The guy's a poser, but I'd never tell him that to his face. I haven't always been the most agreeable man, but I know when to pull my punches. And I absolutely pull my punches with the shitstain who can bring the club down with one phone call.

Unless he crosses the line into purge territory.

"You know I don't work that way," Abyss counters. "It's my reputation on the line if I let junk roll outta Sinful. I put a hundred percent into all my work, mayor or not."

I sigh. "Yeah, I know. Wasn't implying otherwise." I walk to the swinging door separating the workspace from the front lobby and peek out at Asher. "How's he doing?"

"Prospect knows his shit," Spike replies as he gets to work on a standard tune-up. "And he's great with the public."

I observe for another minute or two before turning back to my brothers. "He's been prospecting for a while now. Are we getting close to voting on a patch, or does he need more time?"

Spike shrugs. "Malice and I have been keeping an eye on him. Maybe a few months and a few more runs under his belt before we decide."

"Got it." I scan the shop one last time. "Well, all seems good here. Need anything from me before I move on to Purgatory?"

"Nah," Spike says. "I've got things under control."

"Ya always do, brother."

I take my time riding to the bar. It's almost noon, so I know Rogue is already there working on the books, but I decide to take a small detour.

As I near Naughty/Nice, I slow down so I can pull next to the curb. I immediately spot Cece through the front window, and my lips lift into a grin. She's talking to Trista, the manager Jez and I hired, and they're both laughing. It eases the concern that's weighed heavily on me since Cece found out about the new staff.

Before she catches me staring like a creeper, I pull back onto the road and head to Purgatory. It doesn't take me more than ten minutes to get there, and when I enter the building, I'm surprised to see Waylon, the new manager, standing behind the bar.

He narrows his gaze on me as he tracks my movements. "We're closed," he snaps.

Seriously?

"Considering I fucking own the place, I'm aware," I snap.

The man's eyes widen. "Shit. Sorry man."

"Might wanna pay a bit more attention," I say as I point to the 'President' patch on my cut. Before I continue, I lean across the bar with a hardened expression. "Talk to me like that again, and you'll not only be out of a job, but you'll also be wishing for death."

Waylon's throat bobs when he swallows. "Got it."

I straighten and rock back on my heels. "Rogue in the office?"

He darts his eyes to the hallway and then back to me. "Uh, yeah."

"Word of advice, Waylon," I say with a smirk. "If you're gonna survive at Purgatory, ya might wanna trade in your balls for a bigger set."

With that, I make my way to the office. Rogue glances up from the computer when I enter, but quickly returns to the bar's finances.

"You look like you could use a drink," I comment as I sit in the chair across from him. "Things can't be that bad."

Rogue sighs and leans back in his chair. "Financially, things are fucking fantastic. As for hippie dippy Waylon out there... I'm not sure."

My gut twists, and I sit a little straighter. "What's got you questioning him?"

"It's nothing specific," Rogue admits. "He's great with the patrons, he's always on time for his shifts, he treats the staff with respect."

I snort at that. "I think he needs to be more concerned about treating the owners with respect. Fucker wasn't too friendly when I first walked in."

"And there's the problem." Rogue straightens and leans his elbows on the desk. "He bucks authority."

"How so?"

"Well, take this morning for example. I told him not to come in early, yet when I show up, he's already here."

I arch a brow. "So your problem is he's here too much? I'm not clear on how that's bucking authority or, hell, even a bad thing. You did say you wanted to hire more staff and a manager so you could spend less time here."

Rogue waves a hand dismissively. "Yeah, I know. It's just…" He heaves a sigh. "Fuck, I don't know. It's just a feeling."

And there isn't a Saints Purgatory brother who would be worth his salt if he ignored those *feelings*.

"You can always fire him," I suggest.

He shakes his head. "Nah. It's only been a few weeks." Rogue pushes his glasses up his nose. "I'll keep an eye on him, give it a bit more time."

"Do whatcha gotta do, brother," I tell him. "But don't ignore your gut too long."

"I won't."

"How's the new bartender working out?"

"Great. Skye's a natural bartender, and the customers love her," he says with a grin. "And she's fucking easy to watch work."

I groan. "Dude, do *not* even think about it. She's an employee, not a fuck toy."

"I'm not an idiot, Prez. I won't fuck her, but there's no way in hell I can stop the fantasies that crowd my mind when she's around."

"Just keep it in your pants, Romeo," I order.

"Have you kept it in your pants with Cece?" he counters. "Cause sh—"

"Seems like you've got things handled here," I say as I stand. "I'm out."

His laughter follows me all the way back to the main bar room. I glance at Waylon, who doesn't even seem to notice me as he stocks the shelves of liquor behind the bar. I think about Rogue's *feeling*, but shove it aside as soon as I step outside. I trust Rogue, and if he says it's not time to fire the man, it's not time.

Persuasion Ink is only a block and a half away, so I decide to walk. The sun is shining, and the downtown streets are packed with people going about their normal everyday lives. It's a far cry from the underground world I live in at the clubhouse. And yet, I'd take the clubhouse and my brothers over the sinners in this city any day.

Not over Cece though.

That thought stops me in my tracks. Is it true? Would I really choose her over them? Hopefully, I never have to find out what I'd do because a life without her or them would be equally bleak for very different reasons.

Forcing my feet to move again, I continue down the sidewalk toward the tattoo shop. When I enter, Possum is busy inking a client, as is Animal, and

Justin is sitting at the counter flipping his fucking Zippo open and closed.

Malice put him through his paces in an effort to make sure he could focus enough to handle business, and he proved he can. As long as he doesn't give an indication that he can't, I don't give a damn what he does with the thing. He could light his ass on fire with it, and it's no skin off my back.

"Hey, Prez." Justin greets me as he hops off the stool behind the reception area.

I shake my head at him. "You and that damn lighter."

Justin looks at it and then shoves it in his pocket. "Sorry," he says with a sheepish look.

"It's fine," I tell him. "Just don't let me catch you with it on a run."

"Understood."

I nod. "Got any appointments today, prospect, or are you just observing?"

Justin is artistically talented, but he's not quite ready to take on a full customer load yet.

"I've got one in an hour." He shrugs. "Other than that, observing."

"Kinda hard to observe when you can't see what they're doing," I comment with a tilt of my head toward Animal and Possum.

"Give the kid a break, Prez," Possum calls out. "My girl here didn't want him watching."

"He can watch Animal," I say.

"Nope," Animal says, popping the P. "I hate having him hover. It's annoying."

"I don't know why I bother with this place. Neither of you listens to a damn word I say."

Possum lifts his tattoo gun from the client's skin and turns to look at me. "You making money off the shop, Prez?"

Here we go.

"You know I do."

"Then quit your bitchin'."

Shaking my head, I turn back toward the door. "Don't let these fucks run this place into the ground, Prospect. They do, and it's your head on the chopping block."

Justin's protests are cut off when the door shuts behind me, and I grin. It's fucking fun to mess with the grunts. One of life's simple pleasures.

As I head back to my Harley, I call Cece.

"Hey you," she answers on the fourth ring.

"Still busy as hell?" I ask.

"How'd you know?" I open my mouth to respond, but she groans before I can. "You didn't park out front like a weirdo again did you? You did, didn't you?"

I chuckle. "Guilty."

"You've gotta stop doing that," she huffs out.

"I've only done it once before," I argue.

"And now you've done it two times too many."

"You act like me wanting to see you is a bad thing," I tease.

Cece sighs, and it sounds as if she's trying to reach deep for patience. "Did you need something?"

"Besides just wanting to hear your voice? Yeah. Why don't you come out to the clubhouse tonight after work?"

"You're not coming to my place?"

"Babe, I've been there all week," I remind her. "And I don't mind being there, but the brothers are starting to wonder if I'm ever coming back. I'm worried they're gonna fucking stage a coup soon."

"Omigod," she groans with a laugh. "You are so dramatic."

"Is that a yes?"

Cece blows out a breath. "Yeah, I'll stay there tonight. I don't have to work tomorrow, so we can sleep in or… whatever."

"There will be very little sleeping, trust me on that."

"Promise?"

"Fuck yeah."

"We close at eight. I'll grab a bag and be on my way by eight-thirty."

I disconnect the call and check the time before shoving my cell in my cut.

Just over seven hours, and I'll be dragging Cece off to my room like the caveman she accuses me of being.

CHAPTER TWENTY-FOUR

CECE

"I can't believe I thought I'd remember where the damn clubhouse is."

Talking to myself seems to be my new normal.

What is normal, exactly? Shaking my head, I force my thoughts away from philosophical topics. Normal is whatever the hell I want it to be.

I've been driving on this godforsaken road for what feels like hours. It's the only paved road out of town that goes in the right direction, and I hope it leads to Saints Purgatory. The first time I came out, I was talking to Abyss and Jez and not really watching where we were going. And when I left, I was on the back of Soul's Harley, enjoying the feeling of flying. It doesn't help that the sun set about twenty minutes ago, and it's pitch black out.

Giving up, I pull out my cell and call Soul.

"Babe, where are you?" His deep voice has my girlie parts paying attention.

"Well… that's a good question. I think I'm on the right road. There's only one right?"

"Until you need to turn and head toward the mountain."

"Why couldn't you guys use glow in the dark paint or something to light my way?" Frustration bleeds into my tone.

He laughs. "Because that would fucking defeat the purpose of us not wanting to be found."

"Fine, but I might not make it in time for the party… or *ever*," I say sarcastically.

"Hold on, I'm gonna find Fort." The brothers are in the background, yelling at Soul, but he ignores them. "Yo, Fort. Need ya, brother."

"What's up, Prez?"

Fort's voice isn't as clear as Soul's, but it's loud, so I know he's close.

"Cece's lost. Can you tap into her GPS and see where she is?" Soul asks.

"Sure thing. Let's go to my cave, and I can tap into her."

The distinct sound of a slap fills the car and I chuckle when I hear Fort say 'ow'.

"What's so funny, Ce?" Fort asks.

Fucker put me on speakerphone.

More laughter fills my car.

"Fucker? Really? I remember a certain redhead screa—"

"Do *not* finish that sentence, Soul," I snap.

"Alright children," Fort says with mock authority. "Cece, you're about thirty minutes out. I've got your location locked. I can guide you in, or we ca—"

"Justin just walked in, so I'm sending him back out to you," Soul snaps.

"Before I was *rudely* interrupted," Fort begins. "I was *going* to say, I can send a prospect to meet you." Another thump resonates through the speaker. "Dammit Prez, quit hitting me. You need my brain, remember?"

"I don't need your mouth."

"Boys, boys," I say with what can only be described as a mom voice. "That's enough. Back to your corners." I take a deep breath. "I appreciate the assist. And sending Justin is probably a good idea because it's darker than the inside of an asshole out here."

Laughter echoes through the speakers before Fort speaks again.

"Men, darlin'. We are men, first and foremost. Second, do you spend a lot of time up assholes, and does Soul know about this?"

Another whack.

"Fucking knock it off, Prez," Fort complains.

"Don't ask my woman about being up assholes," Soul growls. "Babe, quit talking about assholes, or when you get here, I'll spank your ass red to match your hair."

I squirm at the thought.

"So, you're, uh, sending Justin then?" I ask, my words and brain scrambled.

"Yep, he's hopping on his bike now," Fort replies.

"I'm gonna keep you on the phone until he gets there," Soul informs me. "And I know exactly what's going on in that dirty little head of yours right now. Don't worry babe, I'll follow through."

Luckily for me, and probably the back of his head, Fort keeps his comments to himself. But I *do* hear him snicker.

"Who all is gonna be there tonight?"

"Everyone," Soul says.

"Even Jez?"

"Yep. She'll be on her way later. She said she had some things to handle first."

"Great! I feel like I haven't seen her in forever."

In reality, it's only been a few days, but when you see a person daily for weeks and then nothing, it's like a piece of you is missing. Jezebel has become like a sister to me, and not seeing her every day sucks.

"Babe, what did yo… say… cutting…"

Soul's words are disjointed as cell reception toggles between perfect and non-existent.

"Fucking cellphones," I mutter.

When I call out to Soul, I don't get a response, but I can hear him and Fort arguing. Sure, it's only bits and pieces, but that's better than dead silence. I keep trying to get their attention, failing miserably.

Light blinds me as it bounces off the rearview mirror, and I squint in an effort to make out what it's coming from.

"Turn off your brights, asshole," I mumble. "Where the hell'd you come from anyway?"

"Babe, what did you say?" Soul's voice is clearer.

"Some asshole just came up behind me with his brights on," I practically shout.

"What? Ce, we can barely hear you. You're still cutting out."

"What are you talking about?"

Soul and Fort speak at the same time, making it almost impossible to make out who is saying what with the shitty reception.

That's it, I'm getting a new plan that covers the middle of fucking nowhere tomorrow or I'll see if Fort has a magical device he can use to amp up my phone's signal. That man is a genius when it comes to technology.

"There's someone beh—"

The car lurches forward when I'm hit from behind. The force of the collision is so strong, my cell phone flies to the floor. I stretch my arm to try and reach the device, but the car lurches again. Even with my seatbelt on, my chest violently hits the steering wheel, and I grunt at the impact.

What the fuck is happening? And where the hell is Justin?

I stomp on the gas in an effort to put distance between us, but the asshole behind me isn't letting up. The vehicle remains within inches of my rear bumper. Fear settles in my gut like a lead balloon, and it's all I can do not to throw up.

I don't want to die. I'm not ready. Please, God, don't let me die.

I continue to search frantically for my phone, and my fingertips graze it just as I'm hit again. Only this time, the car doesn't lurch forward. Instead, I lose control as the car swerves and rolls onto its side. And then I'm hit again, which sends the vehicle careening off the road into the desert sand, where it flips, over and over.

My scream pierces the air, mixing with the horrific sounds of metal scraping and glass breaking as the car continues to roll. As reality sinks in, my blood runs cold. This could really be the end.

It can't be. I'm not ready. This is not how my story ends.

The car finally settles on its roof, leaving me hanging upside down in my seatbelt. I fight to hang on to consciousness, but I'm tired. So damn tired. I give in to the pit of darkness with only one thought on my mind.

Soul, find me, please.

CHAPTER TWENTY-FIVE

SOUL

"JESUS, PREZ, THAT DIDN'T SO—"

"Shut up," I snap at my brother. "Cece! Cece, say something!"

My stomach bottoms out when she moans, and it threatens to shoot straight back up my throat when the moaning stops. I stare at Fort.

"Did she..." I shake my head. "What the fuck did we just hear?"

"Uh, Prez, look at this." Fort points to his computer screen. All I see is the map he pulled up when he hacked her vehicle's GPS system. "Her location is gone."

"What the hell does that mean?" I bark.

Fort's expression darkens. "It means the GPS in her car isn't working. I think... Fuck, Prez, she wrecked."

"How?" I demand. "It's the goddamn desert.

There's little to no traffic and nothing for her to run into. How the hell could she have an accident?"

Even as the words leave my mouth, I know Fort's right. Hell, I heard the same thing he did. But it's as if my brain refuses to process the reality of the situation.

"I thought I heard her say something about some asshole and his brights," Fort says. "But the line was cutting out, so I can't be sure."

He might as well have shoved his hands into my chest and ripped my heart out. If he's right, and Cece wasn't alone out there…

No! No, no, no.

I stare at the screen of my cell. The call is still connected, but I hear nothing. Absolutely fucking nothing.

"C'mon, babe," I mumble. "Say so—"

"Shhh."

I whip my head up to look at Fort. "Did you seri—"

"Listen," he snaps, so I do.

What the fuck is that clicking sound?

Click.

Click.

Click.

Click.

Click.

Click.

A rustling sound comes through the line.

"Cece!" I shout.

More rustling and then, "Prez?"

"Justin?" It registers that the clicking sound was his Zippo.

"Prez, you need to get here," the prospect says, fear in his tone. "I don't know what the fuck happened, but Cece's car is upside down in the fucking desert. Bring Abyss, Prez."

Upside down? Bring Abyss?

I take off running toward the elevator, Fort on my heels. My heart is in my throat, the unknown weighing on me like a thousand-pound boulder.

On my way through the common room, I order, "Malice, Grim, and Abyss! Garage, now! Fort, get everyone here lined out. We're on semi-lockdown until I get back. No one in or out until we get back with…" I swallow past the lump in my throat as it hits me like a freight train that we might not be bringing my girl back. "No one in or out!"

"Got it," Fort says and makes a U-turn to race toward the security room where he can use the intercom.

The elevator door slides open, and I step on. The three brothers going with me step on just as I hit the button to take us above ground.

"What the fuck is going on?" Grim's face is granite-hard.

"Cece's hurt."

"What?" Malice snaps.

I throw my hands up. "I don't know shit, okay. She was on her way here and got lost. I sent Justin after her, and he just told me her car is upside down and to bring the fucking club doc."

"No clue how bad she's hurt?" Abyss asks.

The elevator door slides open, and I race to my Harley. Before I reach it, I switch directions and go to my truck. If I'm bringing Abyss, there's no way Cece's in any condition to be on the back of a bike.

Son of a bitch! What the hell happened?

"Abyss, you're with me. Malice and Grim, take your bikes."

As I jump into the driver's seat, my cell phone pings with a text. I glance at it and see that Justin sent me the coordinates. Fuck, it didn't even cross my mind that I had no clue where we were going. I didn't look at Fort's computer screen that hard when he had her location pulled up.

I forward the text to Malice and Grim, and then shout, "Go!"

The two of them take off out of the garage like rockets. I stomp on the gas and follow behind them, grateful they're not pussy riders. If it wouldn't put them in danger, I'd be leading the pack, but I can't take the chance of kicking up sand in their faces. One injured loved one is enough.

"Love?" Abyss comments.

"What?"

"You said one injured loved one," he says. "Have you told her yet?"

Fuck… this woman and her quirks are contagious.

"Is this really the time for this?" I snap.

He shifts his gaze forward. "Nope."

"Didn't think so," I mutter.

Twenty minutes later, I'm slamming on my brakes next to Cece's flipped car. And for the first time since her moaning stopped, I breathe a sigh of relief.

Cece is sitting next to Justin in the sand. Her face and clothes are bloody, but she's awake.

Thank fuck.

"I'M FINE."

Cece's tone gives away the lie. Between that and the ashen pallor of her skin, I know she's anything but *fine*.

"Forgive me if I don't believe you," I grumble.

"She *is* fine, Prez," Abyss says as he puts all his medical shit away. "Physically at least."

Cece walked away from the crash with a laceration on her head that required ten stitches and a concussion. All in all, she's lucky. I know that, but I can't get the image of her covered in blood out of my head. It doesn't help that she's still wearing her bloody clothes and her cheeks and hair are caked with dried blood.

"See," Cece snaps. "I'm fine."

"Before the two of you get into a full-blown fucking argument, let me give you instructions," Abyss says with a smirk. "Then I'll be out of your hair, and you can fight until your heart's content."

"Instructions?" Cece parrots. "It's a stitched cut and concussion. Nothing too complicated about that."

"No, there's not," Abyss agrees. "But I figured you'd want me to spell out exactly how uncomplicated it is for your man here." He hitches his thumb in my direction and chuckles when I scowl. "Otherwise you're gonna be wrapped in bubble wrap and never let out of this room again."

"I'm not that bad," I mutter.

Both Cece and Abyss give me sidelong glances that tell me they definitely do not agree.

"Whatever." I flick my hand at Abyss. "Well, go on then. Give her the goddamn instructions."

"Cece, keep the stitches dry for twenty-four hours. I know you probably want a shower to wash away all of that," he says and points to the crimson covering her. "But a sponge bath would be better."

"I can live with that," I tease.

Cece huffs out a breath. "I'm sure you can."

"Oh, don't pretend you won't en—"

"As for the concussion," Abyss says loudly. "Soul, keep an eye on her while she sleeps. Wake her up every few hours to make sure she's still doing okay. Cece, if your headache worsens, or you experience dizziness, nausea, or blurry vision, don't be stoic. Tell Soul so he can get me."

"Do you want me to promise you my firstborn, too?"

"I know you're frustrated, but you're lucky," Abyss explains. "Things could've been a lot worse."

"I know."

"He means you could be dead, babe," I tell her. "Do you get that? Do you understand that you could've died tonight?"

"Are you serious?" she snaps, her eyes sparking with anger. "I'm very aware. I was the one run off the road and tossed around like clothes in a dryer!"

"And that's my cue to leave." Abyss walks toward the door, but looks over his shoulder before exiting the room. "If you need anything, let me know."

Once he's gone, I sit down on my bed next to Cece. She tries to scoot away, but I settle my hand on her thigh, and her body sags.

"Talk to me."

She's silent for so long I worry she's not going to say anything. But then she turns and lifts her gaze to meet mine.

"About what, Soul? The fact that I just got over one medical crisis, and here I am recuperating at the clubhouse *again*? Or about the fact that my life was amazing, and then I lost my mom and it went to shit? Oh, wait, no… you want me to talk about the fact that I was just *run off the fucking road* by some lunatic!"

I slowly rub her leg, making sure to keep my movements light and soothing. "Talk about any of it, or all of it." I shrug. "I'll listen to whatever you have to say."

"And if I don't want to talk at all?"

"That's your call."

Cece leans her head against my shoulder and sighs. "I just wanna get cleaned up and sleep."

"Okay."

I help Cece to the bathroom and strip her out of

her filthy clothes. She doesn't resist me taking care of her, which I'm grateful for. After taking my time cleaning the blood and dirt from her skin, I pull one of my t-shirts over her head and guide her back to the bed.

All of this is done in silence, neither of us willing to open our mouths and ruin the peace of the moment.

"It's late, babe," I tell her once she's settled under the comforter. "Why don't you get some sleep, and I'll wake you up in a few hours?"

"I don't want to sleep," she admits. "Can we watch TV or something?"

"Absolutely." I turn on the television and hand her the remote.

"I'm kinda hungry. What snacks do you have in your room?"

I chuckle. "What are you hungry for?" Before she can respond, my cell beeps with a notification. "Hold that thought."

I stare at the text from Grim, my skin burning as the words sink in.

> Grim: Definitely ran off the road. Found tire tracks that don't match hers at the edge and a bumper a mile back toward town.

Me: Take pics and head home. Thanks, G.

"What's wrong?" Cece asks as she scoots up and presses her back against the headboard.

"Nothing."

"Bullshit," she snaps. "I've got a concussion. I'm not stupid." Cece nods at my cell. "Who was that?"

I lock eyes with her and search for any indication that she can't handle the answer. I find nothing. Cece's strong, and keeping things from her, especially information that pertains to her, won't work. It'll push her away, and that's the last thing I want to do.

"Grim," I tell her as I climb onto the mattress next to her.

"And?"

I thread my fingers through hers, although I'm not sure if it's for her benefit or my own. Probably a mix of both, if I'm being honest.

"He said you were definitely run off the road."

"No shit! I knew that already. What I want to know is who did it. Who wants to hurt me?"

"We don't know yet. But we'll find out." She nods, but her expression falls. I press a soft kiss to her lips. "I promise you, Cece, nobody is going to hurt you again. Not on my watch."

"That's just it, Soul," she huffs out. "I can't be on your watch all the time. I've got a business to run, and you've got a club to run."

"No one, Cece," I say again, this time with more conviction in my tone. "I'll make sure of it."

"How, Soul?"

I take a deep breath, giving myself a moment to figure out how to escape her wrath once I tell her exactly how I plan to keep her safe. She's not going to like it, I know, but it's what's best for her.

"Soul?" she prods.

"You're going to move into the clubhouse. I can protect you here."

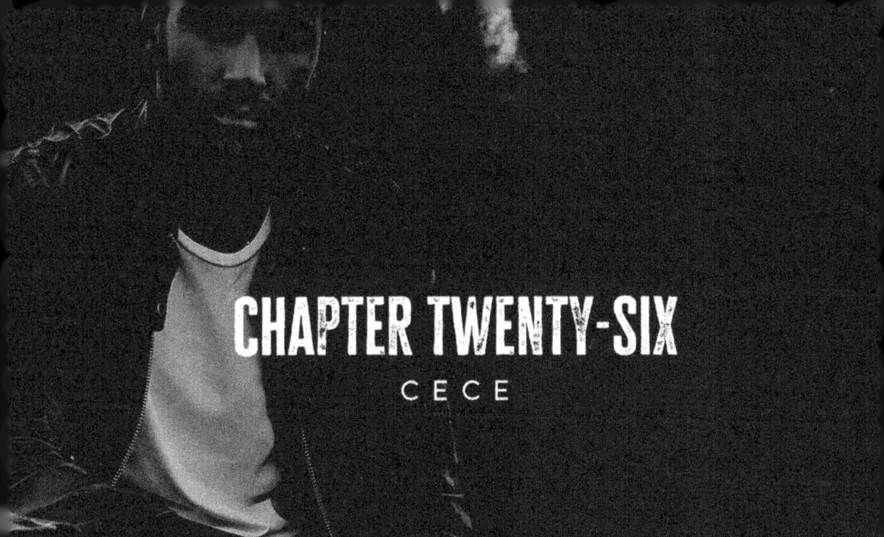

CHAPTER TWENTY-SIX

CECE

"You're going to move into the clubhouse. I can protect you here."

"The hell I am."

I stare at Soul, waiting for him to challenge me. The battle of wills has commenced, neither of us ready to back down. Soul's nostrils flare, and he clenches his jaw. I'll be damned if he thinks he's going to dictate where I live.

"You are staying *here*," he demands with an eerie calmness.

"No, I'm not," I snap. "And you telling me what *I'm* going to do isn't earning you any brownie points."

Soul hangs his head as he draws in a deep breath and then looks at me again. "I almost fucking lost you, babe. You have no idea how that felt. Not knowing what happened, screaming your name, trying to get you to respond… I was powerless." He shakes his head. "I promised you that you wouldn't ever be hurt again, and you were almost *killed.*"

I bite my lip and let his words sink in. He's scared, and I get it. Fuck, I thought I was going to die, but I refuse to live in fear. If anything, I'm more determined to live my life. If the past couple of months have taught me anything, it's that I need to grab life by the damn horns and make it my bitch.

"We talked about this, Soul. I can't have you trying to run my life. If we're going to have a relationship, a *true* relationship, then you're gonna have to bend a little. I can't move in just because you demand it." I grab his hand and squeeze. "That's not me, Soul. I don't need a father, I need a partner. One who will listen to what I'm saying and respect my decisions."

"I need you here where I can watch you, or if I'm not here, the brothers can keep an eye on you," he says before pulling me onto his lap.

"I have a life outside of you and your club. I'm a business owner, Soul. Just like you, I have responsibilities."

"How about a compromise then?"

I'm taken aback by his sudden change of heart. Usually, it would be a much longer argument. I can't help but wonder if he's leading me into a trap.

"What kind of compromise?" I ask hesitantly.

"Nothing too drastic," he says. I move off his lap and stand to face him before he continues. "You don't have to live here, but there will be a guard posted at the house and Naughty/Nice when you're at either location. And if you need to go anywhere, you'll have an escort. It'll be me most of the time, but when I can't, I'll assign someone. And a security system needs installed at the house."

"Nothing too drastic? Are you kidding me?" I tap my foot in frustration. "Guards and escorts? That's not a compromise, Soul. That's a prison without the cell bars."

"No, that's me protecting what's mine." Soul stands, and I take a step back to give him room. "I need to know you're safe."

Towering over me, he cups my cheeks before lowering his head, and his mouth collides with mine. The kiss starts softly but slowly turns demanding, and I moan into his mouth. Our tongues duel for dominance until, as quick as it started, it stops because Soul pulls away.

"Please, babe," he pleads.

"You fight dirty."

"I fight whatever way is going to score me a win." He grins. "And I won't apologize for trying to keep you safe."

"Fine," I huff out. "Anything else?"

Soul's eyes twinkle, and his mouth curls up.

Shit! I just realized my mistake, and now it's too late to take it back.

"Now that you mention it, yeah. You and I are together every night. I don't care where, but we *are* together."

"I can deal with that condition."

"And..."

"And? Seriously?" I shake my head.

"You won't have any more contact with either Dr. Franklin."

"That's the first thing you've said that I agree with."

"Good. Now let's find some food."

THE NEXT COUPLE OF DAYS GO BY IN A BLUR. THE SLIGHT headache I had from the concussion finally went away. You'd think after battling a headache for almost a month from the Lyme Disease that I'd be used to one, but nope. Headaches fucking suck no matter what. I've been irritable and unfortunately, I took my frustrations out on poor Asher, who was dubbed babysitter while everyone else went to work.

"Asher, I swear to God, if you don't quit following me,

I'm going to find a way into your room and stab you in your sleep."

"Damn Ce, you're cranky," Asher replies, but promptly steps back. "Prez told me to watch you, so I'm watching you."

"He said watch, *not* follow my every move.*" I wave my hands in frustration. "Fuck, I can't even walk to the bathroom in peace. Seriously, Asher… let's think about this for a second. This place is like Fort Knox. Do you really think I can't walk from Soul's room to the common room without a damn shadow?"*

"You're right. Sorry."

"I swear if I plan a jailbreak, you'll be the first to know. Give me some space."

"Yeah, you got it Ce. Sorry." He puts his fist out. "Still friends?"

I fist bump him. "Of course."

I don't know when Soul came back to the clubhouse, because I was exhausted and passed out. I didn't even notice when he came to bed, but I wake up to his body wrapped around mine. Desperately needing to go to the bathroom, I wiggle free and manage to do so without waking him.

When I come out of the bathroom, Soul is sitting up and leaning against the headboard.

"Anything you want to tell me?"

"I don't know what you're talking about," I say innocently, batting my eyes at him.

"Really? You threaten one of my prospects, and you didn't think I'd find out?"

"I didn't really threaten Asher."

"You told him you were going to find a way into his room and stab him in his sleep," Soul bites out, although he seems more amused than mad. "Pretty fucking threatening if you ask me, babe."

"He was following me everywhere," I cry. "Literally. Even to the damn bathroom."

Soul swings his legs over the edge of the bed and growls. "The fucking bathroom?"

"Calm down caveman." I straddle his lap and rock my hips. "He didn't go *into* the bathroom with me. I think he learned his lesson."

I'm suddenly flipped onto my back, and my head hits the pillow. Soul grinds his steel-hard cock against my thigh. I spread my legs to give him better access, and he thrusts against my pussy. I groan as he rocks back and forth, dry humping me into a pleasure high.

"Something you need babe?" he teases, applying more pressure.

"Yes!" I cry out as my panties become damp with arousal.

I'm so close to coming that my brain short circuits when my cell phone rings.

"Fuck." Soul stiffens. "Your phone's a damn cock block."

"No, it's a damn pussy block," I growl as I grab the cell from the nightstand. The damn number for the store flashes on the screen. I know I should ignore it, but it might be an emergency.

"Hello?"

"Hey, Cece… It's Trista. I hope I'm not bothering you."

Oh, no, you're just killing whatever hope I had of getting off this morning.

"It's okay," I say with a sigh. "What's up?"

"I was wondering if you could come to the store today. We're very busy and could use the extra set of hands."

Muffled voices come through the phone, and Laura is in the background rattling off a purchase total to a customer.

"Absolutely. I'll get ready and head that way."

"Thanks so much. See you soon." Trista ends the call before I can respond.

Shaking my head, I look at Soul. "Raincheck?"

"You better fucking believe it." He kisses me breathless before tugging me out of bed with him. "You're taking someone with you."

Settling my hands on my hips and scowl as I say, "Babysitter, got it."

"You compromised, remember?" Soul strolls to the bathroom like he doesn't have a care in the world. "Better get ready so you can go," he calls over his shoulder, his tone smug.

Two hours later, Asher's parking the car in front of Naughty/Nice. Before I can even grab the handle of my door, he's there opening it for me. I lift my brows, and it's on the tip of my tongue to chastise him for treating me like I can't take care of myself, but he raises his hand to stop the words from spilling out.

"Sorry Cece, but my mama raised me to have manners."

"I'm sorry. I don't mean to be a bitch." I exit the car and squeeze his arm, guilt hitting me hard. He shouldn't be punished for following orders or for my pissy attitude. "Thanks, Asher. I appreciate it."

I hate that Soul used sexual coercion to get me to agree to a *compromise,* and I'm still upset about my car. But neither of those things are Asher's fault.

Soul had the Camaro towed to Sinful Wheels to see if the guys could repair the damage, and if anyone can fix it, it'll be them. I don't know if I would trust anyone else with such a special project. Another piece of my heart died when I saw the damage, and Soul promised he would do what he could, but it's in the hands of Abyss, Frenzy, and Spike. After what I saw, it'll take a miracle to fix.

Asher explained on our way here that he wouldn't go inside the store unless I wanted or needed him to, so I head in alone. Meanwhile, he's going to spend the day circling around the perimeter or staying close to the vehicle out front.

"Who's the stud?" Trista asks, ogling Asher as he walks in front of the window.

"Asher. He's a prospect with the MC."

"He's cute," Holly says, coming up behind me.

I met Holly shortly after Trista and Laura. So far, I love the ladies who Soul and Jez hired, and I know I need to make my decision soon about whether to cut them loose or keep them on.

"I thought you guys were busy and needed extra hands." I wave my hand around the empty store.

Trista blushes. "Well… when I called we had *two* customers."

Holly laughs and nods at Asher, who's standing like a sentry, facing the street. "We thought you'd need a prison break."

"Trista, I have to say, I'm a little pissed right now," I snap.

"Uh oh," Holly mutters under her breath.

The color drains from Trista's face, and she's

trembling. For a second, I feel guilty, but quickly dismiss it. She has this coming.

"I'm sor—"

"You are a pussy block" I gripe.

It takes a minute for my words to sink in, but when they do, Holly howls with laughter.

"Did you just call her a pussy block? I've heard of cock blocking but not pussy blocking."

"Trista successfully derailed my happy ending this morning." I tap my foot and scowl at her.

"You broke girl code!" Holly frowns at Trista and shakes her head. "How could you?"

"How the hell was I supposed to know she'd be getting sexed up?" With a pout, Trista crosses her arms over her chest.

Holly rolls her eyes. "Honey, when it comes to a man like Soul, you *always* assume she's getting sexed up."

Before I can stop it, a laugh bubbles free and doubles me over with hilarity. Holly joins in, but Trista's eyes are bugging out of her skull as she stares at us like we're crazy.

My sides burn from laughing so hard. "I have a feeling there's never gonna be another dull moment around here." I grin at them both. "I officially welcome you to Naughty/Nice."

CHAPTER TWENTY-SEVEN

SOUL

"Care to fill me in on why you called this meeting?"

I arch a brow at our club attorney as I drum my fingers on the table in his conference room. We typically meet with him at the clubhouse, but with Cece's schedule and the club businesses, I'm in the city more than I'm home.

"I'm pretty sure we pay you enough to avoid the attitude, Jim."

Attorney Staten's shoulders sag. "You do. But I don't have the help I used to around here so impromptu meetings aren't as easy to accommodate."

"If you can't handle our business, I can look el—"

"No, no," Jim rushes to assure me. "Just... what do you need me to do?"

I glance at the clock on the wall, and a fraction of worry teases my mind. Tension seeps into my muscles as I wonder where the hell Grim and Cece are. They're only a few minutes late, but after everything, worst case scenarios are my only thought.

"As soon as the others arrive, I'll ex—"

The door flies open and Grim, followed by Cece, strides in, both of them with their phones in their hands and laughing. Air whooshes from my lungs at the relief that hits me.

"Sure, come right in," Jim grumbles.

I have to sign his words for Grim because, despite our request, our attorney has never learned ASL. He tried, but unless it relates to the law, he's an idiot.

"Cut the shit, Staten." Grim's lips are set in a thin line as he glares at the man. "Your secretary told us to come on back."

"Jim, you already know Grim," I begin. "But I'd like to introduce you to your new client, Cece Parker."

Jim focuses his narrowed gaze on Cece. "Wait a minute. You're Carmella's friend."

Cece smiles brightly at the mention of her best friend. "I am." She steps up to the table and leans across to shake his hand. "It's nice to officially meet you. Carmella always had great things to say."

For the first time since I arrived, Jim's mouth tips up into a smile. "It's nice to meet you, too. How's she doing, by the way?"

"Carmella's doing great. She loves her new job, and it keeps her busy."

"Good, good. I sure do miss her around here, but I'm happy for her."

"I'll be sure to tell her that, Mr. Staten."

"Jim, please," he insists. "Call me Jim."

Cece nods. "Okay, Jim."

She sits in the chair next to me, and Grim walks around the table to sit across from us. Jim shifts so he can include all three of us in the meeting rather than just me and Cece. He might be an idiot who can't communicate with my enforcer, but he doesn't have a death wish, which I can appreciate.

"When you introduced Cece, you said she's my new client," Jim says. "I thought this meeting was about club business."

"It is club business," I tell him. "Cece's with me which makes anything she needs from you club business."

"Understood."

I nod. "I'll let Cece give you the specifics, but the gist of what we need is a wrongful death suit filed against Boulder City Memorial."

"You want to sue a hospital?" Jim's eyes dart back and forth between Cece and me.

"Yes, Sir," Cece replies. "My mother died as a result of a failure to provide appropriate medical care. Between the ER doctor who treated her, or *didn't* treat her, and the hospital director's covering for him, someone needs to be held accountable."

"That's a pretty big accusation, Miss Parker."

"Do you really think I'd bring her to you if we hadn't done our homework?" I growl. "She's stating facts, Jim, not accusations."

"And I assume the information you have to back up your lawsuit was obtained illegally?" Jim asks me.

There's no point in lying to the man. He's the one person outside of the club that knows what Saints Purgatory is about. He knows we're not on the right side of the law.

"It wasn't," I confirm. "But you can use it. Jez is working to pull it all together in a form you can use."

Jim nods. "Okay, good." He focuses on Cece. "Why don't you explain everything that happened to your mother, in as much detail as you can, and I'll ask questions as I need to? That way I can see if this is a frivolous notion or if it's a case I can win."

Over the next hour, Cece takes Jim through her mother's headaches, the trips to the ER, her death… She tells him everything, and I fill in the blanks when necessary. Jim doesn't ask too many questions, and by the time Cece's done, his brows are drawn down and his face is red with indignation.

"If everything you say is true, I'll file the suit pro bono. Doctors shouldn't be able to get away with shit like this," Jim bites out.

"Oh, wow. Um, thank you," Cece says.

"Don't thank me, Miss Parker. I might not be able to do as much as Soul and the club, but I started practicing law to ensure people like the Franklins don't get away with stuff. This is just me doing my part to leave the world a little better than I found it."

My respect and appreciation for Jim Staten rises several notches.

"I only have one last question," he says with curiosity in his tone.

"What's that?" I ask.

"Why aren't you handling this your usual way? Why the lawsuit?"

"Trust me, Jim, we're handling things. But Cece was run off the road a few days ago, and while we can't prove it, we believe Richard Franklin Jr. is responsible. We found a bumper on the road about a mile away from the crash scene, and it matches his vehicle." I reach under the table and rest my hand on Cece's thigh, needing to feel her, to remind myself that she's alive and well. "She deserves some form of justice for all she's been through at the hands of these men."

"I just want to make them suffer the way they've

made me suffer," Cece adds. "It might be petty, but it's the truth."

Grim taps the table to get our attention. His face remained impassive throughout the entire meeting as he took in the conversation with his focus on my hands.

"What is it, Grim?" I ask.

"They will pay." Grim's eyes narrow. "You're going to win this lawsuit for Cece, and they will pay with their money. And then we'll make them pay with their blood. For Cece."

Jim seems to contemplate Grim's statement, almost as if he's deciding whether or not he wants to ask more questions. He must decide against it because he simply nods.

"They'll be served with the papers within the next forty-eight hours."

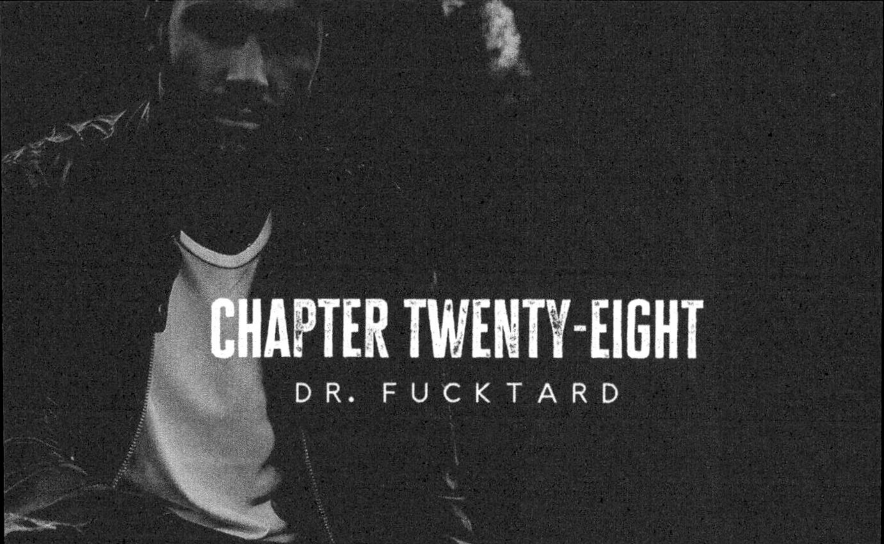

CHAPTER TWENTY-EIGHT

DR. FUCKTARD

"WHAT THE HELL HAVE YOU DONE?"

I stare at my father, ignoring the large manilla envelope he slapped onto his desk. I've avoided his calls for days, but he had me summoned to his office the second I walked into the hospital this morning.

"I'm afraid you're going to have to be a bit more specific."

He bristles, and his face turns a deep red. "Don't get smart with me."

"I have no idea what you think I've done. But I do have a full ER, so if you could fill in the blanks for me so I can get back to work, that would be much appreciated."

"Oh, now you give a shit about your patients?" He shakes his head and hands me the manilla envelope. "Go ahead, open it."

I hesitate for a moment when I see some lawyer's

the sinking sensation in the pit of my stomach and lift the flap to pull out the few pieces of paper inside.

Scanning the document, my temper spikes. "What the fuck?"

"My thoughts exactly," Father snaps. "That's a wrongful death suit filed against the hospital, naming both of us as involved parties, as a result of your negligence with Mrs. Barbara Parker."

"I didn't do anything," I insist. "The woman had a brain tumor and died. How is that my fault?"

"You can't be that stupid," he shouts and then tilts his head. "I don't know what's going on with you, but get your head out of your ass and man up."

"Nothing is going on with me. I work my shifts and bust my ass for patients. And then I go home only to sleep and get up to do it all over again."

"That lawsuit suggests otherwise."

"And it's a bogus lawsuit."

My father narrows his eyes. "Where'd you get that fancy car you were driving this morning?"

I smile proudly. "Oh, I bought it."

"Why?"

Because I lost my bumper in the desert after I ran Mrs. Parker's cunt daughter off the road.

I shrug. "It was time for a change."

He only shakes his head. "No, no. I'm not buying it. Something is going on with you, Ricky. I just hope, for your sake and mine, that you're being smart about whatever it is."

I lower my eyes to the document for a second before lifting them back up and locking my gaze with his.

"Don't you worry about me, Father. I've got everything handled." I toss the papers on his desk. "I promise, that's not a suit we'll lose, and there will be no more problems from the Parker family."

"What have you done, Ricky?"

Failed, like I always do.

But that stops now.

"Nothing, Father," I lie. "I'll meet with the hospital's attorneys and get this all sorted out."

Or not.

Watch out, Cece Parker. I'm coming for you… again.

CHAPTER TWENTY-NINE

CECE

"WHOSE IDEA WAS IT TO DO INVENTORY?" I GRUNT AS I pick up another box.

"Yours, boss lady," Holly says, shaking her ass.

I closed the store early so we can catch up on some much needed cleaning. We also have to do inventory, and I have to look over the books. Rogue handled them while I was out, and I haven't had a chance to review them since coming back to work.

The music is cranked up to max volume, and the pizza I ordered was just delivered. Justin came in a few minutes ago to grab a couple slices, but he's already outside again to patrol

"Where's the clipboard?" Trista shouts over the music.

"Over here," Laura sing-songs.

Watching the ladies dance around and help with inventory brings memories flooding back of when

Mom and I would close the store and do the same thing. I smile at the thought and dig into another box.

"How are things going with Soul?" Trista asks, pulling me from my musing.

"Good."

"Just good?" Holly asks.

"Great." I focus on the clipboard in my hands.

"Good, or great?" Laura asks, getting in on the conversation.

As I tap my pen on the counter, I'm so focused on the inventory logs I'm staring at that I don't realize the three of them are surrounding me.

"Ce, we're waiting," Laura speaks from behind me, and I screech like a banshee.

"That's it! I'm putting a damn bell around your neck."

Laura's cheeks flush as she shrugs, but she doesn't apologize.

"I begged you to, but you said that's workplace harassment." Trista pouts.

"Yeah, but now she's scaring *me,*" I say as I place my hand on my chest to make sure my heart's still beating. "Now it's a matter of workplace safety. One of these days she's going to get punched by someone."

"Why would someone punch me?"

"They call it fight or flight." Holly rolls her eyes.

"Next time you scare someone, instead of just screaming like a little girl, they might throat punch you and ask questions later."

Laura's eyes widen, and her mouth forms a perfect 'O'. Her expression is priceless, and we all laugh.

I tug her close to give her a side hug. "We love ya, girl. You just need to quit sneaking up on us."

"I don't do it on purpose," she mumbles.

"Back to the original topic, Ce," Trista says, shifting our focus.

I squirm like a bug being examined under a microscope. "Let's get back to work."

"Oh, I don't think so."

"Spill woman," Holly orders, laughter in her tone. "We're living vicariously through you."

"Why?" I ask, picking up the clipboard.

"Really? You're shagging a hot ass biker, and you want to know why?" Trista bobs her eyebrows.

"Shagging? Who are you, Austin Powers?" I tease.

"She's deflecting," Holly chimes in.

I toss the clipboard on the counter and throw my arms up. "It's great, okay? Is that what you want to hear?"

"Think we struck a nerve," Laura whispers, but not so quietly that I can't hear her.

Trista comes around the counter and stands in front of me. "We're just teasing you."

"I know." I sigh. "Sorry, we're having fun and getting to know each other, but I'm not sure if this is forever or just fun for now."

"Have you asked him?" Holly questions.

I shake my head. "No. I'm afraid of the answer. What if he doesn't want anything long-term." I fidget with my hands. "He says I'm his, but what the hell does that even mean?"

"Omigod, Omigod, Omigod." Laura bounces on her feet and claps. "You love him!"

"What?" I frantically shake my head. "No… Wait, what?"

Despite my denial, they're all smiling at me. Thinking about all the ways in which Soul's been there for me emotionally, taken care of me physically, and about how he fucks me into oblivion, my mouth curves up.

Trista points at my smile. "Yes, you do! You're beaming."

"No I'm not," I argue, but it's pointless because my stupid grin betrays me.

"You need to tell him," Holly says.

"What if he doesn't feel the same? I'd make an ass out of myself."

"What if he's waiting for you to say it first?" Laura counters softly.

"He probably doesn't want to scare you off," Holly adds.

"I know it's hard putting yourself out there, but it's probably why he hasn't said it either."

Trista purses her lips. "You're both too damn stubborn for your own good."

"Hey! I'm not stubborn," I argue.

Trista chuckles. "I'm not touching that with a ten-foot pole."

"Alright, alright. I'll think about it. Can we please get back to work?"

"You heard the boss-lady," Trista calls out. "Back to work, minions."

By the time the sun is setting, the store is sparkling clean, almost all of the inventory is counted, and I've reviewed the accounting records. I'm impressed by what Rogue did and the improvements he made. Thanks to him, my paperwork time will be cut in half. The guy is a numbers genius, and I owe him a big 'thank you'.

My cell phone rings, breaking my thoughts. I smile when I see that it's Soul calling.

"Hey, caveman. Whatcha doing?"

"You almost done, babe?"

I put the call on speakerphone and set my cell down on top of the box in front of me.

"Almost." I lift the box and carry it to my office. "I only have one more box to count, and I've gotta put some stuff in the safe."

I bend and lower the box to the floor next to my desk.

"Definitely love that view, babe."

Soul's voice seems to echo with the one directly behind me.

I yelp and spin around, almost tripping myself. Soul reaches out to steady me.

"Holy shit! What is it with people wanting to scare me to death today?" I smack his chest.

"Who the fuck scared you? Where was Justin?"

"Calm down, Soul. Laura has a problem with being too quiet when she approaches others."

He smirks. "Still haven't bought her that bell?"

"Nope." I grin. "But now it's a matter of public safety."

Soul tips my chin up and fuses his lips to mine, kissing me until there's no breath left in my body.

"Give me thirty minutes, and I'll be ready to go," I tell him when the kiss ends.

I turn back toward the box and bend over. Soul grabs my hips and grinds his cock against my ass.

"Or we could do something else," he suggests.

"Like what?" I ask, my tone husky.

Soul yanks me up so my back is flat against his chest.

"It'd be better if I fucking showed you," he growls in my ear.

He wraps one arm around my waist while he slowly slides his other hand under my shirt to tweak my nipple through my lace bra. Moaning, I close my eyes and revel in his teasing.

"Feel good, babe?" he whispers as he moves his hand from my waist to my pussy.

I grab his hand and turn around to face him. "What if Justin walks in? I assume he's still patrolling."

"He is, but I warned him to stay the fuck out."

"Sounds like you had this planned before you came in."

Soul shrugs. "Maybe."

"In that case..."

I drop to my knees, catching him off guard.

"Babe, what are you doing?"

I rub his bulge. "I think you know."

Soul sucks in a breath when I unbutton his jeans and free his dick. Soul's shaft is long and thick but thankfully for me, I don't have a gag reflex.

Wrapping my fingers around him, I stroke up and down, and when a bead of precum forms, I swipe it off with the tip of my tongue. My mouth waters from his taste. He's salty and sweet.

Soul moans as he fists his hands in my hair. Surprisingly, he doesn't even try to take control and fuck my mouth. I lick the underside of his cock and massage his balls with my free hand.

"Cece," he grits out.

I peek up at him as I stretch my mouth around his girth and suck him to the back of my throat.

"Fuuuck."

I pull back and swirl my tongue around the tip before sucking him all the way back again. I repeat this several times before he growls and throws his head back. With his hands still in my hair he starts thrusting his hips.

"Pull back, babe," he orders. "I'm gonna come."

I ignore him and dig my nails into his thighs to pull him closer. Soul roars right before cum spurts from him, and I happily swallow it down. Before I release him, I lick him clean. I grab a shirt from the box I carried in earlier and use it to wipe my mouth.

"Guess I'm buying that, huh?" he says as he helps me stand and wraps his arms around me.

"I'd say that's fair."

Soul leans in, but before his lips touch mine, I turn my head and scrunch up my nose.

"What's that smell?"

CHAPTER THIRTY

SOUL

"WHAT'S THAT SMELL?"

"I'm pretty sure that's the smell of satisfaction, babe."

Cece slaps me on the chest as she sniffs the air. "Soul, is that smoke?"

Forcing my thoughts away from her mouth on my dick, I turn away and sniff. I'm instantly catapulted back in time.

"We've gotta go!"

I'm frozen in place, the culmination of two years of planning playing out right in front of me. And I'm fucking frozen."

"Matt, c'mon!" Paul shouts as he yanks on my arm. "We're not who dies tonight. Let's go, man."

Smoke billows around the pews, the swirl of impending destruction mesmerizing. I watch it for a second, listening to the screams of the two men barricaded in the confessional booth. The sound of their fear, mixed with the crack-

ling of wood as the fire begins to spread, knocks me from my stupor.

"Soul!"

Cece's shout yanks me back to the present, and the unmistakable smell of smoke invades my nostrils. My eyes begin to burn, and I grab Cece's hand.

"We gotta go," I bark.

As soon as I open the door, heat smacks me in the face, but I don't see any flames. I tuck Cece behind me so I can shield her from whatever we're running into, and turn toward the back entrance. When we reach the door, I shove it, but it doesn't open.

"Son of a bitch!" I roar, as I pull my cell out of my cut.

I tug Cece back toward the front of the store. Maybe, if we're lucky, there'll be a clear path to the front door. I hit the speed dial for Justin, who's supposed to be on guard duty just outside. Four rings taunt me, and then his voicemail picks up.

Where the fuck are you, Prospect?

We pass the fitting rooms, and any speck of hope I might have had dies. The entire front of the building is burning, and the windows have shattered, allowing air to blow in and feed the fire.

"Soul," Cece cries as she twists her hands in my shirt. "Soul, we have to get outta here."

I turn back toward the office, but an idea forms, and I detour to the bathroom.

"Tell me you have a bucket," I say to Cece.

"A bucket," she repeats. "My store is burni—"

"Cece! A bucket… Do you have one?"

She nods as she starts coughing from the smoke. It's starting to travel through the main shop area to where we are, and we don't have much time.

"Uh, yeah. There's a mop bucket in the closet." She points to a door a few feet away.

"Good." I yank open the door. "I need you to grab a box of clothes. As big a box as you can carry."

"For wh—"

"Just go!"

I shout as I grab the mop bucket and rush to the bathroom. Cece races toward where she keeps the backstock. I fill the bucket and leave the sink running. When she returns, tilt my head to the floor, silently telling her to drop the box.

"Take all the clothes out and soak them in the sink," I instruct. "Get them sopping wet."

As she does that, I step out of the bathroom and toss the water at her office door. I repeat this process six times to get the wood as wet as I can.

"Now what?" Cece demands as she drops the soaking pile of clothes next to me.

I glance toward the front of the store, and panic

sets in when I see the flames licking up the walls of the fitting rooms, which are at the back of the main space. I push the office door open and shove Cece inside.

"Get in the corner, over there." I point to the corner that has the least amount of clutter around it.

"What are you gonna do?"

I grip her shoulders as another coughing fit overtakes her. My lungs burn, and sweat pours out of me, but I do my best to stave off the hacking.

"Cece, just do what I fucking say!"

She seems to freeze, but only for a split second, and then she turns and crouches in the corner. I slide my cell across the floor to her.

"Keep trying to get Justin," I instruct.

She nods and dials. Over and over she calls him, never getting an answer. While she does that, I stick some of the clothes under the office door, which is now closed, blocking the crack. I move to join her, but before I sit, I use several wet sweaters and cover her with them.

We're not who dies tonight.

We're not who dies tonight.

We're not who dies tonight.

I repeat that mantra in my head as I crouch next to her, putting myself between her and the door. If the fire is going to be our end, it's going to take me first.

C'mon, Prospect. Don't fail me now. Where the fucking are you?

"Keep the wet clothes over you," I say as I cover us as best I can. "Try not to in—"

I'm seized by a painful cough, and my insides feel as if they're burning right along with the building.

"Soul, I don't want to die," Cece cries, her voice raspy. "I just found you, and I do—"

"We're not who dies tonight, babe."

With Cece wrapped in my arms, I press my mouth to the top of her head, and she jerkily nods.

We're not who dies tonight.

I have no fucking clue if I'm telling her the truth or not, but I say it again. And again.

We're not who dies tonight.

I say it until my voice is hoarse and my throat is raw. I repeat it until my vision becomes hazy. The fire rages as it climbs the walls, and I know we don't have much time. And yet...

"We're not who dies tonight."

Cece's body sags, and fear claws at me. I hold her tight, knowing she might not feel me surrounding her at all. She might be...

No! Don't go there.

The edges of my vision darken, and I struggle to remain conscious. I fight to stay in the light, but this is an evil I can't purge. One last thought scrolls through my mind before the suffocating darkness wins.

We're fucking dying tonight.

CHAPTER THIRTY-ONE

MARK

"I CHANGED MY MIND."

"Mark," Apple says with a sigh. "We've driven all this way. The least you can do is talk to him. Let him know you're okay."

"He doesn't give a shit," I growl. "He made that pretty fucking clear when he never came back."

"Get over it. We're going."

We hit Boulder City ten minutes ago and are currently cruising down the main street. Nerves settle in my gut when I glance at the GPS because it says we're only five miles from Purgatory.

So fucking close, yet… Shit. Am I ready for this?

My eyes dart around to take in the town, and I notice a Harley parked by the side of a building. The sign reads *Naughty/Nice Boutique*.

"Slow down," I demand.

"We've got five miles to go." Apple points to the GPS even as she lets off the gas.

I glance around to see if any other Harleys are parked close by. I don't spot any, but my attention is pulled to the opposite corner of the building when a sports car peels out, swerving before it straightens out. A few seconds later a different Harley guns down the street, seemingly in pursuit.

"What the hell was that about?" Apple asks.

The closer we get, the more apparent it becomes that something is wrong... very fucking wrong. Smoke billows out of the cracked windows of the boutique.

"Holy fuck! Pull over," I shout.

Apple swerves over to stop at the curb across the street. I grip the handle to shove open the door and jump out of the car before she has it in park.

"Mark, wait!" she yells.

"Call 911!" I call over my shoulder, definitely not waiting.

I try the front door, and in the back of my mind a warning flashes, reminding me that opening the door could do more damage because the influx of air will turn the blaze into a raging inferno. Yanking my hand away, I swivel my head to find another option. I try to look through the windows, but all I can see through the smoke and broken, soot-covered glass is fire. Red hot flames are spreading everywhere.

I scan the street for people, but it's weirdly deserted.

You're not in the big city anymore, dipshit.

My gaze lands on the Harley I originally spotted, and I can't help but wonder who it belongs to and if they're still inside the burning building.

Fuck, what if…

I shake my fears off, keeping them from invading my mind. Whether it's him or someone else, it doesn't matter. What kind of man would I be if I walked away?

I take off in a sprint around the building and look for another way inside. My feet become glued to the pavement when I see a trash dumpster in front of a door at the back of the store.

What the fuck?

I run at the giant hunk of metal and push with all my weight to move it. But it won't budge. I scan the empty lot for anything that could help me.

Think. Think, think, think.

My eyes land on the bottom of the dumpster and hope flares.

Wheels! It has wheels!

I bend down to see why they wouldn't roll the first time I pushed, and I see that they're locked. After flipping the lever to release the lock, I try again.

It moves easily, and I silently thank whatever forces are out in the universe for it not being full of garbage.

I pull the door open, and a blast of heat hits me in the face. Yanking my shirt up to cover my mouth and nose, I cautiously make my way inside.

"Hello?" I shout. "Hey! Anyone in here?"

Stop, drop, and crawl, idiot.

Dropping to my knees, I begin to crawl. The place is filling up with thick black smoke, making it almost impossible to see. I stretch my arms to feel around me, and I've only gone a few feet when my hand hits what I assume is a door. It's warm but slightly damp. I stand and tentatively touch the doorknob. When it doesn't burn me, I twist it and throw open the door.

"Anyone in here?"

A faint moan reaches my ears just as I'm about to give up and go back to searching.

"Hello?" I call out.

Still no answer, but the moaning continues. I race around a desk, toward the sound, and spot what appears to be a pile of wet clothing.

Clothes don't moan.

Peeling the clothes away, layer by layer, reveals a man huddled beneath them. I hunch down to pick him up, and that's when I notice he's wrapped around a woman. I untangle their limbs and pick her up off the floor. Throwing her over my shoulder, I run out the way I came.

Apple is standing outside the building when I emerge. I put the woman down by her and turn to race back inside.

"Stay with her."

"Mark, it's too dangerous. The fire department is on their way."

I shake my head. "There's someone else in there. It'll be too late by the time they get here."

I turn on my heel and run back into the burning building. Dropping to the floor, I crawl back toward the office and open the door. The guy is leaning against the wall when I get to him.

He's much bigger than the woman, and I struggle to get him on my shoulder. After some maneuvering, I have him secure in a fireman's hold. It takes a little longer to get outside due to the extra weight, but I manage.

Spotting Apple sitting on the other side of the alley with the woman's head on her lap, I stumble over and lay the man next to them. I drop to the ground no more than a foot away, and try to catch my breath. As air begins to fill my lungs, a voice I never thought I'd hear again breaks through the fog of the last few minutes.

"Mark?"

CHAPTER THIRTY-TWO

SOUL

"DID HE JUST SAY YOUR NAME?"

I squint at the man whose face is hovering above mine, completely sure that I've died because that's the only way his presence makes sense.

"Mark?" I repeat, my voice raspy from the smoke.

"He did, Mark," a woman says. "He knows you."

"He should know me," the man says. "He's my brother's best friend."

"Holy sh—" A rattling cough wracks my body, and my stomach muscles ache by the time it ends. Using my elbows as leverage, I push myself into a sitting position and stare at the man. "Holy fucking shit," I mutter. "It really is you."

Mark shoves a hand through his hair as his eyes dart to a woman. I follow his gaze and see Cece cradled in the woman's lap. Scrambling to my knees, I crawl toward her, my heart skipping a beat at how still Cece is.

"Cece?" I rasp as I tap her cheek. "Cece, babe, open your eyes."

Cece stirs, and when her eyes flutter open, she immediately seeks me out.

"Soul?"

I cup her cheeks. "Yeah, babe. It's me," I tell her.

Cece scrambles away from Apple and throws her arms around me. She wheezes and coughs as she breathes, but she's breathing and that's the most important thing.

"I thought you were dead," I say with my lips pressed to her head. "Fucking hell, Cece."

"I thought *you* were," she cries before leaning back to look me in the eyes. "Soul, I don't care if you feel the same, but you need to know… I love you. I love you so fucking much. All I could think about when you were hunched over me was that we were going to die, and I hadn't even told you how I feel." Tears spring to her eyes, and the reflection of flames dance in the liquid pools. "If I lost you…" She shakes her head and sniffles. "I lo—"

"I love you, too," I say as I brush hair from her face. "Dammit, Cece, you have to stop trying to die on me. I can't lose you. I lose you, and life stops," I confess as I haul her closer.

As I hold the woman I almost lost, I'm dimly aware of sirens and flashing lights as fire trucks arrive to battle the blaze. Glancing at the rubble that is now Naughty/Nice, I make a mental note to have a *conversation* with the emergency personnel of Boulder City. It shouldn't have taken them this long to respond.

"That's the worst response time I've ever seen," the woman mutters, echoing my thoughts. "I called 911 ten minutes ago."

I face her and see Mark has his arm draped around her shoulder. Who the fuck is this chick, and why is Mark here?

Did they set the fire?

"And you are?" I demand as the events of the last half hour play in my mind like a jumbled-up movie reel.

"Her name's Apple," Mark says. "She's with me."

Apple elbows him in the ribs. "I can speak for myself." She reaches out to shake my hand. "Like he said, I'm Apple. We were on our way to a bar called Purgatory to try and find Paul."

I search Mark's gaze for any hint that Apple's lying, but what I find instead is a mix of exhaustion, determination, and the kind of sadness I haven't seen in anyone since the day Malice realized we knew what was happening to him.

Aw, fuck.

"He goes by Malice now," I tell Mark.

"What?"

"Paul goes by Malice. When you see him, for the love of all that's unholy, do *not* call him Paul. He hates it."

"When I see him?"

Apple smacks his arm. "Yes, dude, when you see him. We didn't drive this fucking far for you to back out."

"Look, Mark, I don't know why you chose now to show up, and I have no clue how Malice will react to seeing you, but I don't particularly care at the moment." I wrap my arm around Cece and pull her close. "You saved our asses, and for that, I'm grateful."

"I saw the Harley," Mark mumbles.

"Huh?"

Apple heaves a sigh. "He saw a Harley parked out front and demanded that I pull over. I assume he thought it was his brother's."

"Oh." I shake my head. "It's mine."

"There was another bike," Mark says and searches our surroundings. "Whoever took off on it was chasing a car that tore out of the alley."

Justin. I fucking forgot about him.

"A prospect, Justin," I explain. "He was chasing a car?"

"Yeah, a sports car," Apple says.

"Soul?"

I glance down at Cece. "Yeah, babe?"

"You don't think it was—"

"That's exactly what I think," I snap.

"What are you talking about?" Mark asks.

"The fire was no accident," I say as I pull my cell phone out of my cut and hit Malice's contact.

"That would explain the dumpster."

I whip my head in Mark's direction. "What dumpster?"

"There was a dumpster shoved up against the back door. I had to move it to get in."

"Yo, Prez," Malice says when he answers my call. "What's up?"

"Go get your car," I demand of Mark. "You're taking us to the clubhouse."

Mark hesitates, but when Apple tugs on his arm, they both run around the building.

"Who are you tal—"

"Malice, Naughty/Nice was set on fire while Cece and I were inside. We're both fine," I rush to add when he starts to ask questions. "I need you to reach out to our contacts in Boulder City and make sure it's reported as an accident."

"But you just said the fire was set," he counters.

"It was. But we're handling this. Do what you gotta do to get it done."

"You got it, Prez," Malice says. "Are you two okay?"

"Yeah, for the most part. Have Abyss on standby to check us out when we get to the clubhouse."

"Will do."

A Volkswagon van enters the parking lot from the road at the back of the boutique. I do a double-take, and sure enough, Apple is driving, and Mark is in the passenger seat.

I tug Cece to the van and continue to bark orders at my VP. "We'll be in a VW van when we arrive. Send Spike to pick up my bike."

"A VW van, Prez? What the fuck is goi—"

"Have Fort get a lock on Justin's location," I bark as if he hadn't spoken. "He took off after Franklin. And reach out to him to see if he needs help. I have no idea if he'll respond, but maybe we'll get lucky."

Once Cece and I are settled in the back of the van, I pull the sliding door closed and smack the back of the driver's seat.

"Let's go," I order. "I'll give you directions as you drive."

"Who the hell are you talking to, Prez?"

Your long-lost brother and his… girlfriend?

"See ya in under an hour, Mal."

I disconnect the call and return my phone to my cut. The upcoming family reunion isn't going to go well, and I have to figure out a way to keep my VP in line and focused on the purge we need to prepare for.

"Punch it, Apple," I say as I lean back on a bean bag.

Does she live in this thing? Does Mark?

Cece scoots to my lap, and I hold her close as we're whisked toward what will surely be a clusterfuck.

My appreciation of Apple rises a notch when she gets us to the clubhouse in forty-five minutes. Who knew that was even possible in this home on wheels?

I direct her to a parking spot on the far side of the garage. As soon as the vehicle stops, Mark jumps out to open the back door. Cece and I file out, and we all trudge toward the elevators.

"You didn't tell him I was coming," Mark comments on the ride underground.

I arch a brow. "You wanna see him, don't you?"

"I don't fucking know," he snaps. "Maybe."

"Too late for maybes, kid."

"In case you haven't noticed, I'm all grown up, Matt."

I stiffen at my given name. "Soul," I snap. "Call me Soul. Matt died in that fire."

"What?" Cece asks, confusion written in her expression.

"Another fire, babe." I kiss the top of her head.

"Do I want to know?" she asks.

I shake my head. "Not now."

She seems satisfied by my answer. Either that or she's too tired to engage.

The elevator settles as it comes to a stop, and I hold my breath when the door slides open.

Malice is standing a few feet in front of it, a scowl on his face. His eyes land on me, and he throws his hands up in the air.

"What the hell, Soul? Why'd you hang up on me? Why wouldn't you tell me wh—"

Malice's face pales, and his shoulders stiffen when Mark steps out from behind me. "What the fuck is he doing here?" he grits out from behind clenched teeth.

I move to grasp Malice's shoulder. "He saved us, brother," I tell him. "I know there's history that needs sorted through, but this isn't the time."

Malice shoves at my chest, but I stand my ground. He tries to move around me, his arms stretched out toward his brother, and I continue to block him.

"Not. Now!" I order. "Stand down, VP."

Malice growls as he cuts his gaze to mine. If looks could kill, I'd be a dead man. Over his shoulder, I see Grim stalking toward us, and Abyss is with him.

"Hey, Cece," Abyss says. "Why don't you come sit down so I can listen to your lungs?"

"No."

"Cece," I growl. "Let him do his thing."

"Soul, I'm no—"

"Cece, go."

She huffs out a breath and stomps around me to go with Abyss. I watch her until she sits on the couch.

"Still remember ASL, Mark?" I ask without looking at the man.

Fuck, when did he become a man?

"Uh, yeah," he responds and steps up next to me.

"Good." I keep my eyes locked on Malice. "Sign for me so I don't have to let go of your brother."

Without hesitation, Mark signs my words. Grim focuses on him, but I can practically feel the murderous heat radiating from my enforcer. I know everyone has questions, and we'll get to them. But not yet.

"Naughty/Nice was torched," I say. "Justin took off after the twat responsible."

"Who?" Grim's fingers are stiff.

I tilt my head and give him a 'who the fuck do you think' look.

"Junior or Senior?"

"Junior," I reply. "Grim, I need you to rally the troops and get Senior here. There's no way he's in the dark about this."

"I'm not leaving." Grim's jaw tics. "The Confessional is my domain."

"I'll handle it."

I whip around, and Rogue is standing there, his eyes sparking fire.

"Whatever," I agree. "I don't give a fuck who gets Senior here, just deal with it while Abyss checks over us."

Rogue nods and turns on his heel to do my bidding. He's in predator mode.

Good. That's what I need from him.

"Malice, you've got two choices," I say, returning my focus back to the older Grandon brother. "You can either get over your shit long enough to handle club business, or you can continue down the rabbit hole of rage and be banished to your suite. Either way, Mark stays until we have a chance to talk." I narrow my eyes. "What's it gonna be, man?"

Malice's eyes slide to Mark and then back to me. He yanks out of my hold and glares. "This isn't finished."

I huff out a laugh. "No shit."

He stabs a finger in Mark's direction. "You, go chill on the couches. I'll have someone bring you a drink."

Mark nods, seemingly too dumbstruck to respond.

"And what should I do?" Apple asks as she steps around on my other side.

Malice cuts his eyes to her, and his nostrils flare.

"Who are you?" Malice asks, and the anger he was exhibiting seconds ago is gone.

"She's with me," Mark snaps, suddenly coming out of his stupor.

Malice smirks. "We'll see about that."

Motherfucker. This isn't a complication I anticipated.

"Keep it in your pants," I growl. "Not the time."

"And not the girl," Apple adds with a slight snarl.

Malice stares at her for a moment before shaking his head. "We'll see."

"I swear to fuck, brother," I bite out. "This is not the time for yo—"

I whirl around at the sound of the elevator door opening, and my blood boils when I see Justin dragging Dr. Richard Franklin Jr. into the common room.

Arching a brow, I cross my arms over my chest.

"Well, well, well… look who the prospect dragged in."

CHAPTER THIRTY-THREE

CECE

"WELL, WELL, WELL... LOOK WHO THE PROSPECT dragged in."

I glance at Soul to see who he's talking to, and fury hits me like a freight train.

"You fucking asshole!"

Pushing Abyss away from me, I jump up from the couch and sprint toward Dr. Fucktard. Soul reaches out to stop me, but I dodge his attempt.

"You tried to kill me... twice!" I scream. "Tried to kill my *man*!"

Blood explodes from his nose when my clenched fist connects with it. I land two more hits before an arm snakes around my waist, and I'm hauled backward.

"Let me go!" I roar as I struggle to break free. Blood drips from my knuckles, but I barely notice. I'm too focused on the douchebag curled up on the floor.

"Whoa there, Rocky."

Tipping my head back, I glare at Animal. I continue to thrash against him, but he's too strong. He's not hurting me, but he *is* pissing me off.

I'm gonna give the doctor the same shit treatment he gave me… Endless suffering.

Soul seems to have frozen in place and is staring at me from a few feet away. Hell, everyone in the room is staring at me. It's quiet, too quiet. The only sound I hear is the moans coming from the bastard on the floor.

They must think I'm insane.

"Let me hurt him," I snarl. "I *need* to hurt him."

Soul finally breaks out of his trance and storms over to yank me out of Animal's hold. He carefully brings my hand up to inspect my knuckles. My chest heaves as I search his face for anger, disgust, *anything* to give me some insight to what he's thinking.

"Fuck, Cece, you hurt?" Soul asks as he wipes the blood from my hand on his shirt.

"I'm fine. My dad taught me how to fight."

I yank my hand out of his grip and whirl around toward the object of my rage. Richard scurries away from me like a crab when I take a menacing step forward.

"Don't let that psycho bitch ne—"

Malice pushes past me and lands a punch to the

doctor's temple, and he slumps unconscious to the floor.

"Grim, take him to the Confessional," Soul orders.

Grim nods with an eerie expression. His eyes are so dark they appear dead, but his smile is oddly gleeful. Uneasy, I take a step back and hit Soul's chest. Grim has always been kind to me, but right now, he's scaring the shit out of me.

"What's the Confessional?" I ask Soul after Grim disappears down one of the halls with Dr. Franklin.

Soul's hand rests on the small of my back. "Come with me." He guides me in the same direction Grim went.

"Soul, what the hell is going on?" I dig in my heels, forcing him to stop walking and look at me. "Tell Grim to bring his ass back here so I can finish what I started."

"I swear on all that's unholy," he grumbles.

"Excuse me?"

"Babe, just come with me," he says with exaggerated patience.

"Do I have a choice?"

"Trust me."

Soul dips his head and brushes his lips against mine. When he steps back, he grabs my hand and takes off again. Knowing it won't do me any good to resist, I let him lead me. We walk down the long hall that I know as the business wing of the clubhouse.

Once we reach the door at the very end of the wing, Soul presses his thumb against the sensor.

"Where are we going?" I ask.

"You'll see."

The door slides into the wall like all the others, and another elevator is a few feet in front of us. Soul enters a code next to the elevator, and a scanner extends out of the wall. He flattens his palm against it, and the elevator door opens.

What else do they have hidden in this place?

Soul tugs me into the elevator. The door automatically closes, and we begin to descend.I gasp, surprised to learn that there's something even farther beneath the Earth's surface.

"We aren't the heroes, Cece," Soul says as he turns to face me fully. "Fuck, we aren't even the good guys. I've explained this to you before." I nod because he seems to want some sort of acknowledgement from me, and he continues. "The Confessional is a room we use to extract information and confessions from sinners."

"Who decided to call the room the Confessional?"

"Grim." Soul smirks. "He's the Grim Reaper after all. I'm the judge, the club is the jury, and Grim is the executioner."

"And how do you extract the information?"

"By any *means* necessary."

My eyebrows shoot up. "*Any* means?"

"Yeah. And babe?" He pauses to take a deep breath. "This is the only time you'll be allowed down here. It's one too many times, in fact. Only members are allowed down here." I open my mouth to snark out a reply, but he holds up a hand to silence me. "The only reason I'm letting you down here now is because he *hurt* you, and you deserve to dole out some justice."

"Can I hurt him some more?" My heart thumps in anticipation.

"He's all yours," he says as the elevator opens, and we step out. "It's time for Dr. Richard Franklin Jr. to confess his sins."

Now that we're off the elevator, I take a minute to look around the large concrete space.It kind of reminds me of a mechanic's workshop. One wall is covered with knives of different sizes and shapes attached to magnetic strips. Another wall has a huge pegboard with hammers, screwdrivers, pliers, and all sorts of other tools I don't know the names of.

I look up and see chains hanging from the ceiling, and I swivel my head to see a table in the corner. It's stainless steel and looks like something you'd find in an operating room. Cabinets and drawers line the last wall, but they're closed so I can't see what they hold… *yet.*

The doctor is sitting in a chair, and his wrists and ankles are bound with leather straps, making it impossible for him to move too much.

Grim, Malice, and Abyss are all lined up against the wall, arms crossed over their chests. I can't help but wonder how Malice and Abyss got down here before us, but now isn't the time for a lesson on the clubhouse layout.

The three of them grin at me and nod encouragingly as I step away from Soul to move closer to the man who single-handedly destroyed my world.

Grim moves to block my path, and I shove at him in an attempt to get him out of my way. He frowns as he pulls his cell out of his cut. His fingers fly over the keys, and then he turns the screen for me to see.

"Just say the word, and I'll make this asshole wish he was never born," I read aloud.

Grabbing his phone, I type out a quick reply.

Thanks, but I need to do this.

He gives me a curt nod as he squeezes my shoulder before stepping aside.

"Gentlemen." I tip my head to Malice and Abyss, who chuckle.

"Time to confess fucker," Soul says as he moves to stand behind me.

"Why… Why are you doing this?" Dr. Franklin's voice shakes with fear.

I read in a book once that people see red when they're angry. I never really understood that until this very second. A dark haze surrounds my vision, almost like I'm looking down a tunnel at night, and the entire inside of the tunnel is painted a burnt orange.

Without thinking, I cock my arm back and slam it forward. My fist connects with the doctor's face and this time, it's Abyss who steps forward to examine my hand.

Tugging my hand out of his, I snap, "I know how to fight." I roll my eyes. "Soul checked when I punched him the first time."

"Duly noted." Abyss grins as he steps aside and sweeps his arm out like a butler inviting someone inside. "By all means, please continue."

The urge to continue pummeling Dr. Franklin is strong, but I want answers first.

I direct my attention back to the dipshit in the chair. "Why didn't you do anything to help my mother?"

"I did!" he cries. "I gave her some medicine and told her to follow up with her doctor."

"Wrong answer," I mutter. "Soul, do you have something I can use to hit him? My hand's starting to hurt."

"No... Wait. Please," Fucktard begs. "I'm a doctor, you can't do this to me! People will be looking for me."

"Nah, they won't." Soul smirks and hands me a tire iron.

I grip the tire iron and smack it against my palm like I see them do in the movies. "I'm going to give you one more chance." My tone is calm, which is in total contrast to the adrenaline swirling through my veins..

"We were busy. If she'd just gon—"

Whack.

Whack.

Whack.

An ear-piercing scream penetrates through the clouds in my brain, and I freeze when the bloody tire iron in my hand comes into focus. I lower my arm, the weight of the weapon becoming almost too much to hold.

"What happened?" I ask no one in particular.

"You bashed my knees, you fucking cunt!"

"Oh, sorry." I shrug. "Maybe you can prescribe yourself some meds and join a support group."

"Medicine won't fix this you bitch," he snarls.

My mind fractures, splitting into multiple pieces, all of which can't determine what's real and what's not. The out of body experience is a first for me, and as weird as it is, I decide to roll with it.

"You ran me off the road and tried to kill me," I huff out. "Then you set my store, *my fucking store,* on fire with me and Soul in it!"

I grab a knife from one of the magnetic strips and stab Dr. Franklin in the thigh. I can see myself doing this like I'm hovering in the air above me, but I have zero control to stop. I thrust the knife into the other thigh, and blood oozes from the wounds to soak his pants.

"Cece!"

I blink several times when Soul's shout registers. Reality seeps into my awareness, and I lift my hand. The light from the numerous bulbs recessed into the ceiling bounces off the wet blade. I shift my eyes from it to Dr. Franklin, taking in the scene.

The knife slips out of my grip to clatter on the floor, and I stumble backward.

Soul catches me before my knees buckle, and hauls me into his chest. "Fuck," he whispers harshly as he slowly turns me to face him. "You okay, babe?"

His hazel eyes darken as they bore into mine.

"Yeah… Yeah, I'm fine." I wheeze as I take a deep

breath, and am reminded that I was in a fire not all that long ago. "I can't believe I just did that."

"Let's get you out of here."

"No, I'm okay."

"We'll finish up," he says as he nods at Abyss, who steps forward.

"Come on Ce, I'll ta—"

I'm fully back in the here and now, and my shock is long gone. Anger bubbles up from my gut and bursts from me like a geyser.

"No!" I shift on my feet, away from Abyss. "No. He took *everything* from me. My mom, my dad's car, my store, my sanity. Fuck, he tried to *kill* us, Soul."

Soul wraps me in his arms, and I inhale his scent, absorb his heat. "I got you, babe. He won't be walking away from this. But I need to take things from here. You're too good to finish it." He squeezes me and presses a kiss to my head. "I won't let your soul be tainted like mine and my brother's. We will *end* him for you."

Grim, Abyss, and Malice surround me, lending me their strength as I fall apart in Soul's arms. I give into my emotions, swearing to myself that this will be the last time I cry because of this piece of shit. When my breath hitches, Soul wipes the tears off my cheeks. I lift my gaze to meet his narrowed one, and anger blazes from his irises.

I twist away from Soul to look at Dr. Fucktard. He's glaring at us, but there's a gag in his mouth that wasn't there before I broke down. A giggle escapes past my lips, and it morphs into a full blown laugh. The sound is maniacal, disturbing, but I feel better because of it. It's as if my laugh is carrying all the pain and hurt caused by this man out of my body.

This man who tore my world apart is broken and bleeding, and I'm the cause of it. I'm the one who inflicted his pain. I'm the one who broke him, who battered him and made him pay for his sins.

And yet…

I can't kill him. Soul's right. I don't have it in me to take a life. But lucky for me, I'm in love with a man whose soul is as black as the Devil's asshole when it comes to people who hurt his family.

And I'm his fucking family.

I lock eyes with Soul, then the others, and nod. I'm *their* family… *because* of Soul.

I glance around the room searching for something to sit on. There's a folding chair leaning against a cabinet, and I move around the men and drag the chair to where I want it. After plopping down, my lips curve into a sinister smile.

Nothing like a front row seat to the purge of the good doctor.

"Make him hurt."

CHAPTER THIRTY-FOUR

SOUL

Make him hurt.

I can do that. I've spent years perfecting my ability to make sinners suffer. But the one thing I've never done is complete a purge when the woman I love is watching.

Fucking hell, I'm hard.

After adjusting myself, I stalk toward Junior. His eyes widen as I get close, and his bottom lip trembles.

"Aw, look guys," I say with a fake sympathetic tone. "He's scared." I tilt my head. "Are you scared, Richard? Do you want your mommy?"

As if on cue, the elevator door slides open, and I glance over my shoulder at the new arrivals.

"Oh, that's right. We got Daddy."

"What is the meaning of this?" Dr. Franklin Sr. demands.

His bravado is cute, and I can't wait to make him see the error of his ways.

"Where do you want him, Prez?" Rogue asks.

"Whaddya think, babe?" I ask without looking at her.

"In the morgue," she replies nonchalantly.

My cock thickens painfully. I swear she's gonna be the death of me.

And what a way to go.

"Malice, grab a chair for our newest guest," I demand. "I suppose he can sit next to his son."

Rogue secures Senior to the chair once Malice has it in place. Then they both move to stand with Grim and Abyss as I turn back around to face the father-son team of sinners.

Senior narrows his eyes. "He needs a doctor," he spits out. "You can't do this to us."

"Abyss," I call over my shoulder. "Do you wanna provide medical care to Junior here?"

"I could," he says casually. "Maybe a lobotomy would do the trick."

My mouth curves into a grin as I glance at Cece to gauge her reaction. Surprisingly, she looks intrigued by the idea.

"It's an option," I say.

"Bring me the ice pick," I demand. Within seconds, the item is in my hand. "Brothers, you can leave."

A loud grunt fills the room, and I roll my eyes.

"Oh, right. I forgot about promising Grim a chance to inflict his brand of pain."

Grim steps up beside me, and the sledgehammer he loves so much is dangling from his hand. I nod to indicate he can go ahead.

"Sit tight, fellas," I tell the doctors. "This won't take long."

Grim lifts his weapon and lunges forward, bringing the sledgehammer down on one of Senior's knees. Senior howls in pain, pleads for him to stop, but what he doesn't know is Grim can't hear him. Grim doesn't give a shit.

The chair tips over, and Senior crashes to the floor. He struggles against the bindings, but Rogue's damn good with a knot. Prick isn't going anywhere.

Grim shifts his attention to Junior. The younger doctor is already broken and bloody, but if I know my enforcer, it's about to get a lot worse.

Grim raises the sledgehammer and just before it hits Junior in the head, he shifts his arm and throws it toward the wall. I rub my hands together like a kid in a candy store. I love it when Grim fucks with their heads.

"Stop," Senior pleads. "J-just stop."

I step toward him and crouch down to look him in the eye, the ice pick dangling from my grasp. "Do you want me to make him stop?" Senior frantically nods. "Oh, okay." I start to turn my head, but then snap my fingers. "Wait a sec, Doc," I say and level my gaze on him. "You didn't stop."

"Stop what?"

"You didn't stop your fucking son," I snarl. "You didn't stop covering for him. You didn't stop, so why should I?"

"I'll stop," he cries. "I promise I'll stop. Do what you want to him, but for the love of God, let me go. I'll stop."

A purge is so much sweeter when they beg.

"Brothers, you're dismissed. I can take it from here."

"But, Prez, we ha—"

"Dis-fucking-missed," I bark, my eyes still on Senior. "They're mine."

There are no further arguments, and I don't move until I hear the elevator close and begin to rise.

I straighten and lift the chair to put Senior back where I want him.

"So, you're telling me that you don't care if I kill your son?"

"Father, please," Junior begs, his voice cracking.

"Ricky isn't worth all this trouble," Senior insists, revealing how incredibly sinful he really is. "Do what you must to him, but please, spare me."

I glance at Cece, who's sitting with her legs

crossed, seemingly calm as can be. "Whaddya think, babe? Should I spare Dr. Fucktard Sr.?"

Cece stands and walks to stand in front of both men. She looks from one to the other before focusing on Junior.

"Ricky, what do you think?" she asks.

Junior sputters, opening and closing his mouth like a fish. Finally, he speaks, and his words are exactly what I expect.

"Kill him," he says. "It's his fault this has all happened."

"My fault?" Senior counters hotly. "You're a lazy piece of shit, Ricky. If you'd just do your damn job, we wouldn't be in this situation."

I nod. "He's right, *Ricky*." I lift the ice pick and move it in front of their faces, taunting them. "If you had taken the time to listen to Mrs. Parker and Cece, a lot of suffering could have been avoided."

"Fine," Junior snaps, spittle flying from his lips. "Is that what you want to hear from me? Fucking fine! I'm lazy. So fucking what?"

Cece lunges for him, but I catch her around the waist. "Ah, ah, ah, babe." I hug her tight to my side. "I told you, I finish this."

"Then finish it, dammit," she snaps. "I can't stand to look at them anymore."

"We're close, Cece. So close."

She glares at me for a minute, her chest heaving, and then turns on her heel and stomps back to her chair. My eyes drop to her ass, and I groan at the way her hips sway. When she sits, my dick practically shouts 'come back'.

I'm so fucking her when this is over.

Refocusing my attention on my victims, I grin. "As I said, we're close boys. There's just one more thing I need, and then this will all be over."

They both perk up at the idea that their nightmare is going to end. And I let them hope. Because their hope fuels my dark soul.

"Anything," Senior says, ever magnanimous. "We'll do anything."

"Good."

I kneel in front of him and untie his bindings. He looks at me with disbelief. When he tries to stand, he's unsteady because of the smashed knee. With a smirk, I shove the ice pick into the thigh of his other leg. He collapses back in the chair, screaming obscenities.

"I'm. Not. Finished," I snarl as I move in front of Junior.

I repeat the process of untying him, but unlike his father, he remains in place. Smart man.

Straightening to my full height, I wipe the blood from the ice pick on my jeans.

"Cece, things are about to get ugly," I say over my shoulder. "You sure you wanna be here for this?"

"About to get ugly?" Junior's tone is incredulous.

"For once, Fucktard is right," Cece says. "Things are already ugly, Soul. Things got ugly the second my mom went to the ER and relied on that prick to help her."

"Didn't answer my question, babe."

"I'm staying. End the ugly, Soul."

My queen's wish is my command.

"Stand up," I order the two men. They exchange a look, but remain seated. I step forward menacingly. "Stand. The fuck. Up!"

Senior rises first, putting all of his weight on his uninjured leg. Junior stands second, and his balance is off thanks to Cece. Her handiwork is a beautiful thing to see.

"It's time to confess your sins," I tell them. I point the ice pick at Senior. "We'll start with you."

"My sins? I don't know what you think I've done."

I stare at him as if considering his words. His eyes flash with that hope I love so much.

"Ya know what?" I jam the ice pick through his eye before he can blink. When he slumps to the floor, I pull the weapon free. "You're right. I just don't like you."

I turn to Junior. "Your turn."

"Wh-what have... You're cr-crazy," he stutters.

"Maybe." I shrug. "But my level of crazy doesn't even begin to match your level of sin."

"What sin?!"

"What sin?" I repeat, arching a brow. "You can't be serious."

"I... b-b-b... I don't kn-know what you want from me."

"I want you to confess. It's pretty simple really." I step into his space. "Repeat after me."

He nods frantically.

"Forgive me, for I have sinned."

"F-forgive me, f-for I ha-have s-s-sinned."

"Not good enough." I press the tip of the ice pick to his temple. "Again."

Junior glances at Cece as if she's going to help him, but finds no sympathy. When he looks back at me, he takes a deep breath.

"F-forgive me, for I have s-sinned."

"Again!" I shout, pressing the tip into his flesh.

He takes several more deep breaths. "Forgive me, for I have sinned."

With all my strength, I shove the ice pick into his skull and watch the life drain from his eyes. I pull the pick free and once again, wipe it clean on my jeans.

"Go forth, sinners' souls, from this world. May

you suffer in darkness, may your home be in Hell, and may the Devil fuck you with his horns."

"What the hell was that?"

I whirl around to find Cece standing a few feet from me.

"The club's version of a death prayer," I answer honestly.

She shifts her gaze to the dead, and shakes her head. "It's more than they deserve."

"It's exactly what they deserve."

Cece takes a step forward, and I reach out to haul her into my chest.

"You're not bothered by this?" I ask her, my eyes staring into hers.

"It's not how I wanna spend my weekends." She shrugs. "But I get it. And I'm glad they're dead."

"Do you still love me, even after seeing this?"

If she says no, this ice pick is going in my own brain.

"I love you, Soul." Cece rises to her tip-toes and presses a kiss to my lips. "All of you. None of this matters to me. Only you."

Air whooshes from my lungs in relief.

"I love you, too. So goddamn much."

I bend to lift her in my arms and carry her to the elevator. She presses her nose to my neck, and alternates between licking and sucking at my skin. I happily let her do whatever the hell she wants because as soon as we get upstairs, I'm taking her to my room and fucking her senseless.

The ride up seems to take longer than usual, but my rock-hard cock is a stark reminder that I'm just an impatient bastard. When the door slides open, I carry her down the hall toward the main room. It takes everything in me to pass my door, but I need to make sure all is well.

When I reach the end of the hall at the common room, I scan the space.

"I wanna go to your room, Soul," Cece whispers in my ear.

"Asher, Justin, Jacob, and Zack," I call out. "Clean up on aisle Confessional."

The four prospects race toward us, but Justin slides to a stop just in front of me.

"VP kicked out his brother and that chick," he tells me. "Thought you should know."

"Thanks, prospect."

He takes off down the hall, and it doesn't take a fraction of a second for me to forget about the last hour entirely. Purging is like that: great in the moment, but quickly forgotten because life goes on and more sinners are always out there, lurking. As long as humans walk the Earth, sinners will thrive.

I search for Malice and see him sitting at the bar. He's gripping a bottle of whiskey and swaying to the point he almost falls off the stool. My gut clenches at the pain I know my best friend is experiencing, but it's not a pain I can fix. The sinner that caused it has already been purged.

This is a demon he has to figure out on his own. I just wish he'd have done it with his brother.

Deciding that the rest of the world can wait until the sun rises, I whirl around and rush down the hall. Cece laughs in my arms as her pupils dilate. Once we're inside my room, I toss her onto the mattress and immediately pounce to straddle her with my knees on either side of her hips.

"Fuck me with the same intensity you used in the Confessional," she says, her voice husky.

I grin. "Do you have sins you need to confess?"

Her mouth tips up wickedly, and her words would bring me to my knees if I weren't already on them.

"Forgive me, Soul, for we are going to sin."

EPILOGUE

CECE

Two months later…

"What do you think?"

After putting the finishing touches on my outfit, I twirl around to show Jez and Heather. I paired dark jeans with my new three-inch heeled leather boots, and both hug me in all the right places.

I love these boots.

"Damn girl!" Jez squeezes my ass. "Perky and round… Just like Soul likes. He's gonna lose his shit when he sees you."

Twisting to look at my tush in the mirror, I smile. Jez is right. These jeans do wonders for my ass. She was also spot-on with the royal blue deep v-neck shirt, with its long lacy sleeves that she picked out from my closet.

"He's not gonna know what to do with you," Heather adds after a cat-call whistle. "And I want a pair of those boots."

"Me too," Jez says.

"I'll have Trista order you both a pair." Checking myself in the mirror again, I fluff my hair with my fingers. I left it down because Soul always says how much he loves my curls. "You sure it's not too much? I mean, you're both wearing jeans and t-shirts. I feel overdressed."

"Honey, you look beautiful." Heather steps up next to me and stares at our reflection in the mirror. "I'd kill for that ass."

"I'd kill for your boobs," Jez says, moving next to us.

"I'd love to be able to tan," I grumble.

None of us can keep a straight face, but Jez is the first to give in to the burst of laughter.

"What? It sucks being a redhead," I complain. "No matter how much sunscreen I use, I burn. You bitches are lucky."

"Minor inconvenience," Heather says with a grin. She grabs my hand and leads me to the bathroom, where my makeup is already set out. "I think we should do a smokey eye and pink lip gloss."

Heather starts applying my makeup, and Jez hops up to sit on the counter.

"How's the hospital doing under new management?" I ask Jez while Heather concentrates on my eyeshadow.

"Great. The changes Dr. DeMarco's made are phenomenal. I'm keeping an eye on things, but so far, so good. And patient satisfaction scores have gone way up."

So many good things have happened since the night the Franklins were *disposed of*. I don't know how the club managed it, but Dr. DeMarco was promoted to Hospital Director of Boulder City Memorial. And I dropped the wrongful death suit immediately after that. It didn't seem right for the one doctor who treated me kindly and appropriately to pay for other's sins.

"How much longer until Naughty/Nice reopens?" Heather asks with a grin. "I can't wait to get in there and shop."

Shuddering, I recall the fire. It still gives me nightmares, but Soul is always there to make things better.

I knew I'd rebuild the boutique with the insurance payout, but my man had *conditions*. So the new location is close to the main street, but on a corner. One of the perks of the location is the doubled square footage. More space equals more clothes, which means more sales.

"I'm not sure. Soul hired the best contractors, and

he's made sure Fort and Lock installed state-of-the-art security and safety features. We won't ever have to worry about being caught off-guard with an emergency again," I explain. "He was *pissed* it took so long for the fire department to respond after the 911 call."

I was more than happy to agree to Soul's terms, and it certainly didn't hurt that we spent several days in bed *compromising*. The one thing we couldn't agree on was whether or not I should open a second location. Soul thinks it's a great idea, but I'm not quite ready to take that leap.

"The grand opening should be in the next month or so," I go on. "We're all excited to get back to work, I can tell ya that. The club is still paying Trista, Holly, and Laura their salaries during the rebuild, but it isn't the same as staying busy, ya know?"

Jez and Heather nod in agreement.

Ping.

"Whose phone is that?" I ask.

Ping.

"Not mine," Jez says as she scoots off the counter.

Ping.

"Not mine either," Heather chimes in as she spins me around to face the mirror.

"Wow," I whisper.

"Wow is right." Jez tugs me into her side for a hug.

"Thanks, Heather!" I pull her into my other side. "My makeup looks amazing."

"I had a beautiful canvas to work with."

"Let's go party!" Jez shakes her ass and smacks mine. "Come on, girls."

"I just need to grab my phone real quick."

It's on my bed, and when I pick it up, I see three text notifications. I tap the screen to open and read them.

Soul: Running late

Soul: I'll meet U in the common room

Soul: Remember to leave UR panties off

A smile spreads across my face as I respond.

Time to give him a taste of his own medicine.

Me: Stay safe

Me: I decided to stay in our room

Me: Naked & waiting

After I hit send, the little dots bounce, so I know he's replying. They disappear, but quickly reappear, and less than a minute passes before his response appears.

Soul: I know UR fucking with me but let's skip the party

Me: Sorry babe… spent too much time getting ready. You'll have to ravish me after the party

Soul's only response is a winky face and tongue emoji, but that's all it takes for him to make me quiver with desire

"Cece's blushing." Jez practically giggles as she points at my face. "Soul must've sent something dirty."

"Or maybe I sent him something dirty." I cock my hip. "Ready to party, ladies?"

"Time to shake our asses!" Heather shimmies.

The common room is packed already, and the music is thumping. Everyone is here other than Soul and Malice.

"Soul said he's running late. Any idea why?" I ask Jez as I follow her to the bar.

Heather bailed the moment she spotted Frenzy, and now he has her shoved against the wall with his tongue jammed down her throat. Jealousy tickles my nerves when she jumps up and wraps her legs around his hips.

Soul better get here fast.

"Nope," Jez says, emphasizing the P.

I raise my brows and side-eye her.

"What?"

I shake my head. "Nothing." I've learned how to tell when Jez is hiding something because she always says 'nope' with obnoxious exaggeration. One thing I haven't figured out yet, is how to get her to spill the details. She's harder to crack than a damn safe.

Asher is working the bar and talking to Nikki and Bunny, but shifts his attention to us when we sit on the stools.

"What can I get you ladies?"

"Beer please." Jez raises a brow at me in question.

"Same, Prospect." While he gets our drinks, I nod toward Frenzy and Heather. "I hope Soul and I are still in love like that someday."

"I don't think that'll be a problem." She smirks.

Jez is definitely hiding something, but I decide to let it go for now. It's time to cut loose and have some fun.

Bunny and Nikki have been watching us since we sat down, but haven't made a move to come closer. *Fuck that*. Us girls have to stick together. The last time we partied, we all had fun dancing together. Time to recreate some memories.

"C'mon ladies, let's dance!" I wave for them to join us before saying to Jez, "Play something we can really move to."

"You got it." Jez reaches for her phone and, after tethering it to the sound system, plays *Ice Ice Baby.*

A collective groan fills the room from the men, but none of them makes a move to change it. Grabbing Bunny and Nikki's hands, I lead them to the dance floor.

"This is my jam!" I shout.

With my hands raised above my head, I let the music take over my body.

SOUL

"YOU DID MAKE SURE THAT TATTOO IS THE ONLY ONE you walked out of the shop with, right?"

I shift my eyes from the road and glare at Malice. He went with me to Sinful Wheels and Persuasion Ink for moral support, but I'm starting to regret that decision.

"I warned Possum that if I found any rodents, roadkill, or anything other than what I asked for, inked on my skin, I'd not only strip his patch, I'd filet him like a goddamned fish."

Malice laughs. "So that's a no, then."

"Fuck off," I snap, focusing on the road. No, I

didn't check every inch of skin, but Possum knows better than to fuck with me.

I hope.

The party at the clubhouse is sure to be in full swing already, and I wanted to be there before it started, but it took Asher longer than anticipated to put the final touches on Cece's Camaro at Sinful Wheels. He did text me that he made it to the clubhouse on time, so Cece wouldn't suspect a thing, so there's that.

"Are you sure about this?" Malice asks me for the tenth time since we took off on our errands this afternoon.

"Do you not like Cece or something?" I counter, annoyed that he can't just be happy for me.

"What?"

"You keep asking me if I'm sure, and I'm just trying to figure out why."

Malice huffs out a breath. "I love Cece." I growl at his words, and he smacks my arm. "You know what I mean. Cece's great. And she makes you happy." He shrugs. "I just can't help but wonder if we're exactly qualified to know how to make anything good stick."

I glance at him out of the corner of my eye, hating that sadness and rage seem to be the two dominant emotions he's capable of lately.

Not lately. He's been this way since we were teens.

"Saints Purgatory stuck," I remind him. "And you can't tell me that the club isn't something good."

A ghost of a smile splits his face, but it disappears so quickly, I wonder if I imagined it. "The club is something good," he admits. "But it's born from pure fucking evil."

Touché.

"Have you heard from Mark?" I ask, diving right into the heart of the matter as I see it.

Malice scoffs. "Fuck Mark. I didn't want to see him when he brought that bitch to the club, and I don't wanna see him now."

"He and *that bitch* saved my life, saved Cece's life."

He waves his hand dismissively. "Yeah, yeah. I'm glad about that." A few seconds pass, and then he grins. "Did you see the tits on her, though? Fucking hell, I didn't know whether to stay pissed that she was associated with my brother or motorboat her damn boobs."

Not knowing what to say to that, I remain silent. In fact, the rest of the drive is quiet, except for the constant string of thoughts in my fucking head.

It's been two months since I rid the world of two more sinners. Sure, there have been others since then, but aside from Father Brine and Deacon Block, the Franklin doctors were the two most important purges of my life. Like the unholy holy men, the docs were eliminated for someone I love, and that's a heady feeling.

After that night, it didn't take me long to convince Cece to move into the clubhouse with me. And it certainly was fun *convincing* her. Together, we decided to keep her mom's house, just in case we ever wanted to get away and be alone. Maybe we'll sell it down the road, but for now, Cece isn't ready to let it go, and I have no intention of forcing the issue.

What Cece wants, what she needs, she gets. As long as I have breath left in my body, I will make damn sure of that.

"You've got everything, right?" Malice asks when I pull into Cece's parking spot in the clubhouse garage.

"Little late to be double checking, don't you think?" I pat my cut and glance over my shoulder at the box in the back seat. "But, yeah. I've got it all"

"And you're su—"

"I'm fucking sure," I bark.

Malice holds his hands up in surrender. "Okay, okay. But seriously, Prez… What kind of friend and brother would I be if I didn't do my due diligence?"

Rolling my eyes, I grab the box before getting out of the Camaro and striding toward the elevator. My VP follows. The ride underground seems to take forever, and it doesn't help that my heart is drumming a steady staccato of nerves. My palms are sweaty, and I swear fucking birds are flying around in my stomach.

The saying is butterflies, dumbass.

When the elevator door slides open, I immediately scan the room for Cece. My eyes land on her, and my cock swells. She's in the middle of the room dancing, and her body is so in tune with the music that it's as if she and the beat are one.

"Go get her, man," Malice says with a push.

I look at Asher, who's behind the bar, and nod. We worked it out ahead of time that when I arrived, he'd cut the music. He grins at me, and does exactly what he's supposed to.

Cece immediately stops moving and glares at Asher. "What the hell, Prospect?"

My mouth tips into a giant grin. It definitely hasn't taken long for my woman to get used to her role as future queen. Which is good, considering…

Asher points at me, and Cece's gaze follows his direction. When she spots me, she takes off at a run and launches herself at me, giving me no choice but to drop the box and catch her.

Cece fuses her mouth to mine, and my tongue darts out to tease the seam of her lips and demand entry. I deepen the kiss, lost in the taste of her.

"Get a room!" Jezebel shouts from across the common area.

I laugh against Cece's lips, but pull back to lock eyes with her. The blue of her irises darkens, and my dick seems to reach out for her, seeking the heat her pussy can provide. And the thought of said pussy being bare under the denim of her jeans… I groan.

"I've got a surprise for you, babe," I say as I set her on her feet.

"I knew something was going on," she cries with a grin. "Jez always pops her P's whe—"

"You told her?" I shout at my twin.

"I didn't tell her shit," she snaps, glaring at me.

"Oh, no, Soul," Cece says. "She didn't say anything. She never does." Her face scrunches up like she finds that fact annoying as hell. "But I've figured out how to tell when she's hiding something. I just never can tell what it is."

My shoulders sag with relief. "Oh. Well, good."

"So…" Cece cocks her hip, and her face lights up with excitement. "You said something about a surprise."

Nodding, I grab her hand and tug her toward the elevator. She practically bounces as we ascend above ground, but when I put a blindfold on her, she pouts.

"No fair," she complains.

"I said I had a surprise, babe. Never said anything about fair."

It takes too damn long for the rest of the members and bunnies to reach the garage, but I wait until everyone is present before doing anything. It was made very clear to me by more than one person that my balls would be in danger if I did what I'm about to do without an audience. And I'm pretty sure we've established that I like my balls.

By the time the entire crowd is gathered around us, Cece is tapping her foot with impatience. It takes every ounce of self-control not to laugh at her. It took a bit, but I learned that laughing at Cece is never a good idea.

"Okay, babe," I begin, slowly guiding her toward the Camaro. When she stumbles, I steady her. "I got ya. Just trust me."

"I do trust you," she huffs out. "I don't trust my own two feet."

I chuckle, but continue the last ten feet before bringing her to a halt.

"Are you ready?" I ask.

Cece nods so I untie the bandanna and pull it away from her face. Her gasp is sharp, and her eyes are wide.

"How? When?" She shakes her head and then looks up at me. "You told me it couldn't be fixed."

I did tell her that. Several weeks after the accident, I knew I wanted this to be part of my plans for her, so I lied. Sue me.

"It wouldn't have been a surprise otherwise," I say. "Besides, I wasn't exactly sure how long it would take them at Sinful Wheels to get all the parts. I wanted it repaired and restored to the same pristine condition it was in before the accident, and that coulda taken a long fucking time."

"I wanna be mad at you," she gripes. "You lied. But I can't. Not when this is the result." Cece throws her arms around me. "Thank you so much, Soul," she says against my chest. "Thank you for giving me a piece of my dad back."

"Anything for you, babe." I kiss the top of her head and hold her for a moment longer. Then I urge her away from me. "There's more."

"More?!" she exclaims. "What more could you possib—" Her lips press together when I take off my cut and hand it to Malice. My shirt goes next. "Uh, Soul… What are you doing? Not that I don't love the view, but…"

"You'll see." I glance over my shoulder at Grim, who pushes his way past Malice to stand in front of Cece. "The big guy wanted to say something first."

Cece's gaze darts to Grim, and she smiles. Of all the brothers, she's gotten the closest with him. She's even learning ASL so they don't have to communicate via their cells for the rest of our lives. But for now, it's still early stages, so Grim pulls out his phone and hands it to her.

Rogue asked me once if it bothered me to not be included in their conversations since it would be so easy for someone to translate for the two of them, and I answered him honestly. Absolutely not. I trust Cece with my life, so why wouldn't I trust her with my family? And the same applies to Grim.

But none of that matters today, because Grim typed up what he wanted to say and showed me this morning. I know exactly what Cece is reading on the screen, and as she reads, I turn around so she sees my back when she's done.

Cece, when I first met you, I probably scared the shit out of you. And for that, I'm sorry. Now that I've gotten to know you, scaring you is the last thing I want to do. You are family. I've always thought that Soul should have a strong woman at his side, and you are that. You are the only woman deserving of the title 'Queen'. So, welcome to the family, Queen. We will protect you with our lives because that's what Saints Purgatory does.

I know the moment she's done reading by the sniffling. Out of the corner of my eye, I see her feet dangle as Grim lifts her up for a hug. I promised my enforcer that this one moment today was his, but I can't resist swinging my gaze to take them in. And when I see Cece sign 'I love you too' and Grim smiles wider than I've seen in years, I know I made the right call.

Grim sets her on her feet and turns her toward me, and I quickly face away from her.

"Oh my god," she whispers. Cece's fingertips trace around the new ink on my back, and goose-bumps break out over my flesh. "It's beautiful, Soul."

An image of what I saw in the mirror after Possum finished the tattoo flashes in my mind. I've had the tattoo of the Saints Purgatory MC logo for years, but he added the words 'Property of Cece, My Queen' today in new top and bottom rockers.

"I want one," she cries. "Promise me you'll take me to get one."

I whirl around and grin. "We can go tomorrow if you're serious." She nods. "Okay, then."

"Is this why you were late to the party?" she asks.

"It's part of it," I admit. "But there's still more, babe."

"No, Soul. It's too much. I'm so grateful for all of it, but no more."

"No can do. I've been planning this for a while, and I'm not done."

She huffs out a breath. "Fine."

She's gonna regret the attitude in about two minutes.

I turn to Malice and take the box he picked up off the floor downstairs before facing Cece with the most serious expression I can muster. It isn't easy because I'm so damn happy, but I give it my best shot.

"Like the tattoo says, you're my queen," I tell her. "And every queen needs the right attire." I lift the lid and take out the leather vest. "You, Cece, need a cut." I hand it to her.

"Oh, wow." She flips it around in her hands. "I love it, Soul. Thank you."

"You're welcome. But there's more." I drop to my knee before she can even open her mouth to argue. Pulling the ring box out of my cut, I begin. "Cece, when Jezebel first asked me to help her friend, I wanted nothing to do with it. But she insisted, and I'll be fucking grateful for the rest of my life that she did." I take a deep breath. "The second I laid eyes on you in that hospital bed, I knew life would never be the same. You were, and are, so goddamn beautiful, and my breath is knocked out of my body any time I look at you." Cece's hands are over her mouth, and tears are sliding down her cheeks. "You are such a bright light, and you make my pitch-black world tolerable. And I want you to be my light for the rest of our lives. I know I'm not perfect, and I'll make mistakes, but if you'll agree to be my old lady, I'll spend every single second of every single day doing anything and everything to make sure you are safe, happy, and so fucking loved."

"Say yes," Asher shouts from the crowd.

"He's the best of us all, Ce," Thorn says.

"Be our queen," Malice barks, and I can't stop my eyes from rolling at his gruffness.

"So, babe, whaddya say? Wanna ride through the rest of this life with me?"

Cece swipes her cheeks, but remains silent. My heart skips one beat, two beats, three.

Fuck, she's gonna say no.

"Cece?"

Finally, *fucking finally,* she speaks.

"On one condition."

She's always warned me payback is a bitch.

My lips twitch. "Only one?"

Cece nods.

"Okay. What's your condition?"

She takes a deep breath, then another and another.

"Outside of club business, the only sinning you do is with me. If you sin, we sin together."

"Done."

After standing and swinging her around in a circle, I set her back down and slide the ring onto her finger. Then I tip my head back and close my eyes.

Forgive us Father, for we are going to sin.

Over and over and over again.

ACKNOWLEDGEMENTS

First, we truly hope that you loved Soul and Cece as much as we do. They took us on an incredible journey, and we loved every minute of it.

Thank you to our amazing beta and sensitivity readers, Amy and Mickaela. Not only did you stick by us through the absolute crazy train of a ride, but Unholy Soul is better because of you both.

A huge shout out to our husbands, who put up with our insane schedules and never-ending phone calls. We know we can be a pain in the ass sometimes, especially when we join forces, so thank you for putting up with it!

Thank you Dr. DeMarco for always answering our medical questions and for not laughing at us when we came up with oddball ideas. Without you, Unholy Soul wouldn't be even remotely medically correct. We know we took creative liberties with a few things, but your knowledge allowed us to determine when we could and couldn't do that.

Thank you Haley for making sure we got details about the Catholic faith as correct as we needed them to be for a work of fiction. We are aware that our ideas and questions weren't always easy to hear, and we appreciate you for your understanding and support.

And most importantly, thank you to our readers! It is because of you all that we are able to write the stories that pop into our heads. It is because of you that we can live our dreams and for that, we are eternally grateful.

Now, who's ready for more of Saints Purgatory MC?!

NEXT IN SAINTS PURGATORY MC

Wrathful Malice
Book 2

There isn't a person in the world who hasn't committed a sin. Some sins are worse than others, but seven of them are deadly. But those seven worst of the worst? They're what drive Saints Purgatory MC to keep fighting.

APPLE

I live my life as a free spirit, a woman determined to carve out her place in the music industry... Hell, in the world. Writing songs and playing gigs is how I survive, and for the most part, it works. Until it doesn't. I never dreamed I'd get sick and be dragged to a motorcycle club for help, but that's where I find myself.

When dark forces come for blood, I don't believe for a second that I'm the target. How can I be when I'm surrounded by men who make their living as vigilantes in a sinner's world? But I'm proven wrong, and that scares me more than I thought possible. My best friend assures me that I'm safe with Saints Purgatory MC, and I want to believe him.

But how am I supposed to trust the brother he hasn't seen in years? Not only with my life, but with my heart?

MALICE

As the Vice President of Saints Purgatory MC, I need to keep a cool head. Unfortunately, fury is my middle name, and there's nothing cool about me. But I've learned how to take that rage and use it to fight the battles that most would run from. I'm talented like that.

With a past that haunts me and a present that's full of sinners, it's a miracle I've done anything at all with my life. The one thing I *don't* do is let people get close. Aside from my club, I don't need anyone. Until my brother shows up with his best friend, and she needs more from me than I've ever willingly given.

I don't know if I can be the man she deserves, but for the first time, I know I'll move heaven and earth to try.

I am Saints Purgatory, and I'm a sinner who takes out the sinful.

ALSO BY

ANDI RHODES & LACY ROSE

Saints Purgatory MC:

Unholy Soul

Wrathful Malice

Grim's Hell

Shadowy Abyss

Rogue's Cross

Thorned Vengeance

Spike's Perdition

ABOUT THE AUTHORS

Andi Rhodes is an author whose passion is creating romance from chaos in all her books! She writes MC (motorcycle club) romance with a generous helping of suspense and doesn't shy away from the more difficult topics. Her books can be triggering for some so consider yourself warned. Andi also ensures each book ends with the couple getting their HEA! Most importantly, Andi is living her real life HEA with her husband and their boxers.

For access to release info, updates, and exclusive content, be sure to sign up for Andi's newsletter at andirhodes.com.

Lacy Rose is an author who loves to write gritty MC (motorcycle club) romance. Lacy loves multiple genres and can be found reading almost anything in her free time. She lives with her husband of 23 years and two children. When she isn't writing, her life is often filled with mayhem from kids' school activities, so she reads and writes in her free time to escape reality. Lacy enjoys sharing her stories with others, and they always have a HEA.

Made in the USA
Columbia, SC
27 June 2023

18225650R00252